So Not Okay

MEAN GIRL MAKEOVER

BOOK 1

By

NANCY RUE

THOMAS NELSON
Since 1798

NASHVILLE DALLAS MEXICO CITY RIO DE JANEIRO

So Not Okay

Published in Nashville, Tennessee, by Tommy Nelson. Tommy Nelson is a registered trademark of Thomas Nelson.

Tommy Nelson titles may be purchased in bulk for educational, business, fund-raising, or sales promotional use. For information, please e-mail SpecialMarkets@ThomasNelson.com.

Library of Congress Cataloging-in-Publication Data

Rue, Nancy N.
So not okay / by Nancy Rue.
pages cm. -- (Mean girl makeover ; book 1)
Summary: In deciding whether to help a bullied classmate, Tori, a quiet sixth grader at Gold Country Middle School, turns to prayer and God's teachings.
ISBN 978-1-4003-2370-8 (softcover : alk. paper)

[1. Bullying--Fiction. 2. Middle schools--Fiction. 3. Schools--Fiction. 4. Christian life--Fiction.] I. Title.
PZ7.R88515Si 2014
[Fic]--dc23

2013049061

Printed in the United States of America

14 15 16 17 18 19 RRD 6 5 4 3 2 1

This book is dedicated to the memory
of my friend Lee Hough,
who never stood by when words
were breaking hearts.

Chapter One

It was a Monday. January 26, to be exact, and I like to be exact. I remember the date because it needs to be circled on a calendar. In red Sharpie.

That's because it was the first time since the start of middle school that Kylie Steppe actually looked at me and apparently saw something besides, well . . . nothing. And it changed, well . . . everything.

My best friend Ophelia Smith and I were leaning against the wall across from the office at Gold Country Middle School waiting for our other best friend, Winnie George, to pick up her slip to get into classes after being absent. The line snaked out the door and down the hall, like half the school had suffered from some kind of epidemic, and Kylie was standing in it. I figured she'd probably been out having her nails done because she had been standing there inspecting them for ten minutes like Sherlock Holmes on a case.

But suddenly she looked up and stared right at me. She was so still, I wondered if she had a pulse.

Ophelia noticed the look too. She hid half her face—not hard to do when your thick yellow hair is like a curtain all the way to your waist—and whispered, "The Alpha Wolf is looking at you, Tori. That's weird."

It really *was* weird because Kylie hadn't shown any signs of noticing me since the first day of sixth grade when she started deciding who was cool and who wasn't. I wasn't. She couldn't prove it. I just wasn't.

I was okay with that. Ophelia and Winnie and I weren't even on Kylie and her Pack's radar. Okay, I know wolves don't use radar. Mrs. Fickus, our English teacher, would say I was mixing my metaphors. The point is: we were like Saran Wrap to the Pack.

But Kylie couldn't seem to *stop* looking at me now. Her nose wrinkled like she smelled something bad, which was totally possible in our school. Between the stinky sneakers and the kids who hadn't been told about deodorant yet, you were better off breathing through your mouth when a bunch of us sixth-graders were crammed together in the halls.

I was considering telling Kylie that I had looked it up and found out the reason boys' sweat could now gag you was because puberty caused their sweat glands to become more active and secrete odor-causing chemicals, when she said, "Why don't you get your eyebrows waxed?"

I opened my mouth to say, *Hello! Because it's painful!* but Ophelia gave me a warning poke in the side. She was right. Kylie wasn't going to listen, so I just shrugged. My mom didn't like it when I did that, but it usually ended conversations I didn't want to be in to begin with.

But that didn't work on Kylie. Clearly, she wasn't done.

"They're starting to grow together in the middle." She gave her splashy little dark brown haircut a toss. "You're gonna have a unibrow. That's so gross."

In front of Kylie in line, her friend Heidi laughed out of her puggy nose. It was only a matter of time before her other friend Riannon would be throwing back her hair—just like Kylie's except mouse-colored—and howling—followed by Izzy and Shelby. That was one of the dozen reasons I thought of them as a pack of wolves closing in on their prey.

I was sure Kylie was going to pull hot wax out of her backpack and come after me with it when our principal Mrs. Yeats parted the kids in the doorway like she was coming through drapes and clapped so hard it made the skin on her upper arms jiggle inside her sleeves. A hush settled over the mob because her chins were wobbling too. That meant the detention slips were about to come out of the pocket of the gold wool vest she always wore.

"If you are not waiting to get a readmit slip," she said in her voice like a French horn, "please move out of the hallway."

"What if we're waiting for someone?" Heidi said.

"Wait for them someplace else."

Mrs. Yeats jiggled back into her office, and Heidi and Riannon stepped out of the line. But Kylie said to them, "It's okay if *you* stay."

That was the thing with the Pack. They thought the rules didn't apply to them, and most of the time they kind of didn't. But they applied to us, so I nodded for Ophelia to follow me away from the office. Besides, I still wasn't convinced Kylie wasn't at least going to break out the tweezers.

"What was *that* about?" Ophelia said as we hurried up the steps to our usual before-school meeting place at the end of the sixth-grade lockers by the window.

"What was *what* about?"

"That whole thing about your eyebrows."

"I have no idea," I said. "I guess Kylie's into eyebrows now."

Ophelia lifted one of hers, which was so blond you could hardly see it. "She waxes so she thinks everybody else has to."

"To be cool. Which I'm so not."

Ophelia dropped her backpack under the window and looked over both shoulders. Kids were clanging their lockers and yelling stuff at each other, so nobody was paying any attention to us, but Ophelia still talked with her teeth together. "Why did she decide to pick on you?"

"She wasn't really picking on me, Phee," I said. "She was just making an observation."

"She said you were gross!"

"She said I was *going* to be gross."

Ophelia blinked her ginormous brown eyes at me. I'd always wanted to measure them to see if they really were bigger than most peoples' or if they just looked that way because her face was tiny.

She started to braid her hair so it wouldn't get caught in her backpack zipper like it did about 80 percent of the time. "I just don't see why she all of a sudden noticed that about your eyebrows. I mean, not that they *are* like a unibrow . . . I'm just sayin' why *you* when she hasn't talked to you since—"

"The last day of school in fifth grade," I said and did my let's-change-the-subject shrug. Ophelia always had a new topic at the ready.

"You *have* to help me with that math homework. It was *so* hard!"

"Okay—"

"I tried to call you last night. Where were you?"

"I was—"

"I was, like, starting to cry because I couldn't get it, and you know my mom is no help, and my dad just gets all yelly with me because I'm such a loser in math—"

"You're not—"

"I am! You have to help me. Please?"

"Phee."

"What?"

"I will."

"I love you!"

She wrapped her arms around me and squeezed a laugh out of me.

"Okay, okay—jeepers."

"I love it when you say that." Ophelia pulled her now-braided hair up on top of her head and let it bounce down. "Where did you get that again?"

"When I had strep throat and Granna came over to stay with me and she had TV Land on the whole day."

"And you watched all those episodes of that one show about the chipmunk."

"Chipmunk? It was *Leave It to Beaver.*"

"I knew it was some cute animal."

"It was a kid! His nickname was Beaver, and he said 'jeepers' all the time. I liked it."

"I love it!"

"So where's your math homework?"

"Oh, yeah."

Ophelia unzipped her backpack, which had so many stickers on it you could hardly tell it was purple, and pawed through what looked like a wastebasket full of papers.

"I hope Winnie's gonna be okay," she said as she dug. "She's having a really hard time at her grandmother's house."

Winnie's dad had lost his job and then her family lost their house. After a lot of listening in on grown-ups' conversations, I figured out that "losing their house" meant they couldn't pay for it and now the bank owned it. The Georges had moved in with Winnie's grandmother, and let's just say, she wasn't like *my* Granna, who rocked grandparenthood.

"Her mom told my mom that's why they gave her a couple of days off from school," I said. "So she could adjust."

"You guys?" said a tiny voice.

I turned in time to see Winnie in a shaft of sunlight, sagging against the end of the lockers.

"I don't think it worked," Ophelia said.

She ran to Winnie and practically knocked her down hugging her. That wasn't hard to do since Winnie's head only came up to both Phee's and my shoulders, and she was always so pale it was like you could almost see through her.

She looked smaller than ever now, and her light blue eyes were all puffy and red around the rims. Her hair was still wet from washing it, so it laid against her round head like an almost-white cap. The only thing that wasn't pale on Winnie was her dark eyebrows.

Again with the eyebrows.

Ophelia led her to me at the window. Winnie dropped her backpack and burst into tears.

"It's that bad at your grandmother's?" I said.

Winnie shook her head about fifty times. "It's those girls."

"What gir—"

"Kylie and them."

"What did they do to you?" Ophelia said.

"Nothing."

"Did they say something evil?"

"No."

I shook my head. "So you're crying because . . . "

"When I came out of the office, they looked at me!"

Winnie's little shoulders went up and down the way people's do when they cry without making any sound. My mom's did that every time we watched the part of *Anne of Green Gables* where Matthew died.

"How did they look at you?" Ophelia said.

"Like you had one big ol' hairy eyebrow growing across your forehead?" I said.

Winnie stopped shaking and blinked at me. "Yes!" She rubbed the space over her nose. "Do I?"

"No. They're just all about eyebrows right now. Who knows why?"

"Because Kylie started having hers waxed, that's why," Ophelia said. "Pretty soon the whole Pack will have theirs done, or they won't be allowed to stay in it."

"For real?" Winnie said.

Ophelia nodded soberly. "I heard they have all these rules they have to follow to stay 'in.' I don't know what they are, but I bet that's gonna be one of them."

Winnie's face crumpled again.

"Why are you crying now?" I said.

"Because you guys would never do that to me."

I shrugged at Ophelia, but she was nodding like she totally got it. She was starting to cry too. Phee was nothing if not dramatic.

I guessed Winnie "having a really hard time" was a 100 percent true.

They both stopped crying by second period when we got to Mr. Jett's social studies class. He wasn't our favorite teacher, but that was okay because most of the time he just gave us an assignment and then patrolled the aisles so we didn't actually have to talk to him that much.

I always finished my work fast and then stared at him, trying to figure out if his glasses and black mustache were connected to his nose and why the top of his hair had all fallen out leaving his head shiny, like maybe his wife waxed it every morning, but the bottom part was still thick. There had to be a scientific explanation for that.

That day he said we'd be watching a movie about poverty and children around the world, and I just about groaned out loud. I asked to go the restroom and came back with a wad of toilet paper for Phee and one for Winnie. Otherwise there would be no end to the snot. Once the two of them started crying, they could turn on and off like faucets for the rest of the day. Me, I was never the crying kind.

Through the whole movie, something was going on in the back of the room where Kylie and her Pack were sitting with their desks in a circle. Mr. Jett was up at the front grading papers, so he either didn't see them or he really needed to get that homework checked. Usually, he was like a security guard or something. I guessed you kind of had to be when you were also the permanent cafeteria monitor.

At first, the Pack was just whispering, so it sounded like baby snakes hissing. Then somebody would snort—probably Heidi—and a word or two would erupt. Like *sheriff* and *evicted*.

Since when did the Pack use vocabulary like *evicted*?

By the time the credits rolled and Mr. Jett turned on the lights so his head shined again and everybody could blink and go "Ow!" the Pack's desks were back in their rows and Kylie was looking like she was about to pop open.

"Someone respond to the movie," Mr. Jett said. "Kylie?"

Her dimples—the ones that looked like two Crater Lakes—got deeper. "That was *so* sad. I don't see how they could do that to those poor people."

Mr. Jett nodded as if Kylie were a saint. Or at least a nun. He adjusted his glasses (and I swore I saw his nose adjust too) and went on to say something about how we Americans don't realize how fortunate we are, and Kylie and the Pack all nodded like they knew exactly what he was talking about.

I didn't see how they could. They were the most "fortunate" people I knew, at least when it came to money and clothes and other stuff. Kylie lived in the biggest house on Church Street, and she had an iPad *and* her own smartphone. Ophelia was probably right about the rules because Heidi and Riannon and Shelby and Izzy all had them too. It was probably on the checklist to get into the Pack.

The bell rang, and all the boys bolted for the door. As I was getting my backpack, I saw Riannon grab Patrick O'Conner's arm and whisper in his ear. His whole round-as-a-Frisbee face turned into one big "oh."

"What do you think she said to him?" Ophelia whispered into *my* ear.

I was about to tell her I didn't know and didn't care, but Patrick turned slowly and looked right at Winnie.

"Dude," he said.

What, "dude"? I wanted to say to him. But Riannon looked exactly like a wolf licking her chops. I decided to keep my mouth shut and my ears open.

~

I didn't have to work too hard at it. All through third-period math and fourth-period science we heard, "Dude," and, "No stinkin' way!" and, "I also heard that she . . ." I picked up pieces that weren't hard to put together. The story was that:

Winnie and her family were evicted from their house—forced out of it by the sheriff because her father stole money from his company.

He was in prison.

The Georges were homeless.

Winnie was wearing clothes that used to be Kylie's that her mom gave away for the poor people in shelters.

It was all 0 percent true.

I didn't have a chance to talk to Winnie about it until we got to the cafeteria for lunch. Fortunately, sixth-graders had the first lunch shift so I only had to wait until eleven-oh-two (to be exact). I once heard Mr. Jett tell another teacher, "They get squirrelly if you don't feed them early."

"Don't pay any attention to anything they're saying, Win," I said when the three of us were gathered at our usual end of the table by the windows.

A chair separated us from the next group of girls. Josie, Ciara, and Brittney were all on the same soccer team and were always talking about goals and offsides and stuff like that. They were totally nice, but we didn't hang out enough for them to be part of *this* discussion.

Winnie squinted at me with still-red eyes. "What who's saying?"

"Kylie and her—"

"Hey, Winnie," Ophelia said. "Would you go get us some napkins? I just slopped ketchup all over me."

I didn't see any ketchup, but Winnie got up and went over to the condiments counter.

"She doesn't know about the gossip," Ophelia said with her teeth pressed together.

"How could she not?" I said. "It's spreading like the flu!"

"Okay, she's *pretending* she doesn't know, so don't throw it in her face."

"Was I doing that?"

Ophelia took a bite out of her hot dog.

"Are *we* supposed to pretend too?" I said.

She nodded.

"You know I stink at that. I can't even lie to my dog."

Ophelia swallowed hard and leaned into the table. "First you. Now Winnie. What is going on all of a sudden?"

I took a bite of my burger and chewed as I surveyed the table in the center of the room, where the Pack sat—right where everybody could see them.

There were five of them, counting Kylie. The tables were made for six, but nobody else ever tried to take that extra chair. How could they, with backpacks and stuff piled up like the Pack was about to jet off on spring break?

Kylie sat in the middle between Heidi and Riannon, her identical bookends. They almost looked exactly like Kylie, too, but that was hard to do. She had these really dark blue eyes with little gold flecks in them that you couldn't imitate like you could a haircut or bracelets or all the other things they copied from her.

Kylie nibbled a pepperoni and swept the room with her eyes like she was looking for trash that needed to be gotten rid of. She looked . . . bored. Yeah, that was it. Like she was wishing something would happen to stir things up.

"She's just restless," I said to Ophelia.

"What does that exactly mean?"

Ophelia was the one who was amazing in English, but even though I was the smart-in-math-and-science person, I knew more words than she did. I was her private dictionary.

"You know, like when you're in church and the sermon's going on forever and you wish somebody would doze off in the pew and fall out into the aisle. Just to liven things up."

"Do you actually do that in church?"

"About 50 percent of the time."

I had actually calculated it. I figured paying attention half the time was more than most people did. I'd seen a lot of them at Emmanuel Church look like Kylie did.

"I don't think we need to stress about Winnie," I said. "Kylie'll be picking on somebody else soon. Like exactly now."

Kylie was watching Evelyn Gottlieb dump her empty plate in the trash. Evelyn had obviously sat on a package of mustard, and it kind of looked like she didn't make it to the bathroom in time. A howl went up from the Pack that got everybody in the whole lunchroom looking to see what was going down.

Ophelia plastered her hand over her mouth. "Poor Evelyn. She doesn't even know."

"Somebody oughta tell her."

But Mrs. Collier-Callahan, our math teacher, was already leading her out the side door. Evelyn still looked clueless, but in a minute she was going to turn the color of a raspberry—as only Evelyn could—and probably start breathing like The Little Engine That Could.

I decided it was a good thing we had English after lunch, because Mrs. Fickus barely let us talk at all, much less laugh. Hopefully by then the Alpha Wolf and her Pack would get distracted by their lip gloss or something and forget about Evelyn's mustard pants and Winnie's homeless situation and, oh, yeah, my unibrow.

"I bet one of the BBAs put that in her chair," Ophelia said.

That was our name for the group of boys in our section who spent most of their time Burping, Belching, and making disgusting noises with their Armpits.

"Yeah," I said. "Did you know the reason boys don't mature as fast as girls is that the two sides of their brain don't come together at the same rate ours do?"

"I don't even know what that means," Ophelia said.

"It means—"

"Here comes Winnie. Don't talk about you-know-what."

Winnie dropped herself into her chair—without the napkins—and stared down at her peanut butter and jelly sandwich.

"I hate them," she said.

So much for not talking about it.

"When I walked past their table, Riannon said I smelled like the inside of the Goodwill store."

"Like she's ever even been in one," I said.

Ophelia glared at me and put her arm around Winnie's shoulders. "You've got us," she said. "Remember?"

I knew the crying was about to start, so I looked over at the Pack. They looked right back. Heidi and Riannon and Izzy dared me with their eyes. Shelby, speaking of pretending, acted like she suddenly noticed a hangnail on her pinkie. Kylie simply twitched her perfect eyebrows. I could just about hear her saying, *What are you going to do about it?*

Ophelia's voice went into that singsong thing that happened when she was trying to cheer everybody up.

"Do you have your essays ready?"

She bugged her big brown eyes at me, which meant, *Work with me here.*

"I do," I said. "I hope we don't have to write any more for the whole rest of the semester. They're so lame. Who *cares* what kind of animal you think you look like?"

Ophelia gave a giggle that was about as real as the hamburger I'd just eaten. "I bet Kylie wrote she was a French poodle or something."

"I'm pretty sure she didn't describe herself as an Alpha Wolf," I said.

Winnie finally smiled. "I said I was a rabbit."

"Perfect!" Phee said.

But that circled-in-red day was far from over. Kylie and the Pack were still looking around the cafeteria like *everyone* was a rabbit and they were on the prowl. What had made them so hungry all of a sudden?

Chapter Two

Most of our six teachers let us talk while they took roll, but Mrs. Fickus wanted us working "bell to bell" in fifth period. When she announced that the first day of school—and in her Southern accent, it sounded like "bayul to bayul"—Andrew Scofield, one of the BBAs, went "ding-ding." And Mrs. Fickus said, "Bless your heart, Andrew, you're having lunch with me tomorrow." After that, he and Patrick O'Conner and Douglas Underhill saved their BBA activities for other classes.

Today Mrs. Fickus told us to get out our essays, and I was all ready to turn mine in—two typed pages thanks to Ophelia's coaching—when she drawled, "Today I'm going to ask several people to read theirs aloud."

"To the class?" Shelby Ryan said.

Even though Shelby was one of her friends, Kylie rolled her eyes all the way up into her head. "Who else are you going to read it out loud to?" she said.

The rest of the Pack laughed, and Shelby looked like she wanted to disappear into a rabbit hole.

"Sarcasm is the lowest form of humor, Miss Steppe," Mrs. Fickus said.

The one and only reason I liked it that she called us *Miss* and *Mr.* was because Kylie's name came out "misstep." Nobody else really got it. I didn't point it out to Kylie.

Of course, Kylie's name didn't go up on the board. It kind of looked like Mrs. Fickus wanted to say the same thing to Shelby herself.

While Winnie was asking for a pass to the nurse, which I couldn't blame her for doing, Ophelia slid a piece of purple paper to the edge of her desk. *How come she always gets away with stuff?* it said in her curlicue handwriting.

I shook my head. I hadn't figured that out either. It didn't seem like it was worth my time.

"Miss Taylor, since you are unusually animated today, let's start with you."

My entire body jerked toward Mrs. Fickus. She was standing so close to me I could see her blue eyeliner and the cracks in her rosy lipstick, but I still said, "Me?"

"You *are* the only Miss Taylor we have in this class."

Yeah. And the only Miss Taylor who hated to talk in front of people more than she hated hearing the BBAs burp the Pledge of Allegiance. About 90 percent more.

But I didn't argue with Mrs. Fickus. (A) I'd never had lunch detention, and I wasn't planning to ever. (B) I didn't argue with teachers. There were plenty of times when I wanted to. I was actually really good at it. But my mother was always telling me that arguing wouldn't make me welcome in most conversations.

She was right about that. Younger kids stared at me like I was nuts when I told them things like atoms are made of quarks. People way older than me got that "isn't she precocious" expression on their faces. People my age rolled their eyes. Early that year when the eye rolling got, like, out of control, I stopped arguing with most people. I just argued in my head.

And right then, as I carried my essay up to the front of the room, I was silently explaining to Mrs. Fickus that I was exactly the opposite of the person who should be first to read their paper out loud, because I wasn't going to set the standard very high. She was a Southerner, the kind that got her hair done at the salon every week. Surely she would have mercy on me if I . . .

But the way she tugged her jacket into place and tapped her seashell-colored nails on her sleeves, I didn't bother.

My knees were actually banging against each other, trying to take each other out, so I was glad I got to stand behind the podium. But my paper was already so damp with sweat from my hands, I could hardly peel the pages apart.

By the time I finished wiping my palms on my jeans and clearing my throat and taking enough breaths to hyperventilate, Mrs. Fickus's eyebrows were pinching together. Talk about a unibrow . . .

"Miss Taylor, is there a problem?"

All I could do was shake my head.

"Then let's get started. This is only a fifty-minute class period."

Somebody snickered in the back. At least it wasn't a howl.

I started to read.

"I checked myself out in the mirror and tried to see what animal looked back at me. I've divided this into features."

I could feel tiny beads of perspiration popping out on my upper lip, but words were actually coming out of my mouth, so I went on.

"Hair. I looked up synonyms for 'brown' in the thesaurus, and the closest to mine was 'cocoa.' Probably the dark chocolate kind, not like Nestlé's. I have a chocolate lab named Nestlé, and we don't have the same color hair. It's thick—mine, not my dog's. My mom says thick is good because hers isn't and requires a lot of product. I looked up *requires*, and I don't think that's true, but I don't argue with my mom that much."

I took a swipe at my upper lip with my tongue and continued. "Back to my hair. My mom keeps it cut in a bob, and I've had adults tell me they wish they had hair like mine. I never know what to say when they tell me that. My mom says 'thank you' is fine, but that seems sort of conceited. So mostly I shrug. My mom doesn't like when I do that, but that's a whole other subject. There is no animal resemblance to my hair."

That snicker erupted from the back of the room again, but Mrs. Fickus snuffed it out with a snap of her fingers. Personally, I didn't see anything funny about my essay, but then it didn't take much to amuse a BBA.

I cleared my throat, blinked down at my paper, and froze.

"Eyebrows," it said.

I could skip this part and go straight to the section about my eyes. Nobody would know. Except Mrs. Fickus later, and then she'd take off on my grade, and my A in English was tottery enough as it was. Nobody would take a chance on howling in here anyway, right?

I gripped the edges of the page. "Eyebrows. They match my hair. I've noticed that not everybody's do. It's about genes, I think, which is something I want to study. My eyebrows are getting thicker, and that makes sense because my hair is thick." I was almost through it. No snickers. No howls. I could do this. "Since not that many animals actually have eyebrows, I moved on to eyes."

I didn't know why I chose that moment to look up. I regretted it the minute I saw the five red, bloated faces all the spitting image of Bob the Tomato as the Wolf Pack held back guffaws.

"Is that all?" Mrs. Fickus said, dragging the *all* into three syllables.

There was clearly a D in her tone. I shook my head, and my lips went into hyperdrive.

"Eyes. My eyes are dark brown and small and shiny. Here's where the animal part comes in. In science last year, we had to keep a list of birds I saw in my backyard, which was almost like cheating because my mom has like fifty bird feeders and I'm not even kidding. I got my dad's binoculars and what I noticed is that my eyes are like theirs. Small and bright and shiny and sort of darty. I wish I had a bird's-eye view like they do, but I'll save that in case we do an essay on what kind of animal I *wish* I was."

I dragged in a breath and refused to look up. I didn't have to. I could hear Heidi's laugh spurting out of her nostrils.

Only Mrs. Fickus's grading gaze kept me going. "Nose. This is where the animal comparison kind of doesn't work. My nose is definitely not a beak. Okay, maybe on a cardinal. I looked it up because we don't have cardinals here, and their beaks are small and kind of turn under like mine does. Theirs are yellow though, and mine isn't. The other thing about my nose is I have a superstrong sense of smell. I know somebody who once lived in my room kept peanut butter in there because it smells so much like it I can almost taste it sometimes. My mom tells me it's my imagination, but as you yourself have said to me, Mrs. Fickus, my imagination muscle is underdeveloped."

I had to stop because I couldn't breathe. Neither could most of the class, evidently. I could feel every single person choking and wheezing so they wouldn't end up in detention. As for me, it was almost worth it to go there right now.

Except that I caught Ophelia out of the corner of my eye. Her face was red, too, only it wasn't from trying to keep from laughing. She was mad. For me. That was the only thing that kept me reading.

"Mouth. I'm just going to go ahead and say it: my mouth is really big, sort of like a baby robin when it opens its beak to get the worm from the mom. It's like too big for its little face. I know this because a mother robin built a nest in our camellia bush last spring, and the ground was still hard from all the cold weather, so my mother went to Safeway and got fishing worms and put some out every day for the mom so she could feed her three kids. Robins grow into their beaks. I haven't grown into my mouth yet."

Half the class let go of their air and collapsed. "Howling" didn't even begin to describe it.

"Now that is enough!" Mrs. Fickus said.

They squeezed themselves back into silence. Mrs. Fickus nodded her helmet head at me.

I looked down at my final paragraph. "The rest of me," I'd written. Thank *heaven* I hadn't used the word *body* or Mrs. Fickus would never have gotten the class back under control.

"I obviously don't have bird wings," I read, "but I'm kind of skinny, so when I stand up really straight my shoulder blades sort of look like wings. I do stand up straight because I'm a little bit taller than average and Granna (that's my grandmother) always tells me not to slump but to be proud of my height. I'll probably get taller because I need to grow into my big bird feet. I wear almost the same size shoe as my mom. But I won't be wearing any of her shoes. We have way different taste in clothes."

Two more sentences.

"So that's how I'm like a bird and not like a bird. And now I'm going to fly off to something else."

I wasn't kidding. I flew back to my seat and sat there so still I didn't even inhale. The only thing moving on me was the sweat trailing down the sides of my face.

Two more people were called up to read, but I didn't hear anything they said.

Actually, I didn't see how anybody else really could either because there was so much grunting and squeaking and asthma-breathing going on as the Pack and the BBAs tried to keep from spewing all over the room.

Two things occurred to me. (A) Nobody had ever laughed at me like that before. If they did, I didn't know it, which is just as good as not having it happen. But (B) they didn't just laugh at *me*. I knew it wasn't all that nice of me, but I was relieved that they laughed at everybody.

That was, until Mrs. Fickus called Miss Iann up to read.

Michelle was the toughest kid in the whole sixth grade, not just our section. That was probably why she was called Mitch. She even called herself that.

I had done a study of Mitch, and I knew why she was the toughest.

(A) She was a head taller than everybody else, especially the boys who were all shrimps anyway.

(B) She hardly ever smiled. Not because she was mad but because it was like she knew adult stuff, so what was there to smile about?

(C) Once, back in third grade, she punched a boy in the face because he called her little brother a "retard." Nobody had messed with her since.

The room got quiet as a funeral. Mitch stood behind the podium and folded her arms across her 49ers sweatshirt and scowled at her paper.

"I'm like a bear," she read. "I'm big, but I can move fast, especially if somebody threatens what I care about. I can smell trouble, and I avoid it if I can. I would sleep all winter if I could. If I'm just allowed to do my own thing and take care of my own stuff, I'm cool."

She lifted her head of spiky brown hair that I was now convinced was grizzly fur and gave the room a look that would have had everybody hiding under their desks if Mrs. Fickus hadn't been there.

"The end."

Nobody laughed. Nobody ever laughed at Mitch.

For the first time ever, I envied her.

Yeah, it was a day that needed to be circled on a calendar, and it wasn't over yet.

~

Actually, I forgot 99 percent of that suitable-for-circling afternoon when my mom took off from work sooner than usual and my dad said we were going to Cirino's for an early dinner.

That was *only* my favorite restaurant in all of Grass Valley, California. Nothing like eggplant parmesan done Sicilian style to make your whole day disappear. Halfway into it, when my stomach was starting to get that bulgy feeling, if you'd mentioned the name Kylie Steppe, I would have said, "Who?"

"Not hungry, are you, Tor?" my dad said.

"I find it highly unfair that she can eat like that and still stay slim as a pencil," Granna said.

She was joining us, of course, and she was late as always. Granna lived across the street at the Bret Harte, which used to be a big fancy hotel, like from 1917 until 1984, and was now a senior residence. I knew that because my dad liked to quiz me on Grass Valley history.

I personally didn't think Granna was old enough to live in a place where everybody else walked with canes and talked too loud and had hair so thin you could see their pink scalps. Sure, she had a messy gray bun, but she always wore comfy pants and shirts with sayings on them and dangly earrings. That night they were ice-cream cones and her T-shirt said, "Oh, Happy Day!" How could you be like that and be old at the same time?

As always she kissed me on the top of my head and said, "Victoria, my pet." I couldn't remember when she didn't do that.

"Mom, it's forty degrees." Dad tilted his head of bushy brown-turning-gray hair. He sort of looked like a bird too. A big one. Maybe an eagle. "Why are you wearing shorts?" he said.

"I wanted to show Victoria my tattoo," Granna said.

I watched my mother's eyes bulge like green marbles. "Your tattoo?"

Granna's eyes, small and brown and birdish like mine, twinkled at me. Wait for it . . . wait for it . . . yeah, there was the wink. That meant, *Play along with me.* I always did.

Granna slid into the booth beside me and rolled the bottom of her khaki shorts up a cuff. For a second I thought the outline of an ice-cream sundae was a real tattoo, so I didn't have to do much acting at first.

"Are you serious?" Mom said.

"As a case of pneumonia," Granna said. She nudged me with her leg.

"Tori, tell me she's not serious."

I nodded, eyes on the really good press-on that was still fresh. That was why Granna was late this time.

"She's serious," I said.

"What did you get, Mom?" Dad said. "A rose?"

Granna cackled. "Do I look like the rose type to you?"

"Come on, Tori, I mean it," Mom said. "What is it?"

"Ice cream. It's so real I want to eat it."

My mother actually got her small self up on her knees on the other side of the booth and peered across the table. I thought her eyes were going to pop out of her head until she figured it out.

"You are both incorrigible," she said and sank back into her seat. She had dragged her white sweater through her lasagna, but I wasn't going to be the one to inform her.

Dad was chuckling.

"I don't see the humor," Mom said, poking him.

"You never see the humor at this time of year," he said.

She sighed. "Why did I ever go into the floral business?"

"Because you're crazy for flowers," Granna said. "You get this way every Valentine's season. February fifteenth you'll be all hyped up about Easter lilies."

That was true, although I'd give it until at least the sixteenth, depending on whether my dad was home or not.

He traveled a lot for work, and Mom was always in a better mood when he was in town. It was like she had a lightbulb inside her face that only turned on when he was around.

Right now her curly, sand-colored hair sagged around her face, which I guessed meant the product had worn off. She had little puffs of bluish skin under her eyes too. But the lightbulb was on, and even brighter than usual.

After Granna placed an order for tiramisu—she always ate her dessert first—I found out what was going on.

"Ladies," Dad said, "I'm going to be home for a while."

"Define *a while*." I glanced at my mom's frown and added, "Please."

"Probably about six months," Dad said. "I've been hired as a consultant on a documentary film on the Empire Mine."

"How perfect is that?" Mom said. I was pretty sure I saw another bulb light up.

It *was* perfect actually, because—

(A) The old Empire Mine that had produced gold for over a hundred years was just on the other side of our back fence, only now it was a historic park and museum.

(B) My dad did history for a living and knew, like, everything about California history. Whenever anybody was making a movie or something about the eighteen hundreds, they hired him to tell them if they were messing up the facts.

And (C) he knew more about the Second Gold Rush than anybody. I looked it up on the Internet once. Dr. Nathan Taylor was the "leading expert."

"I'll be working from home—"

"So I'll be quiet when I get home from school," I said.

"And I'm hiring an assistant, but you probably won't see much of her. We'll be up in my office."

We had a big "bonus room" on our second floor that was Dad's office and library. I had my own curl-up chair in there, but it didn't sound like I'd be visiting him while his assistant was working. I hoped she found her own place to curl up.

Then I felt bad for thinking that. Dad was finally going to be home like other people's dads. And he was the best of anybody's that I knew.

He rubbed his hands together. "I want this film to be about more than just the six million dollars' worth of gold that came out of there."

"That sounds like plenty to talk about to me." Mom smiled at him. Although her mouth wasn't big like mine and Dad's and Granna's, she had a smile that made everybody else want to smile too, especially when she was grinning at Dad.

"Will you bring in something about Lola Montez?" Granna said the way she did every time we talked Grass Valley history.

Both my parents glared at her. Granna nudged me with her elbow, which meant, *Let's get them.*

"We don't need to talk about Lola," Mom said.

"I think Victoria's old enough."

"Mom, *you* aren't even old enough." Dad broke into another chuckle. "Okay, who's up for a history quiz?"

"Not me," Mom said. "My brain is fried."

That didn't stop Dad. "Where was the first flush toilet in Grass Valley installed?"

"Lola's house," Granna said, nudging me again.

"I pass," Mom said.

"Tori?" Dad said.

I smiled smugly. "The Conaway House on South Auburn Street."

Dad and I bumped fists above the table.

"Is the original toilet still there, though?" I said.

"Do you think?"

"No, it would probably smell really gross by now."

"Lovely." Mom looked at Dad. "You realize you are undoing all of my hard work to turn her into a lady."

An image of my eyebrows growing together jumped into my head. No, I definitely wasn't lady material, and I didn't see that as a problem.

"I say we celebrate with dessert." Dad peered at Granna's empty plate. She was currently licking her fingers. "How was the tiramisu?"

"Better than average," Granna said. "You two enjoy. I want to take Tori to the Lazy Dog."

"Two desserts in one night? I can't depend on you to help me turn Tori into a lady either, can I?" Mom said.

Nope. And I was so okay with that.

It was a perfect Grass Valley winter evening. The sky was the kind of dark, sink-into-it blue I'd never seen anyplace else but there, and the air wasn't so much cold as just crispy. There was just enough breeze to stir some gray hairs loose from Granna's bun and make the pine needles whisper. Grass Valley was full of the tallest evergreens ever—except maybe in the Redwood Forest—and they talked all the time.

"It's an exquisite night for a walk," Granna said and kissed me on top of my head again.

Arms hooked together, we strode—there was no other word to use—down the sidewalk on Main to Mill Street, straight toward the Lazy Dog, which had the best chocolate and ice cream on the entire planet.

Granna read from a sign over a new hair salon that had just opened on Mill. "'Be Transformed.'" She chuckled, just the way Dad did, only a little higher. "If I went in there they'd say, 'Sorry, we don't do embalming.'"

"Granna, that's not true!" I said. "You don't look dead. Not even close."

"You always say exactly the right thing, Victoria."

We took seventeen minutes picking out our ice cream and toppings. At least Granna did. I only needed seventeen *seconds* to order two scoops of mint chocolate chip on a waffle cone like usual. Granna always wanted to try something new.

While she was picking out her sprinkles practically one by one, I wandered toward the front of the store to check out the chocolate shapes. Since it was getting close to Valentine's Day, there were a lot of hearts and cupids, but I liked the animals myself. One looked exactly like Nestlé, and Granna would've bought it for me, but I wouldn't be able to bite off his head.

I was on my way to the major jelly bean selection when the bell rang on the door and two people swept in. There was no other way to describe how Kylie Steppe and her mother came into the Lazy Dog. Scarves were flying and shopping bags with tissue paper sticking out of them were rustling, and Mrs. Steppe was swooshing toward the ice-cream counter talking with her arms.

"Pick out what you want," she said. "I'm going to pass. I don't need the calories."

That was a lie. Kylie's mother was so skinny I could see her collarbone sticking out.

"What are you staring at?"

I jumped, nearly losing my top scoop. That would've been the exact wrong thing to do in front of Kylie, who was already looking at me like I was a case of pimples. It made the hair on the back of my neck stand straight up.

"I wasn't staring at anything," I said.

"You were looking at my mom like there's something wrong with her."

I decided not to say, *You mean like she's starving to death?* What would be the point?

"I think there's something wrong with *you,*" Kylie said.

"You ready, Victoria, my pet?"

Granna was suddenly at my elbow holding a supersized sundae with enough whipped cream for all three of us *and* Kylie's mom, who needed it.

Kylie stared at it and then at Granna. When her blue and gold eyes came back to me, her lips were twitching. I couldn't hold it back any longer.

"What?" I said.

"Kylie, do you want ice cream or not?"

Kylie rolled those eyes in the direction of her mother and brushed past me. Out of the side of her mouth, she said, "Victoria, my *pet*?"

It sounded so wrong coming from her lips, suddenly I didn't want my double cone anymore.

But I carried it as I followed Granna back to Main Street and we started down the hill. Normally we would have stopped at every old-timey shop window and analyzed the display. But as soon as we had the Lazy Dog behind us, Granna said, "Do you want to talk about it?"

"Yes," I said, and blurted out the whole thing about Kylie and the Winnie rumors. When I was done, my ice cream was dripping all over my hand.

"You lick, I'll talk," Granna said.

I almost melted with relief, right along with the mint chocolate chip. I could already imagine telling Ophelia exactly what we were going to do for Winnie because Granna said so.

I started in on the sides of the scoops. Granna stopped us on the sidewalk and pointed up at the building in front of us.

"One Sixteen West Main Street," she said. "You know what this was, of course."

I shook my head. This was one of the few buildings Dad hadn't told me the complete history of before I could even read.

Granna made a sound like *tsk-tsk*. "Your father has sadly neglected your historical education." She winked. "This was home to the Lola Montez Theater in the 1930s and '40s."

Lola Montez? I thought we were going to talk about Kylie Steppe and Winnie George.

"I know your parents don't want me sharing what I know about Lola," Granna said as we moved on. "I'm not going to tell you anything rated PG-13 but just to be on the safe side . . ." Her eyes twinkled at me. "What happens with Granna stays with Granna. Okay?"

"Okay," I said, "but—"

"Lola Montez was her stage name. She was actually the Countess of Lansfeld, but that didn't fit her reputation as a dancer. They say her famous Spider Dance was sensational. She performed it all over the world, including here in Grass Valley—right back there at what was then the Alta."

I was still confused, but I had to ask, "What was a Spider Dance?"

"Something the miners liked, that's for sure." The lines at the corners of Granna's eyes crinkled. "The theater was always packed out, and she'd bring in a thousand dollars a show after expenses. That was a lot of money back then."

It sounded like a lot of money now. Still—

"The story has it that the applause drowned out the racket of the stamp mills over at the mine. That's loud."

I stopped trying to interrupt. Granna was going to finish this story. And *then* she'd tell me what I was supposed to do with it. I kept licking.

"There's a picture of her over at the Grass Valley Museum," Granna said. "She was a pretty thing and very calculating."

My ears perked up. "You mean she was good at math like me?"

"She certainly had everybody's number."

Huh?

"Men would visit her at her cottage—it's now the Chamber of Commerce—and they'd find themselves greeted at the door by her pet grizzly."

"She had a bear in her house?" I couldn't help thinking of Mitch.

"She did indeed."

I was starting to like this woman. But I still didn't get it.

"Granna, no offense," I said, "but what does this have to do with what I'm supposed to do about the Winnie situation?"

Granna scraped her plastic spoon at the bottom of the sundae that had somehow disappeared while she talked. "Here's what you need to remember about Lola. Rumors flew about her all the time. Some of it was based in truth; she did have some interesting escapades. But most of it was out of pure spite because Lola dared to be different."

"What did she do about the rumors?" I said.

Granna smiled as if she and Lola had been BFFs. "She just *kept* daring to be different. Now if I don't take you back to Cirino's before it gets dark, I'm going to lose my Victoria privileges. And we can't have that, can we?"

I shook my head—but really? I was as disappointed as I was confused. This was one thing I didn't think I could figure out. And smart as I was, I could usually figure out just about anything.

~

Okay, so there were *two* things I couldn't figure out. The other one was why the unibrow thing kept coming back to me. So I asked my dog Nestlé about it later, after homework. He was lying on the floor with his head on the turtle pillow I gave him because Mom wouldn't let me have him up on the bed. Sometimes I did it anyway, but she always knew.

Dad said mothers have an extra sense that non-mothers don't have, but I didn't think that had been scientifically proven. Mom said the pillow smelled like dog. Well—

(A) Nestlé *was* a dog—and

(B) What was so bad about that smell? It was one of my favorites, right up there with pencils that had just been sharpened and Mom's blackberry cobbler.

"None of those smells is 'ladylike,' Nestlé," I said. "You couldn't make a perfume out of them."

He only moved his eyes to look up at me. I slid off the bed and onto the floor so he could see me better.

"I'm serious," I said. "What do you think about my eyebrows?"

He sniffed my hands. There must have been a miniscule speck of mint chocolate chip left because he licked until I thought my fingerprints were going to come off.

"I'm not sure I can depend on your opinion about these things. I read my essay to you last night, and you didn't laugh at it. You wagged your tail—but that's not laughing at me."

He wagged it now, like a stick thwacking the floor. He could also clear a coffee table with it.

"You know what I can't figure out? I can't figure out why Kylie and the Pack are all of a sudden sniffing out me and Winnie and Evelyn and anyone they can get their claws into. I thought they were bored, y'know, but who gets bored walking into the Lazy Dog? It doesn't bother me that much. It's just weird."

Nestlé rested his head on my leg, sighed, and closed his eyes. I could feel the drool oozing into my pajamas.

"Okay, so it kind of bugged me when they were all laughing at my paper," I said. "Who wants to be laughed at, right? Good thing you never do that."

He rolled onto his back and stuck his legs straight up into the air. I scratched his belly.

"All right, so I laugh when you get peanut butter stuck in the roof of your mouth, but that's different."

He moaned. I decided that meant he agreed.

So I crawled into bed and thanked God *that* day was finally over.

Yeah, well, little did I know that day had already started changing everything.

Chapter Three

The next day, Tuesday, I was still trying to decide how I was supposed to tell Winnie to dare to be different. Winnie never dared to do anything. She picked the right topic for her essay because she did remind me of a little white rabbit sometimes. She could hardly go to the restroom alone. Lola Montez she was not.

So I was starting the day with a bad 'tude.

That was our P.E. teacher Mr. Zabriski's word. He used it on people who got lazy running around the track.

"Let's watch those 'tudes, people!" he'd yell.

It took me a whole first period one day to figure out he meant "attitudes."

I was pretty glad that this semester our physical education class was devoted to "Getting a Healthy Start" and that Mr. Zabriski's wife was teaching it. I liked being away from his yelling.

It didn't help my 'tude that on my way to our before-school meeting place, I had to pass the Pack's "den," which was right inside the front entrance by an old trophy case nobody looked into anymore.

I always thought it didn't make sense to be on display like the trophies if you wanted to talk about private stuff. But I guess it worked for them because when the Pack didn't want anybody else to know what they were saying, they just turned their bodies into this tight little knot and everybody knew not to get within three yards of them. Not that I ever wanted to anyway. They never looked like they were having that much fun.

That day I heard the words "new girl" spoken by the Alpha Wolf as if she were tasting mud.

"Did you *see* her?" Kylie said to the girls knotted around her.

"I did," Izzy said. She was a little rounder than Kylie's other friends and right now her cheeks were neon red, the way Ophelia's little sister Juliet's were before they discovered she had a milk allergy. "I was in the office when her dad checked her in."

All eyes turned to Izzy. I made my way ultra slowly up the steps so I could listen. I wasn't sure why I was doing that. I just did it.

"She has the greasiest hair," Izzy said. "It's like she hasn't washed it in like a week. Maybe more. And—"

"I *know.*" I glanced down to see Kylie's eyes flash. "And she's wearing this sweatshirt that comes down to her knees. And she talks like this—REALLY LOUD!"

"Nuh-uh!" Shelby said.

Riannon pointed herself at Shelby. Everything about Riannon was pointy so that wasn't hard for her to do. Her eyes were green—way greener than my mom's because she wore contacts that I was pretty sure were tinted to look like they came out of Emerald City—and when she drilled them at somebody, it was like they got closer together over her nose.

"Kylie wouldn't say it if it wasn't true," she said to Shelby.

"I know—"

"What's her name?" Heidi wrinkled her little pug nose and said it like Shelby hadn't even started her sentence. Huh. Members of the Pack could even be invisible to each other.

Speaking of being invisible, it felt like it was time for me to get out of sight before they caught me lurking. As I rounded the bend in the stairs, I heard Izzy say, "I didn't hear what her name was," and Kylie say, "Who *cares*? She's probably not even going to be in our section. She's probably special ed."

I felt bad for the new girl with the greasy hair and the loud voice. But it sure sounded like the spotlight was going to be off Winnie that day. My 'tude improved 88 percent.

~

I was right. And Kylie, it turned out, was wrong.

I was right because Winnie became nonexistent again as far as the Pack was concerned. No one glanced at my eyebrows again either. We were Saran Wrap again.

As for the new girl, she *was* in our section. Mrs. Zabriski introduced her to our health class as Ginger Hollingberry, and the BBAs laughed like a trio of orangutans, which made no sense to me. What made even less sense was that Ginger laughed this sort of burro laugh right along with them.

In fact, she didn't act in any way like you'd expect a new girl to. Even though she did have flat reddish hair that could've done with some of Mom's product (starting with shampoo), and she wore a faded navy blue sweatshirt that must have been her dad's, and she talked like we all needed hearing aids, she didn't seem like she (A) knew any of that about herself or (B) realized it made her totally different from everybody else in the room.

All Ginger did was laugh when nothing was funny and raise her hand to answer questions she didn't know the answers to and ask questions *everybody* knew the answers to. Exactly twelve times louder than anyone else.

Talk about daring to be different.

Between third and fourth periods, when I was at my locker, I turned around to find Ginger about five inches from my face. Jeepers, the breath. Listerine, anyone?

"Hi," I said.

"Hi," Ginger said back.

"I'm trying to meet everybody in the class." She moved even closer. "Are you Lori?"

"Tori," I said.

"Oh. That's cool."

She didn't show any signs of moving, so I said, "And you're Ginger."

"Yeah. My real name's Virginia, but they call me Ginger. Because of my red hair."

"Mine's really Victoria," I said.

"Oh. We're both Vs. That's cool."

I wondered if there was anything she didn't think was cool. Including getting right into somebody's space and yet still yelling like Granna's friends down at the Bret Harte.

"The bell's gonna ring," I said. "You know the way to the science room?"

"Yeah," she said. "I'll show you."

She took off down the hall like *I* was the new kid. I'd lived in Grass Valley since I was one, so I didn't know how I would've acted in her place. But I made a note to self: *if I ever am the new kid, don't get all up in people's grill work.*

For the next two days, some people were polite to her and then ran the other way, including me. The BBAs laughed right in her face, and she acted like it was all hilarious. As for Kylie and the Wolf Pack, they acted like whatever was "wrong" with Ginger was contagious. And still Ginger didn't get it.

Until the next day in science class.

~

Mr. V was the cool teacher. We all called him Mr. V because no one else could pronounce his last name.

Vasiliev.

I never saw what was so hard about it. It was *Vas*—rhymed with *mass*—and *il*—like when you're sick, you know, *ill*—then *eee*—rhymed with *bee*—and *ev*—like in *whatev. Vas-ill-ee-ev.*

I would've called him that because I thought he'd be impressed, but I knew for a fact that would set the BBAs off. Within seconds, they'd be burping it—*Vas-ill-ee-ev*—and that was just wrong.

Mr. V caught the soccer ball some people were throwing around and tossed it between his hands as he perched on his high stool. He didn't demand absolute silence like Mrs. Fickus, but most people paid attention to Mr. V just because. I was one of those.

He smiled a lot, but his grin never looked the same twice. I guess that was because (A) his mouth was sort of like elastic and (B) he didn't try to keep it under control like most teachers did.

"Don't you think Mr. V's hot?" I'd heard Kylie ask her Pack at least fifty-one times.

I wasn't even sure a teacher could be hot, but I didn't bother telling *her* that.

"Hold your applause when I announce this," Mr. V said now. "It's time for another small-group project."

The BBAs whistled and clapped, and not because they loved doing small group projects. Just because Mr. V said not to.

"Yay!" Ophelia said to me. "I love these!"

"We're gonna be a group, right?" Winnie said. Winnie needed a lot of us telling her everything was okay these days. Probably because everything was not okay at Grandma's house.

"Are you serious? Of course we are!" Ophelia said with exclamation points. The three of us were always a group—plus one.

I couldn't wait to see what the assignment was. Science was my absolute favorite subject, because (A) everything had a reason and (B) I could always figure out what it was and (C) it was 100 percent logical, so you never really had to argue about the results. No shrugging needed.

Last time Mr. V said, "Choose a body system and find out everything you can about it." So our group picked the nervous system because it's the most complicated. Of course the BBAs chose the excretory system so they could talk about poop. The Pack took the skin, and all they talked about in their presentation was zits and how to prevent them. (Like any of them had ever had or would ever have a zit in their lives. Probably another one of those requirements for being in the Pack.)

"I think this calls for a drumroll," Mr. V said now.

We turned our index fingers into drumsticks and hammered on our desks. Back in BBA world, it sounded like a rock band going out of control.

Mr. V put his hand up, and it mostly stopped. I leaned forward in my desk, actually holding my breath.

Wait for it . . .

"This is a little different from your other projects."

I could do different.

"I want your group to ask a question about . . ."

He hopped off the stool, dropped the soccer ball on his desk, and went to the dry-erase board. He was killin' me.

He wrote with a thick orange marker, and the class read the words as they took shape.

"The . . . human . . . being . . . dot-dot (they actually said *dot-dot* instead of *colon)*: mind . . . or . . . body."

The class was totally silent for the first time since . . . well, never.

"Your question has to be something you don't already know the answer to," Mr. V said. "Your assignment is to discover that answer and present it to the class."

He rolled the marker between his palms and grinned at us. Personally, I didn't know what he was smiling about. That had to be the worst assignment ever.

Heidi raised her hand. She was looking at Kylie, who was mouthing words to her.

"What is she, a ventriloquist?" Ophelia whispered to me.

"Heidi!" Mr. V said. He always smiled biggest when somebody asked a question.

"This is probably a lame question—"

Douglas snorted. "Probably."

"Shut *up*!" Heidi said to him. Which, from what I'd observed before, meant "I love that you noticed me."

Barf.

"The term 'lame question' is an oxymoron," Mr. V said.

Heidi looked at him with nothing on her face for a second and then tossed her hair back. "Okay, whatever. We don't get it."

"I get it!" Ginger waved her entire arm like we did in kindergarten when we all wanted to be the first one to recite the alphabet.

Patrick held his nose. Mr. V just smiled at her.

"Tell us what you get, Ginger."

"Well," she said in her usual megaphone voice, "you want us to explore and think and not just regurg . . . reglug . . . I forget the word, but you don't want us to just find out facts and vomit them out."

"Gro-oss!" Kylie said. She turned to the Pack with her hands spread out like, "Did she seriously say that in front of me?"

"*Regurgitate* is the word you're looking for," Mr. V said, his eyes doing some kind of fun dance. "And you are exactly right, Ginger. This not a report." He looked at the whole class. "This is a study, and I want you to do it on something you really want to know more about."

"What if we already know everything we wanna know about the human body?" Douglas said. The look he gave Patrick and Andrew was a big clue that he was thinking something disgusting.

"Then ask something about the mind," Mr. V said.

"Huh?"

Mr. V let one side of his mouth go up. "Don't you want to know how girls think?"

Douglas's face lit up. "Hey, can that be our question?"

"You'll have to refine it some but, yeah, you can go with that."

Kylie raised one finger. Picking up her whole arm was obviously too much trouble.

"Kylie?"

"What should our group do?"

"Your group should figure out something awesome."

"Not fair!" Shelby said.

But the Pack shut her up with a unanimous stare. She let her hair-almost-like Kylie's cover her face as she looked down. Her part even turned red.

I would have sat there analyzing how hard it must be to learn and follow all the Pack rules, but I was too jumbled up by Mr. V's assignment. I studied stuff and figured it out all the time—but not for a grade.

"Okay, form your groups and start brainstorming," Mr. V said.

"What if we already got our question?" Patrick said without raising his hand at all.

"I'll be around to approve your question and give you the sheet on how to do your proposal."

"What proposal?" Ginger said, waving half of her body.

Mr. V smiled at her exactly the way he did at Kylie and Heidi and probably his own mom. How did he do that?

"Form your question first. Then I'll explain. But don't drag your feet, guys. The proposal's due by February 17."

Ophelia and Winnie turned their desks toward mine, leaving a space in our circle for Mitch. She was the plus one.

She had joined us on the very first assignment after she walked around the room checking out all the groups.

"I'm working with you guys," she told us back then. "You don't mess around like everybody else."

We let her be in our group because (A) it never occurred to us to say no to Mitch and (B) she always did her share of the work. In every other group, there was at least one kid who just sat around doing nothing and still got credit for the project. Not in ours.

"We doing this like we always do?" Mitch said.

We all nodded.

Our group had a good system. Mitch and I came up with the topic, and then we all did the research, except not so much Ophelia. She went off on too many what my dad called "bunny trails."

Winnie mostly wrote up our report, with some help from Ophelia, but Phee's big part was coming up with a very cool way to present it to the class. She knew not to give me an acting part. Like when we talked for the various parts of the brain, I just held the signs up over their heads.

Everybody else was really good at that, even Mitch, which you wouldn't expect because she didn't say that much the rest of the time. She was scary quiet, until you got to know her some. Still, I was always careful not to argue with *her.*

"So what question are we gonna ask?" Ophelia said, looking at me.

Mitch said something, but whatever it was got drowned out by Ginger's voice.

"There *would* be room if you moved your stuff."

Everybody stopped what they were doing and stared. Ginger was standing just outside the Pack circle, pointing to the chair where someone had dropped a pink-sparkled backpack. Who knew which one of the wolves it belonged to, since they all had matching ones. It was still sliding down in the chair, like somebody had just dropped it there.

"Mr. Vacillate said we could have six in a group and you only have five."

"Mr. *Who*?" Kylie said, not to Ginger but to Riannon.

A laugh came out of Heidi's nose. Let the howling begin.

I looked at Mr. V, but he was sitting with the BBAs, explaining with his hands.

"I need a group," Ginger said.

"Then go find one," Riannon said.

Kylie turned her head so that a panel of dark hair fell across her face as she got her glossy lips close to Riannon. "She's big enough. She could be a group all by herself."

Riannon threw her head back and let her shrill laugh rip.

"Why are you being so mean to me?" Ginger said.

"Because you won't leave us alone unless we, like, spell it out for you," Kylie said.

She nodded to Shelby, who looked at her with her plumped-up lips hanging open for a second before she said to Ginger, "We. Do. Not. Want. You. In. Our. Group."

"That new girl needs to get a thicker skin," Mitch said to *our* group. "Mr. V sure isn't gonna rescue her."

I was suddenly bristly. *It's not his fault!* I wanted to say to her. *He doesn't even know what's going on because the BBAs are taking up all his time. If he knew, he'd stop it.*

But like I said, I didn't argue with Mitch.

A few rows over, Evelyn was waving *both* of her arms. "Mr. Vee-ee, Brittney and I need help!"

"Just keep throwing out ideas," Mr. V said. "You're not going to come up with something right away. This is a higher level of thinking—"

"We have ours, Mr. V," Izzy said.

Kylie smiled, something she almost never did except at boys and teachers, and displayed the Crater Lake dimples. "Come see us, Mr. V."

Evelyn seemed like she wanted to point out that she and Brittney had asked first, but she deflated like a party balloon. Was it just me or was the Pack getting control over everybody?

"Ginger's about to cry," Winnie said.

Mitch didn't even give Ginger a glance. "Yeah, well, like I said, she needs to—"

"Anybody have any ideas?" I said.

Ophelia chewed on her left thumbnail. "I don't think I can do 'higher level of thinking.'"

I wasn't sure I could either. My grades and test scores proved I was smart, but this might be a level I couldn't reach. What if I couldn't do this? Now *that* was weird. Since when did I doubt that I could do just about anything?

Chapter Four

I brainstormed for a study question with Nestlé on Saturday while it rained. Dad was pretending to read but was actually taking a snorey nap in the recliner in the living room, and Mom was at her shop selling people flower arrangements and doing a wedding. It seemed like a depressing day to get married.

It turned out to be a depressing day to do anything. Every idea I came up with was lame. Nestlé didn't even wag his tail when I read him the list:

"Why do guys have low voices and girls have high voices? What's that about?"

"Why doesn't my grandmother's skin fit her anymore?"

"If the appendix doesn't really do anything, why do we have one?"

"Some questions weren't meant to be answered," Dad mumbled from behind *The Maidu Tribe.*

"I have to find one that is," I said. "It's for science class."

While he pried his eyes open I explained our assignment. I had the faint hope that he would call Mr. V and tell him the project was too hard for sixth-graders, but that pretty much died as Dad sat up straighter in the chair and got that *This is phenomenal!* look in his eyes.

So I said, "What should we do?"

Dad tilted his bushy head. "I know what *I* would do. I would ask why the United States government signed peace treaties with the Maidu that guaranteed them large reservations to live on, and then hid the treaties and didn't give the Maidu a single acre of land."

I tried really hard not to roll my eyes. "Dad, that's a history question. I need something about the body or the mind."

"Okay, so how about 'Why do people do bad things?' No, I guess that's a spiritual question."

"Thanks, Dad," I said. "I'm gonna keep working on it. Can I make popcorn?"

The more I thought about it, the worse my ideas were. I told Ophelia about some of them on the phone Saturday night, and she went all drama queen on me. She did that sometimes, probably because her whole family was into acting. She always wanted to try out for parts in the movies my dad consulted on.

"If we get up there and start talking about boys' Adam's apples and stuff, we might as well plan to change schools right after," she said in her theater voice.

"I didn't say we should—"

"And do you know where your appendix *is*"?

"It's down—"

"I'm not gonna point to that in front of those boy creatures, are you?"

"No—"

"And your grandmother's *skin*? What were you *thinking*?"

"Do *you* have any ideas?" I said.

I didn't usually get all prickly with Phee, but jeepers.

"I'm not the idea person." I could almost see her lower lip folding out like a sofa. "I'm the presentation person."

"Well, we gotta think of something to present."

The fuzzy sound of Ophelia sighing came through the phone. "Sorry, Tor. I don't know why I'm all freaked out about this."

"I am too," I said. "And I don't know why either."

~

So that made two questions nagging at me when I sat in church the next day. (A) What were we going to do for this stupid project? and (B) Why was I sifting every idea through what the Pack and the BBAs were going to say filter? A week ago that wouldn't even have crossed my mind.

Granna slid into the pew beside me, tucking me between her and Dad. Of course she kissed me on top of my head and of course she was ten minutes late. Our pastor, who we all called Jake because he didn't want to be called anything else, was already starting the sermon.

"In today's Gospel," he said.

Granna gave me one of her elbow jabs. "What was the Gospel? I missed it."

I could smell why. She had pancake syrup on her breath. They always served a big breakfast at the Bret Harte on Sunday mornings.

"We all know the story of the Good Samaritan . . ."

"Got it." Granna's eyes twinkled at me. "This is one of those 'You tell 'em, Jesus' stories. I like these."

Mom leaned forward on the other side of Dad and gave me a look. Like I was the one talking barely below a street voice in church. I looked at Granna and put a finger to my lips. She nodded like she got it. She usually did. Except when she thought a story about the Spider Dance lady would help me with the Wolf Pack.

Dad nudged me. Was I wearing a sign that said, *Hey, poke me!*?

"See the girl in the third row? Dark hair?" he whispered.

I saw the back of a bunch of curls. "Uh-huh," I whispered back.

"That's Lydia."

"Who's Lydia?"

"My assistant."

"She goes to church here?"

"Looks that way."

Mom shoved her shoulder into Dad's. At least I wasn't the only one getting bruised up.

"Shh," Dad said to me.

Really? *Really?*

It didn't surprise me actually. My parents didn't talk a lot about God at home except for us saying the blessing at the table and Mom telling a friend on the phone that she'd pray for her. But we went to church most Sundays and I was expected to show respect for God by being quiet like a lady and paying attention to what was going on.

Nobody was making it easy that day. Besides all the nudging and poking and jabbing and shushing, Granna kept grunting at whatever Jake was saying. I tried to pay attention, but I got all hung up on whether the Samaritan guy was an actual doctor.

When the service was over, Granna said to me, "Victoria, my pet, I hope you were listening because that was the perfect story for your situation."

I thought Lola Montez was supposed to be my perfect solution. But I said, "Yeah, Granna."

I was relieved that she moved on to where we were going for lunch.

~

It was just as hard to concentrate on coming up with a science project at school as it was at home. That was because the Pack went from acting like Ginger was carrying the H1N1 virus to turning on her like she was their next meal and they were out to take her down. Ophelia and Winnie and I watched it all from our place—where Wolf radar couldn't detect us.

Every morning I'd see them in their den, heads all bent together, going over the day's battle plan. I knew that's what they were up to even though I couldn't hear what they were saying as I hurried up the steps. Maybe I didn't want to.

But I sure saw what they came up with. Everybody did.

Except the teachers.

Izzy and Shelby grabbed Ginger's backpack while she was opening her locker and dumped it into the trash can on top of somebody's rotten banana. Where was Mr. Zabriski with some yelling about 'tudes?

Between classes Ginger ended up with gum in her hair at least three times. Once she had to go to the nurse and came back to fifth period with a small chunk cut out of her already pretty sad do. Mrs. Fickus didn't appear to notice—this the woman who could spot a wrong comma from fifty paces.

The Pack must have had a bunch of inside jokes about Ginger because in science when we were supposed to be working in our groups, Kylie and the rest of them would go wild laughing whenever Ginger looked their way. And Mr. V would say, "I'm glad you're enjoying your project so much, but let's try to keep it down to a roar." Like the rest of the teachers, he just wasn't seeing it.

And it didn't stop even in the cafeteria. Ginger would go by the

Pack, and they would all imitate the way she walked—sort of like a bulldozer—and the way she yelled everything. Then when she turned around they would "forget" to stop doing it and laugh. Only it didn't sound like laughing to me, or even howling. It was more like the sixth-grade version of *neener-neener-neener* we used to do on the playground in first grade.

Thursday at lunch Ginger really lost it.

"Stop it!" she screamed at them.

"Stop what?" Heidi said.

"That! Making fun of me. It hurts my feelings!"

Kylie did an eye roll so dramatic it made Ophelia look like an amateur. "We were just *kidding*," she said. "People don't tease you unless they like you."

Ginger's face brightened up. "You like me?"

"No," Kylie said. And then they all turned away from her at exactly the same second in exactly the same way and neenered until I thought they were all going to pass out.

I wished they would.

When I looked back to see how Ginger was taking it, she was gone.

"That was horrible," Ophelia whispered.

Winnie's eyes were already leaking. "I'm so glad they're not picking on me anymore. I couldn't handle *that.*"

Ophelia put both hands on Winnie's. "They wouldn't. Because you don't bring it on yourself."

I stared at her.

"Ginger kind of does," Ophelia said. "I'm not saying what Kylie and those girls are doing is okay, but it wouldn't be happening if Ginger wasn't so . . . I don't know."

The bell rang, and Ophelia and Winnie gathered up their trash. I just sat there.

"You coming, Tori?" Winnie said.

"Go ahead. I'll be there in a minute," I said.

Ophelia gave my neck a quick squeeze. "Don't be late or Mrs. Fickus'll give you lunch detention."

I didn't answer, but I was thinking I'd rather *have* detention than have to eat watching something like that again. My stomach was doing one belly flop after another.

I pulled my English notebook out of my backpack and tore out a sheet of paper. My pen hovered over it until Mr. Jett called from the doorway, "Let's go, Tori. The bell's about to ring." I scribbled, "Don't pay attention to anything they say," and folded the paper. And then I had no idea what to do with it, so I stuck it into my notebook and took off for fifth period.

My 'tude needed some major adjusting when I got home from school that afternoon. A cup of hot chocolate should take care of that. I was allowed to make it myself as long as I used the microwave.

"It's way better when you heat up the milk on the stove," I told Nestlé as he trailed me down the hall and through the living room and dining room, his toenails clicking on the hardwood parts between the rugs. "Maybe when I'm in seventh grade, Mom will let me—"

Both my mouth and my feet stopped in the kitchen doorway. Nestlé pushed past me and wagged his way over to the curly-haired person who was standing at the counter in front of the coffeepot. I didn't wag. I stared.

She looked at me just over the top of Nestlé's head and said, "I'm Lydia. Your dad's research assistant. You must be Tori."

No, I must be somebody else. Somebody whose dad wouldn't tell her that his assistant was the size of Ophelia's six-year-old sister Bianca and had short arms and legs and a head that seemed to be too big for the rest of her. *My* father would have prepared me so I didn't just stand there with my chin hitting my chest.

"Nice to meet you too," she said. Her tone was dry. Her voice itself . . . I expected her to start singing about the Yellow Brick Road.

"Sorry," I blurted out. "My dad didn't tell me you were a . . . midget."

"That's because I'm not. Technically I'm a dwarf, but we prefer to be called 'little people.'"

That's all she could say at the moment because Nestlé was leaning against her and squishing her against the cabinet. He pushed so hard she ended up sitting down on a step stool I hadn't seen since I could finally reach the sink in the bathroom. I guess she'd need that to get to the coffeepot.

"You think you could get him off me?" Lydia said.

"Sorry," I said again. I snapped my fingers at Nestlé.

He looked at me, then back at her, like he was trying to make a decision.

"Really? He's crushing me."

"Sorry." Had I said it at least forty times already?

I grabbed Nestlé's collar and dragged him away from her. Lydia stood up and climbed to the top of the step stool.

"I like dogs," she said. "I just don't like to be *smushed* by them."

"Sorry."

Okay. It was official. I had lost my entire vocabulary except for that one word. Too bad, because now that the initial shock was over, there were about eighty questions I wanted to ask this "little person." Maybe I would have asked at least one if she hadn't said, "In about thirty seconds, I'm going to be walking through here with two cups of hot coffee. I think it would be a good idea if you got Bruiser out of the room first."

Of course I said, "Sorry. And his name's not Bruiser. It's Nestlé."

"Oh," she said. "Clever."

And then I stood there and watched as she filled two mugs that were bigger than her hands. She turned to me and lowered her chin. "So, dog? Out?"

I bit my tongue so I wouldn't say the apology word again and dragged Nestlé to the back door and shoved him out. By the time I turned around, Lydia had already rounded the corner into the dining room.

My dad was toast.

Chapter Five

But I forgot to talk to Dad about Lydia—or even to tell Phee—because the next day, Friday, was not a good day.

First of all, the Pack versus Ginger thing was really getting to me. As in, it was hard to concentrate with all that going on.

Izzy or Shelby or Heidi kept calling her by her nickname, which they'd decided was "Gingerbread," until her face turned as red as her hair, and she whirled around and said, "What?"

Then they went after her.

"You must eat a lot of gingerbread, right?"

"So what did you do with the money your mom gave you for shampoo?"

Or the worst: "Why are you looking at us? You're a freak."

I tried *not* to observe any more, but I couldn't help watching because I couldn't believe it was happening. And from that, one thing struck me as strange.

It was almost never Kylie who actually said that stuff to Ginger. I saw her whisper to Riannon, who whispered to one of the other three and that person would deliver the message into Ginger's face. Kylie only smiled like she'd just been elected president.

Ginger's skin wasn't getting any thicker.

But I had a problem of my own. Our group still hadn't thought of a question for the project in science, even though we had fifteen minutes out of fourth period every day to work together.

All the other groups had theirs, and Kylie's Pack had already presented their proposal to Mr. V. He had the groups do those back in the lab, not in front of the whole class, but it was hard not to overhear the Pack's since they did it as a cheer. Complete with pom-poms.

And their question? *Why are some people more beautiful than others?*

"Do you *believe* Mr. V is letting them use that?" Ophelia whispered to our group while the Pack was still going *rah-rah-rah.*

"Yes," Mitch said. The word came out like a grunt. "He just thinks everybody's wonderful."

Mr. V wasn't going to think we were so wonderful if we didn't come up with a question. "I got an idea," Mitch said.

"You do?" I thought Winnie was going to hug her. That's how desperate we were because . . . you just didn't hug Mitch.

"'Why can't girls play football?'"

"Because they're girls," Ophelia said.

"I think that's her suggestion for a question," I said.

"A-a-a-nd I don't think that's going to work."

We all looked up at Mr. V. I was ready to hug *him.* I did *not* want to spend the next three weeks thinking about boys in gigantic shoulder pads and helmets that made them look like extraterrestrials.

Mr. V half sat on an empty desktop. "I think you're making it too hard on yourselves."

I didn't point out that we weren't the ones making it hard. It was *his* assignment.

Jeepers, I was even getting prickly with Mr. V.

"Look around you. Notice what bothers you, what you can't wrap your mind around."

When he left us to deal with something involving armpits in the BBA group, Ophelia whispered, "What was he even talking about?"

Winnie started to cry. I was getting close to that myself. And I hardly ever cried.

~

So, talk about your 'tudes—mine was not good when we got to sixth period. Spanish was my worst subject anyway and I really needed to pay attention, but instead of my mind wrapping around it, whatever that actually meant, it kept wandering off into the land of *What if we never think of anything and we get an F? What if I get taken out of the smart section? What if—*

"Señorita Tori!"

I did some kind of spasm and knocked my notebook off my desk. Mrs. Bernstein picked it up and handed it to me. I didn't look at her face. Didn't have to. I knew her velvet black eyebrows were in upside-down Vs and her eyes were drilling into me over her really sharp cheekbones.

"Por qué (la something) . . . Señorita (el something) . . . trabajar ahora?"

I couldn't remember the word for *what* so I said, "Cómo?"

"'How'?" Mrs. Bernstein said. Her lips wobbled like she couldn't keep from laughing. At me.

All I could do was shrug.

She shrugged back.

She was imitating me? In front of the class?

She wasn't the only one. In the row next to me, Kylie was doing exactly the same thing. Mrs. Bernstein looked down at her, ponytail flopping as she turned her head. "Do you know what that means, Kylie?" she said, doing another really big version of my shrug. Like, up to her gold hoop earrings.

"No, ma'am," Kylie said."I was trying to figure it out."

"When you do, let me know." Mrs. Bernstein pressed a brown finger on my open Spanish book. "We're on number sixteen in case you want to catch up."

"Sorry," I said.

"Lo siento." Mrs. Bernstein's sarcastic voice was as pointy as her cheekbones. "That makes everything okay. It's right up there with, 'It's all good.'"

Kylie laughed. Not her Leader of the Pack laugh. It was the kind of laugh one grown-up shares with another when they know something the little kids don't know.

All I knew was that it wasn't "all good."

I opened my notebook—while I was waiting for my face to return to its normal temperature—and I was surprised that I couldn't exactly see the homework I'd done there. My eyes were all blurry. I blinked the way Riannon did when she was announcing to the world that she had something in her contact lens. I was so not going to cry.

I turned the page to find number sixteen. The note I'd written to Ginger was folded there.

Mrs. Bernstein had gone back to the front of the room and was hiking herself up onto the front edge of her desk so that the sandals she even wore in winter could flop around. Good. She was too far away to see that I had a note. Her reading it out loud to the class—not what I needed right then.

But as I tucked the note farther back in my notebook, I realized

I knew something I didn't know before sixth period started. I knew why Ginger didn't just "get a thicker skin."

~

Over the weekend, I wanted to talk to Mom about everything that was going on, but with Valentine's Day only a week away, she was at her shop from way early in the morning until I was ready to go to bed. By then, all she could do was give me a hug and say, "Hang in there, Tor. This'll be over soon." And remind me to wear something besides my unladylike—but favorite—Einstein sweatshirt.

Ophelia and her family had gone to Lake Tahoe. Not to ski, but to see two Shakespeare plays. She was excited because all six of the kids and their mom and dad were dressing in Renaissance costumes. They would probably have better ones than the actors, thanks to their mom. I knew Phee would come back to school Monday saying stuff like "alas" and "forsooth." It wasn't my thing, but I kind of loved that about her. She definitely dared to be different—but only with Winnie and me.

Dad was constantly reading and talking on the phone and Skyping and squinting at his computer. I went up to his office a couple of times to my curl-up chair, but I didn't feel like talking to him. Not even about him letting me feel *awkward* with Lydia, who probably now thought I was the rudest kid on the planet.

I talked to Nestlé a lot, but he basically just wanted his belly rubbed 24/7. I would have been glad to get back to school if it hadn't turned into one big wolf den there.

And on Monday, it got way worse. We're talking fifty percent worse, to be exact.

I was so grumpy the first three periods even Ophelia stopped telling me stuff about the Shakespeare weekend. If Winnie had asked me if I was okay one more time, *I* probably would have made her cry, and she was doing enough of that already.

So I wasn't in the best place fourth period when Mr. V. came over to our group and said, eyes doing no dance at all, "I'm a little disappointed in you guys. What's going on with you?"

Winnie, of course, burst into tears and Mitch got all grunty and Ophelia waved her arms around for no apparent reason and muttered, "Alas." I could feel all of them waiting for me to say something, but a sob bigger than any of Winnie's erupted from the Pack side of the room. Even Mr. V looked.

"A-a-a-ll right, what's going on?" he said—in that drawly way he used when people were going over the edge.

"That Ginger chick freaked out," Douglas told him, voice breaking into an octave only dogs can hear.

"Where *is* Ginger?" Mr. V said.

Evelyn raised her hand. "She left, Mr. V."

Mr. V went to the doorway, moving a little faster than usual, which wasn't that fast since he never really hurried anywhere. As soon as his back was turned, the Pack all collapsed against each other, except for Heidi, who kept her eyes on Mr. V—obviously in case he turned around.

As for *my* eyes . . . they were filling up like cups of salt water, and I couldn't see how I could stop them from overflowing. I was so done with the whole room.

I got up, grabbed the pass, and headed for the door.

"Excuse me, Mr. V," I managed to choke out. "I need to use the restroom."

"Sure," he said, although I wasn't sure he actually heard me. He was peering down the hall the other way.

The urge to cry was gone by the time I got to the girls' bathroom. It wasn't the same for Ginger.

I found her curled into a ball under one of the sinks, sobbing into her knees. From the smell of the place, she had just lost her breakfast in one of the stalls. Good thing I didn't really have to go in there.

I just didn't know where I did need to go. It was like I was divided into two parts. One part wanted to pretend I didn't see her and bolt out the door. The other part felt like I should at least ask her if she was okay. That seemed stupid though because anybody could see she wasn't.

There must have been another part of me. That part crawled under the sink and sat beside her with my back pressed against the cold tiles.

Now to think of what to say.

"I hate them," Ginger said. "I hate them so much."

That was easy.

"They're awful to you," I said.

"I don't even know what I did wrong."

I thought about what Ophelia said, about how maybe Ginger brought it on herself, but I decided not to give Ginger the list.

"They just like to pick on people," I said instead.

Ginger raised her face from her knees. Jeepers. She looked like she'd been stung by about twenty bees and was allergic to all of them.

"Have they ever picked on you?" she said, like she hoped the answer was yes.

"Twice," I said.

"Why did they stop?"

I wasn't sure they had, actually. Not after Friday in Spanish class. But I said, "They found somebody else to pick on."

"Me?"

"There was somebody else between you and me." I was thinking of Winnie, who in Ginger's shoes would have flushed herself down the toilet by now.

Ginger swiped off a tear from under her eye. "Do you think there will be somebody else soon?"

"I don't know," I said.

The tear was replaced by three more. "I tried to be friends with them."

"Why?"

She looked at me like I was nuts. "Because they're the popular girls. Doesn't everybody want to be friends with them?"

"I don't. I want to be friends with people who want to be friends with me."

She stared at the knees she was hugging. "That's the problem. Nobody wants to be friends with me."

I couldn't argue with that.

"I don't even know how to make friends. This is my twelfth school since first grade."

"Jeepers. How come?"

"Because my dad's a construction worker and him and me and my brother have to move wherever the work is."

"What about your mom?"

"She died."

It must have happened a long time ago because she didn't start crying again. Maybe she'd used up all the tears she had for that.

"I always try to make friends, but it never works. My dad says to just be nice to people and helpful and they'll like you. I do that, but they just act like I have leprosy."

Something stabbed me in the chest. At first I thought it was guilt because I'd acted like that toward her some myself. But this was more like something was trying to cut me open. Like Ginger's heart breaking was happening to me too.

"We should go back to class," I said.

"I can't," Ginger said.

"You kind of have to, or you'll get in trouble. Even Mr. V doesn't let people cut."

She shook her head, the way Ophelia's two-year-old sister did just before she burst into *I don't want to! I don't want to!* I had to stop Ginger before she got to that because I *really* wouldn't know what to do then. Ophelia was way better at that than me.

"I'll walk with you," I said.

She finally nodded and uncurled herself from under the sink, and we went back to Mr. V's class.

The room was quiet, and everybody had their books open and their pens moving. Mr. V looked up, but he just nodded at me like I'd done something wonderful and pointed to the assignment on the board.

As I slid into my desk, I knew some other people didn't think I was wonderful. I glanced over my shoulder and the entire Pack was watching me, practically panting.

I rolled my eyes and turned back around. On top of my science book was a piece of pink paper folded into a triangle.

I looked at Ophelia, but she was alternating between chewing her braid and gnawing her fingernails as she wrote in her notebook. Besides, if it had been from her it would have been purple.

A voice whispered in my head not to open it, but I did. One word in and I wished I had listened.

If you don't hate Gingerbread, you must love it. And we can't stand Gingerbread Lovers.

I tore the note into tiny pieces until it looked like confetti and dumped them into the trash can when nobody was looking. Maybe Ginger didn't know how to get out of their spotlight, but I did.

I mean, right?

Chapter Six

The Pack's spotlight only seemed to turn brighter until Ginger had to be blinded by it.

Staring at her until she looked like she was going to shrivel like a grape that gets left in the bottom of the produce drawer for too long.

"Accidentally" shoving her in the hallway and pretending they didn't even notice her bouncing against the wall or falling into somebody who went, "Why don't you watch where you're going?"

Forming a "casual" line across the cafeteria door so she couldn't get in. I followed to see where she went to eat her lunch. She carried her brown bag into the girls' restroom.

I also noticed that she was toting all her books and notebooks in her backpack. "Methinks she looks like a camel," Ophelia, who was still in Shakespeare mode, whispered to me as we walked behind Ginger on the way to fifth period Tuesday. "Why is she dragging all her stuff around with her?"

You didn't have to be a genius to figure that out. The Pack wasn't letting her go to her locker.

I stopped Ophelia outside Mrs. Fickus's room. Winnie slipped in beside her.

"Do you know where Ginger ate her lunch today?" I said.

They shook their heads.

"In the restroom."

Winnie put her hand over her mouth like she was going to be sick.

"Why?" Ophelia said.

"Because of the Pack. We should—"

"Wait." Ophelia's hand was on my arm so fast I almost heard it go *schwing.* "You're not thinking you should invite her to have lunch with us, are you?"

"She's not that bad," I said. "I talked to her yesterday—"

"And now Kylie and those girls are looking at *you* the same way they do Ginger." Winnie's already tiny voice was practically disappearing. "What if they start looking at Ophelia and me too?"

I didn't have an argument for that. The Alpha Wolf's looks every time I went to the pencil sharpener had started to make the hair on the back of my neck stand up.

Mrs. Fickus stuck her helmet head out the door and told us without even moving her rosy-lipstick lips that the bell was about to ring.

"Please stay away from Ginger," Ophelia said when she was gone. "Let's just us three be friends, like always. Okay?"

I didn't point out that not much was "like always" anymore. I just said, "Okay."

For a minute, it was worth it to see both of them smile.

~

The only thing that made *me* smile for the rest of the day was that I was going to go out with Granna after school. I would even take a Lola Montez story right then.

But during sixth period I got a note from the office telling me to go ahead and walk home because my grandmother had a doctor's appointment.

I analyzed that right away.

I had been going to Granna's appointments with her since I was a toddler. I knew all the doctors' names and what kinds of stickers and Band-Aids each of them gave out and what all Granna's jokes were with them. So why suddenly did she need to go by herself?

(A) It wasn't time for any of her regular checkups—what she called "The Doctor's Excuse to Get Money Out of You for Telling You That You're Fine." Which, of course, she already knew.

(B) She liked having me there so I could see her prove to them that she might be old (something I never agreed with in the first place), but she was as healthy as a teenager. There was always ice cream at the Lazy Dog afterward to celebrate "Yet Another Victory Over Medicine."

That added up to the whole thing being strange and me being disappointed.

Then when I got home, Nestlé didn't even greet me at the back door. Not like he usually did, with his voice all whimpering and his tail banging against the kitchen chair and knocking over the newspaper Dad had left there at breakfast. He just peeked around the corner of the snack bar and sort of nodded and then went back into the kitchen to whatever was more exciting than me.

It was Lydia.

She held two coffee mugs over her head, like that was going to keep them out of Nestlé's reach, and said, "Look, dog, if I spill this we're both going to be sorry. And you don't want me to be sorry."

"Nestlé!" I said.

He turned his head to give me a glance that said, *Don't you see I'm busy here?* Lydia tried to take that opportunity to slip by him, but

Nestlé whipped back around and knocked his nose right into the cup in her left hand.

It was like watching one of those paper towel commercials where the spill happens in slow motion. And just like I *was* watching TV, I stood there and witnessed coffee spraying everywhere and the mug smashing to the floor and Nestlé trying to play in the puddle while Lydia turned her whole body to face the refrigerator with the other cup shoved against her chest.

"Get. Him. Out of here," she said.

"Do you want me to help—"

"Yes—get him out!"

I grabbed Nestlé's collar and dragged him through the coffee and the pieces of what I was pretty sure was Dad's favorite mug with the handle shaped like an old gold miner's mustache. That of course made the whole mess worse, but I sure wasn't going to offer to clean it up again. Lydia might be a "little person," but she had a big voice when it came to giving orders.

And so far, that was all I'd ever heard her do. I wasn't sure I liked her any more than she liked me.

Outside, Nestlé bounded to the back corner of the fence around the lower part of our yard and barked for our next-door neighbor to come out and give him a treat.

"He's not even home right now, Nut Bar," I said.

But Nestlé sat there, wagging his tail back and forth through the wet leaves and whining. He reminded me of Ginger before she figured out the Pack didn't want her in their den.

I shivered. And it wasn't even that cold.

I could have taken the wrap-around porch to the front door and gone back inside, but I knew Nestlé would head right for wherever Lydia was. And wherever Lydia was, *I* felt like Clifford the Big Red Dog.

I started to sit on one of the metal chairs on the patio, but it was wet, just like everything else in Grass Valley in the winter. Besides, I needed to get farther from the house. I considered taking Nestlé for a walk around the Sunrise Lane loop, but his leash was inside. Where else . . .

That was when my gaze drifted upward, and I remembered the Spot.

Our yard was divided into two parts: the lower part where the house was and a higher part like a shelf that you could get to only on a path that curved up to it on the other side of the fence. The way-cooler-than-anybody-else's yard thing about the Spot was the tiny log cabin up there. The cabin wasn't big enough to live in, and it was too far from the house to store anything. Even if you did, it had a dirt floor so stuff would get wet in the winter.

As I pried open the rusted-closed gate, memories rushed in. I did my first real science project up there when I was in fourth grade: a weather station where I could actually check rainfall and barometric pressure and wind velocity. I got first prize in the science fair for my grade level, and then I brought it back and set it up in the cabin again until the raccoons got it.

I wasn't too upset about that because by then I was doing other experiments up there, and only some of them were actually for school. It was cool to see how many different breeds of spiders I could identify and whether kudzu could grow in the dark because it took over every place else. I proved that it didn't, which as I looked back on it, was probably a good thing. I didn't think my mom would want kudzu coming down the hill and choking out her cucumbers.

Until that afternoon, as I picked my way from the path and across the upper yard to the cabin, I hadn't been to the cabin since September. I didn't argue, of course, when my mom said I shouldn't go up there anymore. Something about a girl my age needing to get past the bug-collecting stage. I'd forgotten about it until now, when suddenly, I didn't have anyplace else to think.

As I stood there with my hand on the cabin door, ready to push it open, the first thing I had to think about was whether to go in. Mom (and Dad) had made it pretty clear that I wasn't supposed to, in that voice they saved for when I needed to know it wasn't just a suggestion.

But I decided (A) being "more like a girl my age" wasn't going to help me solve any problems right now; and (B) I couldn't think of anyplace else where I could be whoever I was.

I wasn't even sure where that came from because I never even thought about who I was before. Being up there just made me remember how I used to get all into a project and didn't worry if the BBAs were going to tell me it was lame or the Pack would roll their eyes back into their brains. I didn't think they even did that stuff back in fourth and fifth grades. It used to be easier. And it felt easier again up in the Spot.

At least I knew I wasn't a person who argued with that this-is-not-a-suggestion voice. So I didn't go into the cabin. I just sat on a rock overlooking the lower yard and the house and wrapped my arms around myself. Nestlé sat beside me and leaned his thick body into mine. For a few minutes, we just listened to the pines sing a low song about how a storm was brewing, and pretty soon the who-am-I feeling went away and then I felt smart enough again to take my problems one by one.

Problem #1. Maybe Granna didn't want me to go with her to the doctor because (A) she was going to have to put on one of those gowns and she didn't want me to be embarrassed or (B) . . .

I couldn't think of a B, so I moved on.

Problem #2. Maybe I could (A) time my hot chocolate runs so I wasn't in the kitchen the same time Lydia was or (B) I could go back to going to Granna's every afternoon after school like I did 'til this year. That led me back to Problem #1, so I kept going.

Problem #3. I could try to convince Ophelia and Winnie that we should at least let Ginger sit with us at lunch so she didn't have to eat next to the toilets by saying (A) . . .

Another shiver went through me, hard enough to make Nestlé whimper.

It was the first time ever that I couldn't even think of an (A).

I gave up on the Spot and went back into the house through the front door and ran straight to my room. Just in case Lydia was getting more coffee.

~

The next day, Wednesday, I tried to focus on Winnie and Ophelia, who really were the best friends ever. I let Phee go on and on before school about how she wanted to be in the Empire Mine film—even though I'd told her like a hundred times that my dad didn't have anything to do with picking the actors—and I listened while Winnie talked—okay, cried—about how her grandmother was telling her mom what a bad job she was doing raising her. I even let them both hug me, and I'm not the hugging kind.

But I still couldn't help seeing that the Wolf Pack attack on Ginger was escalating. It's not like they didn't make it obvious.

Before first period even started, Izzy dropped a plastic zip-up case full of little containers on Ginger's desk, with her sitting right there.

Izzy looked back at Kylie the way Nestlé looked at me when I told him to "stay" and he did. *Did I do it right? Did I? Huh? Huh? Was I good?* I expected Izzy to start drooling when Kylie gave her the nod.

"What is all that stuff?" Ophelia whispered to me.

All I could see was a miniature deodorant and a comb. That was enough. Ginger was slowly unzipping the bag, and I wanted to yell, *Don't do it, Ginger! It's a trick!*

Ginger looked inside it and jumped like something had sprung out at her. She zipped the case back up and went to Mrs. Zabriski's desk.

"She's not gonna *tell*, is she?" Ophelia hissed in my ear.

It felt like the whole room was holding its breath.

"May I have the pass to the restroom?" Ginger's voice sounded dead.

Mrs. Zabriski inserted a pencil behind one of her ears that stuck out from her supershort haircut like little doors. "Why don't you go *between* classes, Ginger?"

Ginger didn't answer.

Mrs. Zabriski sighed the way only teachers who don't really like kids can sigh and handed her the pass. "This is the last time," she said.

Ginger took it and went for the door. On the way, she dropped the zippered case on Shelby's desk.

"You can have this back," she said and left.

"Now you know why we can't invite her to lunch," Ophelia wrote in a note to me.

I didn't write back, and not just because Mrs. Zabriski had a bad 'tude herself that day. I knew what Phee was talking about. But every time the Pack did something worse to Ginger, memories bit at me. Like Kylie laughing with Mrs. Bernstein over my Spanish mistakes. Kylie wrinkling her nose at my eyebrows. Kylie making fun of Granna.

Every time the Alpha Wolf bared her fangs at Ginger, I felt like they were going through me too.

When Ginger came back from the restroom she put her head down on her desk and didn't move. She did that second and third periods too, and Mr. Jett and Mrs. C-C didn't say a word to her.

Anybody else would have gotten the message from Ginger that she was done with them. But the Pack made signs in the shapes of gingerbread people with stuff written on them like "Don't Touch the Gingerbread!" and "Gingerbread Alert: It's Poisonous!" and handed them out between second and third periods. It was so bad, Ginger didn't even take her test in math class. I knew, because I was watching her.

In fourth period, Mr. V gave us our usual fifteen minutes to meet in our groups after he took the roll. We barely had our desks circled up when Kylie raised her whole arm. The entire class turned around. For her to hold up more than a finger was that unusual.

"Yo, Kylie," Mr. V said, smiling at her with his elastic mouth.

"I don't mean to tattle but, um, Ginger isn't doing anything. I thought we were supposed to be working in our groups."

If I had had antennae, they would have gone up because (A) since when did she care if people were doing their assignment? and (B) since when did she do her dirty work herself?

Like everybody else in the room, I turned in my seat to see where Kylie was pointing. For once she was telling the truth. Ginger sat alone in the back of the room with her head on a desk that was pushed against an old dry-erase board Mr. V didn't use anymore. On it, somebody had written "Stale Gingerbread is gross" with an arrow pointing down to her.

Just like somebody had lit the end of one of those long dynamite fuses in an old cartoon, the laughter fizzled from one end of the room to the other, getting louder and hotter as it raced toward Ginger and the big boom everybody seemed to hope for.

But I was the one who exploded. Or somebody who took over Me who didn't like to talk in front of a bunch of people stood up and said, "She's not doing anything because she doesn't have a group."

I felt Winnie tug on my sweatshirt, but the other Me said, "She can be in ours."

I wasn't sure who choked harder—the Pack or the BBAs or the rest of the class that usually kept their heads down and their mouths shut. I just knew it wasn't my friends or Mitch, because when I looked down at them, they were way beyond moving at all.

They just stared at me like their faces had been shocked frozen.

Chapter Seven

Mr. V was the first to speak.

"All *right*, Tori!" he said. "Way to be a team player!"

He put up his hand to high-five me, and I was surprised my palm didn't slide off his. I was already sweating that hard.

"Ginger!" he said. "Get your stuff together and come let these ladies bring you up to speed. And, Evelyn, would you erase that board for me? I don't know what that's about."

Mitch grunted. She was the only one who stayed in her desk in our circle as Ginger made her way across the room to us.

Winnie was already standing in front of Mr. V, her little voice begging, "Please let me do a project on my own. We haven't started on ours anyway . . ."

"This is a group project, Win," Mr. V said. "One person doesn't make a group."

Winnie grabbed the bathroom pass and fled like the Pack was already after her.

Meanwhile, Ophelia was crouched beside my desk and from the

way she was talking, I was convinced her top teeth were welded to the bottom ones.

"Why did you do that? You *know* we don't want her in our group!"

"It's fine with me," Mitch said, "as long as she does the work."

"It's not fine with me. Winnie is going to have a total meltdown. Why did you *do* that, Tori?"

Ginger saved me from answering by dumping her overloaded backpack onto the floor beside the empty desk Mr. V had pulled into our circle. Ophelia tightened her teeth so hard I had to practically lean right out of the desk to hear that she was talking at all.

"If you weren't my best friend, Winnie and I would start our own group right *now*," she said.

Winnie returned, swollen-eyed, from the restroom, and Ophelia got back in her seat and began to make lunch out of the end of her braid.

"So what's your question?" Ginger said.

"We don't have one yet," I said.

"I have one," Ophelia muttered.

~

I didn't find out what that was until after school when I called her to get help on the writing assignment Mrs. Fickus gave us fifth period. *If you were a plant or a flower, what would you be?* Right then I was thinking *poison ivy* because Ophelia had barely looked at me the rest of the day after science. I was sick of those lame topics, but at least it gave me an excuse to call her and get us back to where we were.

I had never needed an excuse before.

Three Shakespeare-named Smith kids answered the phone and passed it to the next one before I finally got Ophelia. Unlike at school, she suddenly had a lot to say to me. She was so freaked out, I was sure she had eaten several mouthfuls of her hair before I called.

"Did you call about the English paper?" she said.

"That and—"

"I'm not helping you with that until you tell me why you picked that Ginger person over Winnie and me."

"I didn't—"

"You invited her into our group without even asking us!"

"I didn't know I was going to say it until I did it."

Ophelia went on like I hadn't even uttered a syllable. "I don't have anything against Ginger. I kind of feel sorry for her. But that doesn't mean we have to be friends with her. And you know what's gonna happen now. Kylie's gonna *think* we're friends with Ginger, so she's going to start treating us exactly the same way she does her."

"Kylie doesn't even—"

"And it isn't going to just be them *looking* at us, like Winnie said. I didn't say this in front of her because she would totally have a breakdown, but we're gonna get gum in our hair and signs on our backs and have to eat our lunch in the toilet—"

"Well, not actually *in* the toilet—"

"It's one thing if she's in our group. We can't get out of that now. But just so you know, I don't think we should hang out with her any other time than in science class."

"Okay. But she's not really that bad, Phee." My voice must have gone all high because Nestlé was cocking his head at me like I was hurting his ears.

"But *they* think she is!" Phee said.

"I thought you didn't care what they think."

"I do when it means they're going to turn on us. Even if you don't care about me anymore, I still care about you."

"*What?*" I said.

"I can't talk about this," Ophelia said. And with a very loud click, she hung up.

I knew that was Drama Queen Ophelia kicking in, and any other time I would have given it five minutes and called her back so she could enjoy an even more dramatic scene of us making up.

But this wasn't any other time.

I was suddenly so lonely even Nestlé pressing his head into my thigh didn't help. I almost hated Valentine's Day for keeping my mom away from me, and I almost hated that when I called Granna, the person who answered her phone said she was resting, which she, like, never did. Before I could think of anything else to almost hate, I marched up the steps to my dad's office. If Lydia was there I would ask her if I could have ten minutes alone with my father.

Lydia wasn't there. It was the first break I'd caught in days.

"I was just about to get a coffee," Dad said. "You interested in some hot chocolate?"

Until I shook my head I hadn't realized just how miserable I was. I saw it in *his* eyes as they dropped at their corners. He motioned me to my curl-up chair, sat himself down in the one across from it, and picked up his pipe. He didn't light it because Mom wouldn't let him smoke it. He just liked to hold it in his mouth when he was figuring something out. I evidently needed figuring out.

"So what's on your mind, Tor?" he said.

I gave him the whole story, most of it anyway. I tried to stick to the facts; like, I left out the part about Ophelia. I'd save that for Mom. Valentine's Day would be over in exactly four days.

Dad nodded through the whole thing, and when I was through, he just kept nodding for a few more minutes until I thought his head might just bob off. Finally, he put down his pipe and leaned forward with his hands folded between his knees.

"First of all, I think you did the right thing."

"Thanks, but what do I do?"

"Have I ever told you about the Maidu tribe of Native Americans?"

What?

"They lived here in Grass Valley long before it was Grass Valley."

I didn't bother to tell him I knew that. I was too disappointed that he didn't get it. I might as well sit through the story and go back to Nestlé. At least he listened to me.

"The Maidu elected their chiefs based on how much they were liked. Today we'd say 'by how popular they were.' Anytime their chief did something they didn't like, they exercised their right to remove him and put in somebody else." Dad put up a hand like I was about to interrupt, which I wasn't. "Now, they didn't have another election. They just consulted one another, just like we'd do over coffee down at the Briar Patch, and agreed on who was in." He shook his head sadly. "That happened to Chief Wemah when he tried to lead the tribe through the tough times during the Gold Rush. They made a big mistake there. It led to their ruin. I think they could have—"

"Thanks, Dad," I said.

I bit the inside of my cheek so I wouldn't say, *That really doesn't help and neither did Granna's story about Lola Montez.* I didn't want to (A) hurt his feelings and (B) get Granna in trouble.

I even started to stand up, but Dad scooted forward a little more like we were just getting to the good part.

"It must be human nature to try to get power over other people, Tor," he said. "I told you the other day about the US government forcing the Maidu into a peace treaty and then never honoring it."

"Uh-huh."

"And yet the Maidu were just as cruel to each other when it came to who had the power." Dad smiled like he was actually smiling at somebody else. "Reverend Jake calls that 'original sin.' I think that's what you're seeing with these girls you're dealing with."

Jeepers, he *had* been listening. I scooted to the edge of my chair too and was about to say, "So what do I do about it, Dad?" when somebody made a sound in the doorway.

"Sorry," Lydia said. "I didn't mean to interrupt. I'll just go get us some coffee while you—"

"That's okay," I said and pretty much leaped out of my curl-up chair. I didn't know how much of all that Lydia had heard, but I didn't want her to hear any more. She already thought I was a big enough loser.

I got past her without knocking her down, and collected Nestlé from my room, and ran with him up to the Spot. Maybe up there I could analyze the facts about the Maidu and their popularity contests and see if it could help.

But after thirty minutes of sitting there outside the cabin with Nestlé licking the snowflakes off my face as they hit, all I could figure out was (A) there had always been mean people and (B) the mean people had the most power.

Between that and the fact that my feet were frozen into stumps, I left the Spot and went back to the house.

~

We didn't get a snow day off Thursday. The streets were cleared and the buses were running, and that didn't help my 'tude at all. Ophelia did throw her skinny arms around my neck when I got to our meeting place by the window and said, "Okay. I think it'll be all right with Ginger in our group, and I'll help you figure out what kind of plant you are because I don't understand the math homework at *all* and I'm going to fail and never get into college."

That was the Phee I knew. It made me think for the next couple of hours that we were going to be okay.

Then we got to fourth period.

Mr. V told us our group could have the whole time to work on our project since Ginger had just joined us. Shelby came out from behind her hair and raised her hand to ask if that was fair—probably because Kylie told her to—and Mr. V said, "When did anybody ever promise you 'fair'?"

It was a strange answer, but I didn't have time to analyze it. The first thing Ginger did when we sat down was ask Mr. V if she could use the restroom pass.

"Why do you do that every single day in here?" Mitch said to her.

Ginger looked around our little group. The only people who looked back were Mitch and me, and we must have looked pretty trustworthy because she said in a hoarse whisper, "Because Kylie and those girls won't let me in the restroom between classes."

"What do you mean they won't let you? You're bigger than every one of them." Mitch glanced over her shoulder at the Pack as if she were double-checking their size. "Yeah. You could push right through them."

"Could we just get to work?" Ophelia said.

"What work?" Mitch said. "We don't even have a question."

"I've got one," Ginger said. "I just thought of it."

Mitch grunted. Winnie whimpered. Ophelia muttered something between her teeth.

Had everybody forgotten how to talk in real words?

"What is it?" I said to Ginger.

"Why are some people mean? Is there a part of the brain that makes them that way?"

Mr. V. stopped on his way back from the BBAs and put his hand on Ginger's shoulder.

"Not bad," he said. "Not bad at all. In fact, it's awesome. What does the group think?"

Ophelia didn't look at him. She was too busy burning a hole into me with her eyes. Winnie was tearing up again.

Only Mitch spoke. "You said it had to be a question we didn't already know the answer to."

"Yea-a-ah," Mr. V said. "Do you know the answer to that, Mitch?"

"Yes. Some people are just born that way. End of story."

Without moving her head, she cut her eyes toward the Pack who were all innocently labeling the parts of the scientific method on a worksheet.

"That's one of the theories you could test," Mr. V said. "I'm thinking you should go with this, ladies. It's a decent question, and you're running short on time. Your proposal is due Tuesday."

"Okay," I said. And then Ophelia kicked me under the desk and I added, "We'll talk about it."

"What's to talk about?" Mitch said when Mr. V went back to the BBAs. "We got a question. We do the work. Simple as that."

"You *know* what *they* are going to do if we get up there and start talking about mean people," Ophelia said.

"Uh-huh," Winnie said.

"They're so lame they probably won't even know we're talking about them," Mitch said.

"Ophelia's kind of right," I said to Ginger. "Doing a whole project could make things even worse for you."

Ginger's shoulders sagged. "I don't see how they could be much worse. If you want me to, I'll go back to not being in a group—"

"Let's look at this logically," I said quickly. Ophelia was way too nice to say, *That's a great idea, Ginger, you go.* But just in case . . .

I held up one finger at a time as I went through the letters.

"*A*—we don't have time to think of another question. *B*—if we don't make our report sound like it's about them, they're not going to stand up and admit they're mean—"

Mitch gave the version of the grunt that I thought meant she approved.

"And *C*—we shouldn't talk about it here where they can hear everything we're saying."

"But where can we talk about it?" Winnie glanced at the Pack. "They're everywhere."

"They're not at my house," that other Me said. "We could meet there after school every day until we're done with the project."

Ophelia grabbed my arm and squeezed it. "You have to ask your mom, and she's so busy right now. And your dad's working at home, right, so we might disturb him."

And when did she become the boss of me?

"I'll call my mom at lunch," I said, "but *A*—she always wants me to bring friends home. And *B*—we could have a whole party in our house and my dad wouldn't know it because he gets all focused and stuff."

"I like the way you talk," Ginger said, smiling at me. Her teeth were about the color of butter, but she looked almost happy for the first time since she got to Gold Country Middle School. "You know, with *A* and *B*. It sounds like a real scientist."

"She's the smartest one in the class," Winnie said.

Any other time I would've felt pretty good about that. But when fourth period ended and everybody tore out of there for lunch, Ophelia grabbed me and dragged me to the back corner of the room.

"You invited her to your *house*?" she said. I wasn't sure she was ever going to get her teeth unstuck again. "You promised we didn't have to hang out with her except for the project!"

"This *is* for the project."

"You're just trying to ruin our lives!"

"That's a hyperbole," I said. Too bad Mrs. Fickus wasn't there to hear that.

"I'm not being a drama queen." Ophelia flipped her braid over her shoulder. Nobody could say *that* wasn't dramatic. "If Kylie and the Pack find out we're all going to your house with Ginger, we'll all be in a worse place than Ginger is now."

"Why would they find out? It's not like we're announcing it to the whole class."

"They'll know. They know everybody's business."

I forced myself not to roll my eyes. "It's just 'til the project's over, and then you won't ever have to even look at her again."

"You're making it sound like I'm the one who's mean."

I didn't know what to say to that, so I shrugged.

"We used to talk about everything before," she said. "Are we even still best friends?"

"Yes!" I said. "Why are you even asking me that?"

"I have to make sure. I wouldn't do this for somebody that wasn't my best friend."

"All we're doing is a science project," I said.

"Do you promise?" Her eyes were filling up with big dewy tears.

Which was why I said, "I promise."

She threw her arms around me and squealed, "I love you!"

Jeepers.

Chapter Eight

Snow was falling again in big fat flakes that stuck like cat paw prints to my kitchen bay window as our group got around the table after school. With the five cups of hot chocolate I made in the microwave and the package of Oreos Mom told me on the phone we could have (once I promised we wouldn't disturb Dad or leave our chocolate-dried-up-in-the-bottom mugs all over the place) and the outside all sparkly with frost, it could've been like one of those winter afternoons you read about in books.

All we needed was a fire in the fireplace—except who has a fireplace in their kitchen?—and a smile on somebody's face—except everybody looked like they had a hair ball they couldn't cough up.

Maybe not Ginger. She seemed kind of excited. Her eyes, which I noticed for the first time were like a pair of blueberries, got all round, and she kept looking at me and giving me the butter yellow smile.

"What are you so happy about?" Mitch said to her as I was putting the last mug of cocoa on the table in front of Ophelia.

"I haven't been invited to anybody's house since I moved here," she said.

Ophelia ignored the hot chocolate. "This isn't exactly a party."

Mitch pulled up the corner of her Valentine place mat. "Sort of looks like a party."

"My mom does this stuff for every holiday," I said.

"The ones shaped like four-leaf clovers are my favorites," Winnie said.

"Could we just get started?" Ophelia glanced at her wrist like she was wearing a watch, which she wasn't. "I don't have that much time."

I knew for a fact that Ophelia didn't have to be home until six and that since it was snowing her dad would be picking her up so she didn't even have to walk the exactly five minutes it took to get from my house to hers.

But she kept staring at me, bug-eyed, so I pulled out the paper Mr. V had given us to fill in for our proposal. The only thing I had written on it was our question.

"Step two," I read.

That was as far as I got. Nestlé, who had finally finished sniffing everybody and putting his slobbery ball into each person's lap trying to convince somebody it was their job to play with him, jumped from his rug and bounded across the kitchen. I didn't have to hear the coffee cups clicking together to know Lydia had arrived.

Winnie withered like she'd just seen a troll, and Ophelia stared with her chin practically hitting her chest. Even Mitch didn't move for a minute.

"Tori!" Ginger said. "You have a dwarf!"

"No, she did not just say that," Ophelia muttered to me.

She did. Which seemed to give Mitch permission to open up too.

"Why does she limp?" she said.

"So!" I said, in a voice that made Ginger's sound like a whisper. "How are we supposed to prove or not prove that there's a part of the brain that makes a person mean?"

"I can help you with that."

Lydia left the mugs on the counter and came over to the table, and Mitch was right. She did have sort of a limp that made her rock from side to side when she walked. With only a glare, she lowered Nestlé back to his rug and then stood at the table with her chin barely clearing the top so that all I could see was her wide face and her gigantic mop of dark curls. Even tiny Winnie had to look down at her.

"How can you help?" Mitch said. "Are you mean?"

I bit my lip so I wouldn't say, "Well, kind of."

"I bet people have been mean *to* you!" That came from Ophelia who seemed to have forgotten she'd taken a vow of silence. Her brown eyes were all bright and interested.

Lydia opened her mouth to answer, but Ginger cut her right off. "I don't see how you can help us unless you're a brain scientist."

It was sort of a relief to know I wasn't the only one who turned into a babbler when Lydia was around.

But Lydia looked at Ginger the way she'd never looked at me. As in, like Ginger might be an intelligent human being.

"I'm not a brain scientist," she said, "but I'm a professional researcher. I know how to put a research project together."

"Why would you help us?" Mitch said.

Ophelia raised her hand. Lydia did sort of make you want to wait your turn before you talked.

"Yes . . . ?" Lydia said.

"Who—"

"Name?"

"Oh, sorry. Ophelia."

"Go on."

Ophelia fiddled with the end of her braid. "So, not to be rude or anything, but, um, who are you?"

"She's my dad's assistant," I said.

"And my *name*"—long, pointy look at me—"is Lydia."

Mom would've been getting on me about not making introductions, but jeepers.

Ginger waved her arm. "I'm Ginger."

Everyone told Lydia their names. Winnie squeaked hers. Ginger continued to wave her arm the whole time, but Lydia didn't even look like she wanted to roll her eyes. Instead, she turned to me and jerked her head toward the empty chair.

"Do you mind?"

"No!" Ginger said. "Do you need a pillow to sit on or something?"

She was already halfway out of her seat, probably planning to grab one of Mom's heart-shaped cushions from the living room, which practically had "These are just to look at!" written all over them. But Lydia was pulling *The Second Gold Rush* by Nathan Taylor, PhD, from the snack bar where Dad had left it. I couldn't believe she was actually going to use it for a booster seat, but she did, and I sure wasn't going to tell her she couldn't.

How could somebody that small seem so . . . powerful?

When she was finally settled, she folded her hands on the table in a way that made me think of the word *tidy* and nodded at the sheet in front of me. She nodded a lot.

"So you want to find out whether being mean is nature or nurture," she said.

"We do?" Ginger said.

Ophelia's already big eyes got bigger. "I don't even know what that means."

"It means is there something wrong with mean people's brains or were they brought up that way?" Mitch grunted. "I already told you what I think."

"Which is?" Lydia said. "Oh, and that was impressive by the way. It takes guys with doctoral degrees entire books just to get the question right. You said it all in seventeen words."

I counted. She was right.

"I think some people come out mean."

Ginger cocked her head at Mitch. "Have you ever seen a mean baby?"

A sound bubbled out of Lydia that sounded like a little kid gurgling. Maybe a grown-up little kid.

"I like it," Lydia said. "You're going to get some lively debate going while you're working on this."

"Fighting with each other is good?" Winnie wasn't squeaking now but that could change at any minute. She was half hidden behind Ophelia's right shoulder.

"Debating's not fighting. It's healthy banter. Here's what I suggest to get you started." Lydia was still looking at Mr. V's proposal sheet. "Are you meeting here tomorrow?"

"Monday," I said. "Tomorrow's kind of like Valentine's Day, only it isn't—it's really Saturday, but my dad and I always—never mind. We're meeting Monday."

Lydia didn't act like I'd just done the kindergarten babbling thing. She just said, "And would you like my help?"

"Hello, yes!" Ginger said. Well, bellowed.

Nestlé looked at me like, "Why does she have to do that? I'm trying to sleep here."

Mitch gave her approval grunt, and Winnie nodded and actually came out from behind Ophelia. Even Ophelia herself said, "Yes.

Because if you don't, this is gonna be a total disaster and we're all gonna get Fs and that isn't even gonna be the worst part."

"Do I want to know what the worst part is?" Lydia said.

"No," I said.

Ginger obviously thought Lydia was the best thing ever. Winnie wasn't doing her mouse imitation. Ophelia was getting that "you fascinate me" thing going on. Now I was the only who was ready to kick somebody under the table.

I wasn't sure making Lydia the leader of our group was a good idea at *all.* How was I supposed to work for thirteen days with somebody who didn't like me?

And then Ophelia swiveled herself toward me while everybody else was offering Lydia Oreos and she said, right into my ear, "Wouldn't this be perfect if it wasn't for . . . you know."

How was I supposed to work for thirteen days with somebody who didn't like me, again? I should just ask Ginger.

"Okay," I said. "Where do you want us to start?"

"I suggest that each of you come back Monday with a situation where someone has been mean to you. The kind of mean you're studying here."

Ginger went with the hand waving again. "I can tell you mine right now."

"Monday's good," Lydia said.

"That's our last time to work on this before we have to turn in the proposal," Mitch said.

Lydia glanced at the sheet. "I see that. Guess we'll have to get right to work Monday then."

She climbed down from her chair and picked up the book.

"I'll do that for you," Ginger said, and she tripped over Nestlé trying to get to Lydia.

"Thank you," Lydia said to her. "But just so you know, I *can* do most things for myself and I prefer to. I think we all do."

She smiled at Ginger, something I had never seen her do before.

At least *somebody* liked Ginger.

Which was good because Ophelia's *not* liking Ginger was out of control. As soon as Mitch and Ginger piled into Winnie's mom's car to go home, Ophelia hauled me to my bedroom and closed the door, leaving Nestlé whining in the hall. After Ophelia started in, I didn't even hear him anymore.

"I think it's really cool and everything that Linda is gonna help us," she said.

"Lydia," I said.

"What*ever*! It'll probably keep us from getting an F. But, Tori, what are we gonna do about *her*?"

"Who?"

"You *know* who I mean!"

Ophelia sat down on my bed so hard all the cushions and throw pillows tumbled over on themselves.

"We can't put her up in front of the class with us. Did you *see* her today?" She did an exaggerated imitation of Ginger waving her arms. "She's gonna do that, and she's gonna interrupt everybody and—" Phee shuddered. "It is going to be horrible."

"So we don't give her a presentation part. I won't be up there either."

Ophelia flung herself back on the bed and crossed her arms over her face. I would have told her she had just gone beyond drama queen if she hadn't started crying.

"You don't get it!" she said. "This is awful, and it's just going to go on and on and on way after this stupid project is over."

"Come on, Phee," I said. "It doesn't have to be *that* bad."

She let a few sobs go before she suddenly sat up and looked at me really hard. "You're right," she said. "It doesn't."

She let that hang in the air like I was supposed to know what she was going to say next. I didn't. I wasn't even sure who I was talking to.

"You have to be the one who stands up in front of the Pack and the BBAs and tell them what makes them mean."

"That's not how we always do it—"

"Nothing is like how we always do it anymore."

I had to give her that.

She was crying again. "If you do the presentation part by yourself, maybe it'll be okay. And you owe it to us."

"Why?"

"Because." She folded her arms hard. "You got us into this."

She looked toward the window. The lights of a car flashed across the frosty glass.

"My dad's here," she said. "Do you promise?"

"I already promised we would just include Ginger for the project."

"I know, but you have to promise this too. You can't make Winnie stand up there, and for sure *not* Ginger and not me. You and Mitch maybe—only it isn't Mitch's fault . . ."

"Jeepers, Phee, come *on*!"

"Promise, Tori. You already made things bad enough. You can't make it worse. If you're really my friend and Winnie's and not Ginger's like you said, then you'll do this."

I didn't say anything, not until I heard her dad blow the car horn. By then, the tears had stopped rolling down Ophelia's cheeks. Her big round eyes were squinted into long dashes, and for a minute, my best friend looked almost like a wolf.

"I hate standing up in front of people," I said.

"I know. But if you want—"

"Okay," I said and shrugged.

And only because I didn't want her to finish that sentence.

The horn blew again, and Ophelia hugged me while I stood there all stiff and then she left.

Nestlé hurried into the room and gave my hand a do-you-still-love-me nudge.

"I thought I was gonna have a hard time thinking of something for Lydia's assignment," I said to him, "because nobody was ever really mean to me." My voice broke in half as I whispered, "Until just now."

Chapter Nine

The next day was Friday the thirteenth.

I was probably the only person in the sixth grade at Gold Country Middle School who thought of it that way because everybody else saw it as Valentine's Day. The actual Valentine's Day was the day after that, but what was the fun of that if you weren't at school?

Of course, it wasn't as much fun as it was in elementary school. Back then, everybody got a Valentine from everybody else, and even though they weren't supposed to have parties in the classroom, the teachers and the mothers always figured out a way to have one, like taking us on a field trip to the Empire Mine that day and then serving us cupcakes or candy from the Lazy Dog.

But Valentine's Day was completely different in middle school. We didn't have those individual mailboxes we spent a week making out of shoe boxes and paper lace thingies and too much glue. Anybody who wanted to give somebody a Valentine had to pass it to them in the hall or stick it in through the vent slot in their locker. Or text them.

Ophelia and Winnie and I all gave each other homemade cards.

Mine from Ophelia said on the inside: "Thanks for promising. I love you." It kind of made me not want to eat the cupcake she gave me at lunch. I choked it down because (A) she was sitting right there and (B) her mom never skimped on the Red Hots.

What I really didn't expect was the pile of envelopes that fell out of my locker when I opened it after lunch. It was like a landslide of pink and red. I didn't have time to see who they were from because the bell was about ring and we were headed for Mrs. No-Tolerance-for-Tardies class, so I unzipped my backpack to stuff them in. There were about five more already in there. Jeepers. Winnie and Ophelia went all out.

But when I found a stack of them on my desk in English, my radar went into effect. Even my BFF wouldn't go *this* all out.

I looked around for Mrs. Fickus, but she was still standing outside the door. I shoved all the envelopes but one into my pack. There was just enough time to read it before the bell rang, so I pulled out the card, which had been made on a computer. On the front was a picture of a heart with a crack down the middle of it. I opened it.

Big mistake.

"You're breaking everybody's heart by even showing up at school," it said. "You reek like moldy gingerbread."

My mouth suddenly tasted bitter. Like after you eat kale.

I wasn't going to be opening any more of *those*.

For about seven seconds, I wondered if it *did* come from Phee. It wasn't a logical assumption, but (A) she was at least fifty percent less happy with me than usual and (B) everything was changing so . . .

Yeah, seven seconds later I got logical again. No way. I picked up my backpack and headed for the garbage can. I didn't even care if I was out of my seat when the bell rang and I got lunch detention. I wasn't going to sit all period with a load of trash.

But I didn't even get halfway out of my desk when Ophelia grabbed my arm and shoved another computer printed card close to my face.

"Look at this!" she hissed to me between her teeth.

She was already crying so hard she had bubbles coming out of her nostrils.

"You need a Kleenex," I whispered to her.

"Read it!"

The bell rang in time to cover that outburst. Mrs. Fickus opened her laptop to take roll, and Ophelia threw her head down onto her arms on her desk. I could feel eyes watching me like the ones in cartoons when they turn out the lights.

I reached down and unzipped my backpack so I could stuff Ophelia's card in with the rest of the trash, but she grabbed my wrist with a snotty hand and squeezed hard.

Jeepers.

"Take out your vocabulary homework," Mrs. Fickus said.

Zippers unzipped and notebooks appeared on desks. I crammed the card into the pocket of my pack as I pulled out my homework. As soon as I opened my notebook, Ophelia slid another card on top of it.

When I turned to glare at her, I saw that she had at least five more on *her* notebook, all of them opened. She took in a raggedy breath, and I knew if I didn't at least pretend to read the thing she was going to have a meltdown right there in English class.

I tilted my notebook up, pressed the card against it, and opened it.

"You should just cross February 14 off every calendar you ever get because who's ever going to love somebody that stinks like rotten gingerbread all the time?"

My first thought was, *And Mrs. Fickus thinks* my *imagination muscle needs developing.*

I didn't get a chance to have a second thought because a shadow with a helmet for a head fell across my desk.

My life was over.

"All right, y'all," Mrs. Fickus said. "There is a box by the door. I will give you two minutes to put every Valentine you have in your possession into that box. You may pick them up at the end of class."

Yes, my life was over. I had died and gone to heaven.

I was the first one at the box, even though I had to sidle past Mrs. Fickus, who was still standing over me like I had *invented* Valentines and this was all my fault. Before anybody else could even get out of their rows, I had dumped every pink and red envelope. Then I turned around, expecting to see Ophelia and Winnie behind me. But I ran straight into Riannon.

Her face came into a green-eyed point so sharp I knew if I touched it I'd need first aid.

"You had to mess it up for everybody, didn't you?" Somehow the words came out without her even moving her lips. Ophelia had nothing on her.

I answered her with a shrug—no surprise there—and went back to my seat. I bulged my eyes at Ophelia, but she looked away. Winnie was shaking all over, just like a baby bunny.

It didn't occur to me until Mrs. Fickus went back to the vocabulary homework that she wasn't going to check everybody's backpacks and purses to make sure all the Valentines had been put in the box. I was an idiot.

"Kylie," Mrs. Fickus said.

Or maybe I *had* gone to heaven.

"Would you please collect the homework? Class, please pass your papers to the front of your row."

I tore mine out of my notebook. Before I could even tap Mitch, who was sitting in front of me, to take it, Kylie's pink sweater brushed my arm as she passed. How she did it I never figured out, but she made a small piece of paper come out of her sleeve and land on my notebook without even pausing on her way up the aisle.

If it had been folded, I wouldn't have opened it. If it had landed upside down, I wouldn't have turned it over. But it was staring me in the face and my eyes read it before I could stop them.

"If you don't get every one of those Valentines out of here before Mrs. F. sees them, we will take YOU out."

The sick feeling in my stomach told me they didn't mean out for ice cream.

What it did mean, I wasn't sure. I tried to focus on the punctuation sheet Mitch passed back to me, but the commas and the colons ran around on the page like the thoughts in my head.

I'm not scared of them.

But I never had anybody threaten me before.

What are they gonna do? Take away my birthday?

They just took away Valentine's Day.

If I do what they say, I'm a loser.

If I don't do what they say . . .

There was only one way to finish that thought: *I would make it harder for Ophelia and Winnie. And maybe even Ginger.*

~

When the bell rang, I went with a compromise. I scooped the envelopes out of the bottom of the box. But as soon as I got out into the hall, I dumped them into the first trash can I came to and made sure the swinging lid was still swinging when the Wolf Pack went by.

Without waiting for Ophelia and Winnie, I headed straight for my locker to see if there were any more evil cards in there so I could take them to Spanish class and tear them up into Mrs. Bernstein's wastebasket in front of Kylie. That's how mad I was. But when I got to my locker, Ginger stood at her open one, staring inside.

I wondered why the Pack wasn't blocking her way. But then she plastered her hands over her nose and mouth and acted like she was about to lose her lunch. One whiff and I knew why.

The stench of mold is one smell you don't forget, and I hadn't. I did an experiment with cheese up in the Spot one time and forgot about it. The next time I went in the cabin, it was gag-worthy. The stink coming out of Ginger's locker was even worse.

"I think I'm gonna be sick," she said.

I pointed to the trash can, and as she ran off choking, I pinched my nose with my fingers and looked inside at a plate piled with cookies. I could only stand there for a few seconds or I was going to be joining Ginger at the trash can, but I got enough of a look to notice three things: (A) they were ginger cookies (I knew because Granna made them every Christmas); (B) they were shaped like hearts that had been twisted and distorted until they belonged in a horror movie; and (C) they were half-covered in something blue and fuzzy.

It took a while for mold to grow that much, unless somebody really knew what they were doing. That meant "somebody" went to a lot of trouble for this. But the bigger question was—

"How did they get in here?" I said to Ginger, who hadn't thrown up after all.

"I guess it was when I left my locker door open."

"You left it open?"

"After English Heidi told me I could come here, that they weren't gonna bother me anymore."

"Uh-huh," I said, instead of "And you actually believed them?"

"And when I opened it, Mr. V. called me to the end of the hall and said he wanted to talk to me." Ginger's eyes watered.

"What did he say?"

"He just asked me how things were going in our group, and I started to tell him and then he said I should go to my locker and get to class. And when I came back, here they were."

I looked down the empty hall.

"We have to go or we're gonna be late," I said. "I'll just dump these—"

"No, let me!"

Ginger grabbed the plate and pulled it out. The paper plate collapsed and moldy, horror-movie cookies hit the floor with sickening plops.

"Oh, nuh-*uh*!" I said.

No As, Bs, or Cs came to my head. The only thing that was going to happen was that we were going to pick up these . . . things with our hands and throw them away and be late to Mrs. Bernstein's class and go in there reeking like leftovers somebody stuck in the back of the refrigerator six weeks ago. That was what was going to happen.

"You go to class," Ginger said. "You shouldn't be late."

"What about you?" I said.

She blinked her blueberry eyes at me. I didn't see how she wasn't crying.

"What about me?" she said, as if that was the stupidest question anyone had ever asked her. "I'll clean it up and then I'll go to the nurse's office and be sick in her bathroom and she'll let me go home early."

There was another one of those seven-second things where I teetered. Phee would never speak to me again if I helped Ginger, no question about that. And if the Pack found out, I'd be the next one with moldy baked goods in my locker. But I already knew how this felt. And it was *so* not okay.

I shook my head. "I'm staying."

But she gave me a little push with a clammy hand.

"Go," she said. Her face was stronger than I'd ever seen it. "Please."

So I went. All the way I thought that Ginger must have been through things like this before because she knew just what to do. And nobody had ever stopped it.

~

All through Spanish class Kylie's lookouts kept their eyes on the door while the rest of the class was writing the numbers to a hundred in Spanish. I was almost to sixty, and Ginger still hadn't arrived. I was relieved that the nurse probably had sent her home.

For people who couldn't stand Ginger, the Pack seemed disappointed that she didn't show up. Kylie looked like she wanted to pinch someone's nose off.

Of course, she always kind of looked like that.

When the last bell rang and Mrs. Bernstein stepped into the hall, everybody ran out—it was Friday after all—except Kylie and the Pack. I took my time leaving, mostly because I didn't want to talk to Ophelia and have to cross my heart and hope to die a dozen more times.

The Pack was so focused they talked like I wasn't even there.

"What am I supposed to do with *these* now?" Izzy said. She pulled a bunch of dead flowers out of her backpack and waved them around. My mom would've been all over that with a lecture about caring for living things.

"Not my problem," Kylie said to Riannon, who said it to Heidi, who turned to Izzy and said, "Do whatever you want with them, I guess."

"Should I put them in her locker?"

"How are you going to get the door open, genius?" Riannon said.

I knew it was her because her voice was pointy. By then, I was pretending to rearrange the contents of my backpack.

"I could ask Mr. V again—"

"Shhhhhhhhh!"

Apparently I wasn't pretending hard enough. I slung my backpack over my shoulder and hurried out, not just to get away from them, but because now *I* felt sick.

Mr. *V* was in on it? He kept Ginger occupied so they could put those disgusting cookies in her locker?

How was that even possible? (A) He wouldn't and (B) he wouldn't and (C) he just wouldn't.

But he had.

For the first time I thought maybe Ophelia was right. Maybe we should go back to hiding under the radar if a teacher, a cool teacher like Mr. V, thought this was all funny too.

The hall seemed like a tunnel as I walked down it. I knew other kids were there, but I couldn't hear them. The only sound was the voice in my head.

You could do it, you know. You could tell Mr. V that Ginger wasn't doing any work in the group and he would take her out of it.

You could think up another topic and even do the whole project yourself so nobody would be mad.

You could pretend meanness doesn't exist.

Instead of trying to figure out where it comes from.

I found myself at the bottom of the stairs, between the main office and the front door. I had to shake myself inside to get back to the real. Dad was picking me up. We were going to the Lazy Dog for our traditional Valentine's Day sundae. Mostly to celebrate Mom being not-a-crazy-person after tomorrow.

Even though I'd just made a huge decision, I didn't feel like eating chocolate sauce and whipped cream.

Chapter Ten

The next day, on actual Valentine's Day, I told Nestlé, "I'm having a hard time loving *anybody* today."

He cocked his cocoa-colored head at me.

"Except you, of course. Do I even have to say that?"

Apparently so because he put his paws up on my bed, which I hadn't even gotten out of yet because (A) it was Saturday and (B) I didn't have anything to do and (C) I couldn't *think* of anything to do.

Maybe Mrs. Fickus was right. Maybe my imagination muscle *had* turned flabby.

I sat up and listened hard. No sounds of coffee grinding and toast popping up were coming from the kitchen. One peek out the window assured me Mom was already gone. With the Valentine's rush I wasn't even sure she had come home the night before.

Could there be a few more things going on? I felt anxious, like I was about to take a test I forgot to study for. Which, like, never happened.

"Come on," I whispered to Nestlé.

I patted the bed, but he was already up there, turning himself around . . . and around . . . and around until he finally curled into a ball that reminded me of a Reese's peanut butter cup. With a big growly sigh, he rested his head on my leg and moved just his eyes to let me know I could start with the petting any time.

I stroked the smooth place between his eyes and just like I knew it would, having him all warm and heavy up there with me calmed things down.

Except for my thoughts about Ginger and Ophelia and Winnie. And worse, about Kylie and Shelby and all the rest of them who morphed into a single mean face in my brain.

"It's like they're one person," I said to Nestlé, "and Kylie's the head and the rest of them are her hands and feet." It was such a big person, it was kind of hard to remember there were only five of them making it up.

I wished Winnie and Ophelia and I were like one body. We used to be in a way.

I flopped back onto the pillows, and Nestlé scooted his way up so his head was on my chest. I tried to think of the ceiling as a piece of paper I could write some numbers on.

Three of us.

Five in the Pack.

Attacking *one*—Ginger.

Okay, maybe *four* if you counted the Saint Valentine's Day Massacre of Winnie, Ophelia, and me.

Nine altogether.

But how many girls were in our class?

I tried to remember but (A) I didn't really pay that much attention to anybody but us and (B) Nestlé was trying to lick my ear. Even I couldn't think with a tongue in my auditory canal.

I wriggled out from under him and let him fall asleep there. I dug through the project supplies in the bottom of my closet and pulled out a piece of big paper and some markers. With a sweep of my arm, I cleared my desk and went to work.

When I was through I found some tape and stuck the paper to the door of my closet and sat on the edge of the bed to look at it. Nestlé sat up too and leaned into me.

"It's a chart," I told him. "Of all the girls in our section. Who knew there were fifteen of us and only twelve boys? I thought there were at least a hundred of those creatures." I looked at Nestlé, who looked back. "I know you're a boy," I said, "but you don't count as a creature."

He seemed content with that and stretched out to sleep again. After today there would be no more getting up on the bed until Mom's Easter rush started. He had to take advantage of it while he could.

I let him snooze and studied the chart in silence.

The Pack	Brainy Girls	Athletes/Dancers	Indies	Target
Kylie	Me	Brittney	Evelyn	Ginger
Riannon	Ophelia	Josie	Mitch	
Heidi	Winnie	Quinby		
Shelby		Ciara		
Izzy				

I had to do the next part out loud, whether Nestlé was listening or not.

"So there's one target. And there are five wolves attacking her. Although, if Kylie wanted to, she could turn on Shelby or Izzy at any time. I've seen her do it." I tilted my head at the chart. "If Kylie decided Ginger wasn't any fun to torment anymore, would Riannon or Heidi even do it?"

"Mathematically speaking," I said to Nestlé, "it doesn't make sense that 33 percent of the girls in our section should have 100 percent of the power over 7 percent of the girls, when there's another 60 percent just standing around."

Too bad the Kylie and her pack weren't that good at math.

But I was.

~

The Wolf Pack was quiet Monday at school, even in science class where they were allowed to be the noisiest.

"I'm glad they're leaving us alone," Winnie whispered when our group circled up for our fifteen minutes of project time.

"For now," Ophelia said.

Winnie's tiny face crumpled. "What do you mean, 'for now'?"

Ophelia used her hair as a blond shade so she could peek through at the Pack. "They're planning something."

I didn't think she should have told Winnie that. The poor kid slid so far down into her desk all I could see were her eyes and the top of her almost-white head. But I had to agree with Phee. All the Wolf heads were bowed together like they were praying. Which I was pretty sure they weren't.

"Where's—" Ophelia pointed at Ginger's empty desk.

"Bathroom," Mitch said.

"How's it going, ladies?"

I felt Mr. V behind me, but I didn't turn around to look at him. I'd been making it a point *not* to look at him. His elastic smile wouldn't seem real to me, now that I knew he'd been in on the moldy cookie prank. Just hearing his voice brought all the disappointment up like it was yesterday's lunch.

"Is there a problem?"

Ophelia chewed at the ends of a hunk of hair. "There kind of is."

"Do you want to kind of tell me about it?" He slipped into Ginger's desk.

Ophelia looked at me, but I just stared back at her.

"Anybody?" Mr. V said.

"It's Ginger," Ophelia said. "We only have fifteen minutes to work together in class and she spends most of it in the bathroom."

"I never refuse you girls a trip to the restroom. Somebody else just went too—"

"We work at Tori's house after school though," Winnie said, "so we'll get our project done."

Ophelia looked like she wanted to bop Winnie over the head with her science book.

"You're really into it then." Mr. V let his mouth go into a grin. How could somebody that cool and nice be taken in by the Wolf Pack?

"Here's our Ginger," he said.

He unfolded himself from her desk and did a big swoosh thing with his arm like she'd just arrived on a red carpet. She didn't even look at him. I didn't blame her.

"I want that too!"

That came from Heidi, who had strolled in behind Ginger. Mr. V went over to swoosh her into her desk, and Ginger dropped into hers. Her face was paler than Winnie's hair.

"Since we have like seven seconds left," Ophelia said to me, "you should ask if everybody did their research so we can do our proposal this afternoon."

Why did I never notice before how bossy Ophelia was? I almost told her if she wanted to know she could ask them herself, but Winnie was already half crying so I said, "Did everybody do their research?"

All heads nodded.

"My mom made us brownies for our meeting," I said.

"Cool," Mitch said.

Nobody else said anything.

Maybe this was something even chocolate couldn't fix.

~

Lydia already had the brownies on the table and real hot cocoa heating on the stove when we got to my house that afternoon. Mom had replaced the Valentine's place mats with the ones shaped like silhouettes of George Washington and Abraham Lincoln. The brownies were on a plate that had part of the Gettysburg Address on it.

"Didn't you tell your mom this wasn't a party?" Ophelia whispered to me while everybody was piling their jackets on the coat-tree.

I just shrugged. Speaking of being over people.

I really wasn't "over" Ophelia. I just wanted the real one back.

When we were all settled with what sure *tasted* like a party, I pushed the proposal sheet to the middle of the table. "We're on step four: what basic facts have you found that you need to learn more about before you can answer your question?" I shrugged. "We all did our research, so I guess we should go around the table and say what we found out."

I thought Ginger would shoot her hand up before I even got the words out, but she had been totally quiet all afternoon. We hadn't heard the foghorn voice one time.

Mitch told us she'd go first, and she pulled out a picture of a brain and showed us what part handled judgment and making decisions and self-control.

"There's no part for 'mean,'" she said. "But stuff can go wrong and make people all twisted. That's what I'm looking up next."

"So you still think it's all about the brain," Lydia said.

"It is," Mitch said.

"Let's call that a hypothesis."

"You mean, like on a triangle?" Winnie said.

Lydia actually giggled. "No, honey, that's a hypotenuse. Not to be confused with hypothermia or hippopotamus."

Winnie's whole face twinkled. I had to give it to Lydia. I hadn't seen Winnie do much of anything but whimper for weeks now.

"I'll do mine," Winnie said. "I looked up whether more boys are meaner than girls."

"Right," Lydia said. "So you'll know whether it has anything to do with gender."

"That's whether you're male or female," Ophelia said.

Like we didn't all know that. But at least she was trying to impress Lydia instead of griping about Ginger.

"And what did you find out, Win?" I said.

Almost invisible lines formed between her eyebrows like ditto marks. "It said boys used to be meaner, but now girls are catching up. Only their mean is different from boys' mean." Her eyes ran down the page. "Oh, so my next thing I'm going to look up is how mean is different in girls and boys. Is that okay?"

"Sounds good to me, Win!" I said.

I didn't usually speak in exclamation points like Ophelia, but I was feeling so relieved that the whole thing was going well, they just sort of popped up at the ends of my sentences.

"What did you find out, Phee?" I said.

"I was supposed to find as many definitions for the word *mean* as I could." Ophelia's brown eyes got huge. "There are, like, fifty of them. One of them was . . . here it is, 'small.' I didn't get that."

Lydia laughed again, this time letting her big head of curls drop against the back of the chair. "I hope it didn't say all things that are small are mean!"

"You're totally not!" Phee said. "You're one of the nicest people I ever met. I mean, I don't know you that well, but you're taking time off work to help us when you don't even have to. That's just so . . . nice!"

Ophelia was switching back and forth so fast between Evil Phee and Good Phee, I was starting to get dizzy.

"I'm not always so nice," Lydia said. "But I do try not to be mean. So where are you going from here?"

Ophelia blinked her big brown eyes. "Home."

"She means what are you going to look up next?" I said.

"Um, I guess I'm gonna figure out which definitions we're talking about?"

Lydia nodded at each person around the table. We all ended up nodding too, but I didn't think any of us knew why.

"You're a smart little tribelet," she said. "I'm impressed."

"Tribelet?" Winnie said. "That's so cute!"

"What does that mean?" Mitch said.

But Ophelia said, "Ginger hasn't told us what she found out yet."

At least she didn't call her "that Ginger girl" like she wasn't even there.

Although she might just as well not have been there. Until that minute, Ginger hadn't even really made eye contact with anybody. Now she glanced up at Lydia and dropped her gaze right back to the brownie she hadn't so much as nibbled.

"What were you supposed to look up?" Ophelia said.

"I was supposed to find five reasons psych—psy—counselor people think kids bully."

"And?"

I couldn't help it. I kicked Phee under the table. I mean, jeepers.

Ginger just shook her head.

"What's up, Ginger?" Lydia said.

"I lost it," Ginger said.

How could she lose it? She carried everything with her in her backpack.

"Let's backtrack." Lydia's voice was patient. "When do you remember having it last?"

"When I got to science."

"So you left it there?" Ophelia said.

Ginger was shaking her head.

"What did you do with it in science class?" Lydia said.

"You took it to the bathroom with you."

We all looked at Mitch.

"How do you even know that?" Ophelia said.

"Because. I time it every day to see how fast she asks for the bathroom pass."

"Why don't you say it *to* her instead of *about* her," Lydia said.

Mitch turned to Ginger. "You broke the record today. Six seconds."

"So you took your folder with you?" I said.

"I wanted to go over my part while I was in there. I was excited about telling you guys."

"I don't get it," Ophelia said.

But I did. It all came together like the last few pieces of one of those gigantic jigsaw puzzles you do when everybody comes for Christmas.

Ginger taking the pass and the folder with her to the restroom.

Heidi asking Mr. V if she could go too because she knew he always said yes to the girls.

Ginger coming back all white-faced and quiet.

Heidi coming back like she just won a beauty contest.

Or like she just did something to Ginger's folder.

"Heidi threw it in the trash, didn't she?" I said.

"No," Ginger said. "She threw it in the toilet. After she used it."

"I *so* did not need to hear that!" Ophelia shook her hands like something was stuck to them that she couldn't get off.

"I think we all needed to hear it," Lydia said. "Isn't that what your project is about?"

Ginger didn't answer because she had covered her face with her chunky hands and was crying into them. But Mitch grunted a yes, and Winnie bobbed her head up and down, and I said, "Ya think?" as I got up to get Kleenex for Ginger.

"How are we supposed to do our proposal done without her part?" Ophelia said.

Lydia just looked at her the way she looked at Nestlé when he was about to do something bad.

"Okay, Ginger . . ." Ophelia said, looking like it hurt to say her name. "How are we supposed to get this done without your part?"

"Do you remember any of it?" I said, handing her the Kleenex box.

"I remember all of it."

Lydia looked around the table. "Who's going to write this down?"

Winnie raised her hand and clicked her pen.

"Give it a shot, Ginge," Lydia said.

Ginger squeezed her eyes shut and dragged in a breath Dad probably heard up in his office. "Reason number one: because they're bullied at home so they need someone to take their anger out on. Reason number two: because they're insecure—they don't think they're worth anything so they're proving all the time that they are by getting power over other people. Reason number three: because they get away with bossing everybody around at home so they think they can do it anyplace. Reason number four: because they're afraid of people who are different so they try to squish them down. Reason number five: because they're afraid other people will hurt them so they hurt other people first."

Ginger sagged like she was out of air and opened her eyes.

"Jeepers," I said.

"Did you get all that, Winnie?" Lydia said.

Winnie was still scribbling, but she nodded.

Mitch didn't even grunt. She just said, "That was awesome."

"I'm not done," Ginger said. "Next I'm gonna find out why people think that stuff. Y'know, like do their parents teach them that or what."

Huh. And the Wolf Pack had thought she wasn't smart enough for our section.

"This is a killer proposal," I said. "So, Phee, how are we gonna present it to Mr. V?"

Before it was even out of my mouth I remembered, and before I remembered, she was saying, "I don't know. How are *you* going to present it to Mr. V?"

"It's not a big deal," Mitch said. "Not like the real project."

"But Kylie and them had pom-poms." The whimper was creeping back into Winnie's voice.

Even though I kind of wanted to shake *Ophelia* like a pom-pom right then, I shrugged and said, "I guess I'll just read it to him."

"We could take turns," Winnie whimpered, as if she would rather have a cavity filled.

"I'll do it," Ginger said. "Since I messed up and let Heidi throw my folder in the toilet . . ."

"You didn't 'let' her do anything."

We all sat up straight in our chairs when Lydia said it. Even

Ophelia. Lydia's eyes were blazing, but it was her voice that made me hold my breath. It wasn't a voice you ignored.

"What that girl did is not your fault, Ginger. If you had fought her, you'd probably be suspended right now. If you'd grabbed it out of her hand, she would have run back to the teacher and told him a whole sob story about how she was just trying to help you and you yadayadayada. If *you* had told the teacher, you'd be labeled a tattletale. I don't even have to know this girl to be able to tell you she has a power you don't understand." Lydia leaned forward, and everybody else did too. She seemed bigger than us at that moment. "But you're *going* to understand it. That's what you're all about here, and that's why I'm helping you."

Nobody argued. Not even me. Because about halfway through that I got the feeling Lydia had seen that same scene go down herself. And that she had watched some important paper of hers get flushed down a drain.

Yet now it didn't seem like anybody could have power over Lydia.

Ginger sat up tall in her chair. Her face was blotchy, but the blueberry eyes were shiny even in the middle of the red crying rings. Winnie finished writing and handed the paper to Ginger.

"How are we gonna make sure our whole proposal doesn't get pee—doesn't get destroyed?" Ophelia said.

Mitch held out her hand. "I'll keep it."

"Good choice," Lydia said. "For now."

While everybody else was getting their coats on, Ophelia dragged me into the bathroom. She looked like she wanted to flush *me* down the toilet.

"*You* were supposed to present to Mr. V," she said.

I parked myself on the edge of the tub. "What is your deal? You don't have to do it. You don't even hardly have to be there. Kylie can think you had nothing to do with any of it."

"Why are you all mad at *me*?"

Because you're almost treating Ginger as bad as they are. That's what I wanted to say. But Ophelia wasn't really waiting for an answer.

"She's probably gonna do the whole proposal from memory, and Mr. V's going to think it's amazing," I said. "It kind of is."

"Are you starting to *like* her?"

"I don't know."

"Okay." Both of her palms were facing me. "I'm not going to stop being your best friend because you can't get her out of our group and you're not presenting the proposal. But I'm still upset. You're being really selfish, Tori."

I was getting annoyed.

"You heard all that stuff she said about the reasons and what Lydia said about Heidi being powerful. And Heidi isn't even as powerful as Kylie!" Ophelia grabbed my arm. "What if they do all that stuff to *us*? That's what I'm so scared of."

"Hey, Ophelia," said a voice outside the door, followed by heavy banging. It was Phee's brother. "Did you fall in the toilet? Dad's waitin' for ya."

"You can't do this to us," Ophelia said to me.

And then she flipped her hair around and left.

I just stood there and did a little hair flipping myself. Because what about what everybody was doing to Ginger?

Chapter Eleven

The next day, Tuesday, Ginger did present our proposal to Mr. V totally from memory. Although Ophelia pouted so hard I could have sat on her lower lip, Mr. V praised us like we were getting the Nobel Prize, but not just for that. He also thought *what* we were saying was awesome and that we were going to say some important stuff the whole class needed to hear. He said *we* were awesome, and even though it had taken us a while to hit our stride, we were really on a roll.

Yeah, and he said it all so loud the entire room heard it all the way from the lab. I knew that because the minute I left the classroom at the end of the period to go to lunch, I felt warm breath right around my ear. It didn't smell like Ophelia's grape cough drops or the Downy Winnie's mom used in her laundry.

It smelled like strawberry shampoo and brand-new clothes and the gum only the Pack got away with chewing.

"You do this project and you are so dead," the peppermint breath said into my ear.

With a flip of splashy hair, the breath owner was gone. I didn't even have time to see which one of the Pack it was.

After that, I took my time getting to the cafeteria. I even considered going into the restroom and having lunch with Ginger. For about half of a second.

It wasn't that I was scared to face the Pack. I just wanted to get alone and figure out what "dead" meant.

"Let's get a move on, Tori," Mr. Jett said behind me. "What's with you and falling behind lately?"

What was with *him* always being the one to catch me doing it? I picked up a little speed, hoping he'd pass me so I could slow down again and think, but he ushered me into the lunchroom like we were going to a wedding. I'd have to define "dead" later. But I couldn't get Ophelia's words to leave me alone: *What if they do all that stuff to us? That's what I'm so scared of.*

~

Our group didn't meet at my house after school that day because: (A) we didn't have anything to talk about until everybody finished the rest of their research and (B) I had a date with my mom. Thinking about that got me through the rest of the classes, which wasn't easy with Ophelia acting all stiff and Winnie looking like Gumby between the two of us and the Pack firing arrows at me with their eyes. And Ginger suddenly acting like we were attached with Velcro.

I am not even kidding.

From the start of lunch on, you'd have thought we'd signed a BFF treaty.

As she followed me from class to class, she asked me exactly thirty-two questions about Lydia, Nestlé, my dad, my mom, and my last four science projects. Before I could even answer one, she moved on to the next so I stopped even trying. She didn't seem to notice.

She asked Mrs. Fickus if she could move her seat to sit near me in English. Mrs. Fickus said she wouldn't change her seating chart. It was the first time I thought I might like Mrs. Fickus.

It wasn't that I didn't like Ginger, even the way Ophelia didn't like her, which was more like not liking what could happen . . . Anyway, I just didn't want to get in trouble, which is what happened in Spanish when Mrs. Bernstein did let Ginger change her seat to sit in front of me, and she whispered questions to me the entire class period. When I finally looked at her to say, "Shhhhh!" Mrs. Bernstein got all over *me* for talking in class.

And then she shook her head at Kylie, and Kylie shook hers back.

Big throw ups.

Ginger smelled kind of like laundry that sat around too long before it got washed, and her voice could lead you through the San Francisco fog. That was definitely irritating as a stiff tag in the back of a new T-shirt, but I could've just shrugged that off. I mean, she *was* smart. She came up with stuff I never even thought about, like:

Do you think Lydia's parents are little people too? How does that work?

What do you think came first? Black Labs, chocolate Labs, or yellow Labs?

And . . .

What's your dream science project of all time? The one you want to do really bad?

I could totally have gotten into a discussion with her about any of those—if she ever hit the pause button long enough for me to get a word in—but if I did, it would make things even worse with Ophelia.

And they were bad enough as it was.

Every time I even looked like I was going to answer Ginger,

Ophelia pinched my thigh. I was going to have to take stock of my bruises later. Every time Ginger started walking beside me, Ophelia pulled on my backpack until I basically had to stop or it was going to fall off.

After school, I ran for the door. All I wanted to do was talk to Mom.

But Phee cornered me there. I mean, really, she got in front of me so my shoulders were between the wall and the last locker.

"Ginger is hanging around you all the time," she said.

"I noticed," I said.

"So did the Pack." Ophelia's eyes were big brown pools of worry. "They think you're friends with her."

"How do you know that?"

"Hey—Victoria."

I saw it in Ophelia's eyes before I even recognized the voice. Kylie was approaching.

I stepped in front of Phee and opened my locker. Out of the corner of my eye—I thought that was called peripheral vision—I saw that Kylie had only Riannon with her. Two of us, two of them. That could work.

"Vic*tor*ia," she said again, this time with the accent on the *tor* like it was a bad word or something.

I ignored her and pulled my jacket out of my locker. Ophelia was now in the corner staring at the floor like maybe there was a trapdoor she could go through. Me? I didn't feel scared. I was just annoyed.

"Hey! I'm talking to you . . ." Kylie stopped a couple of feet from me. Riannon was so close behind her I thought they might be stuck together. "Vic*tor*ia, my pet."

I jerked and banged my elbow on my locker door. "Don't call me that," I said.

"Why not?" Kylie looked at me all innocent. "It's your name, right?"

"No."

"Then how come that old lady called you that?"

"That was my—"

I stopped myself. I'd watched Ginger let herself be dragged in by Kylie, and I wasn't doing it.

So I pulled my math book out of my locker and slammed the door. Then I squatted down to put my books in my backpack.

"Oh. Hi, Phee-Phee." Kylie's voice went so shrill it hurt the one filling I had in my back molar. "I didn't see you there, Phee-Phee."

The only person who called Ophelia that was her toddler sister Hero. She always yelled it from her car seat when Phee's mom picked her up. I waited for Ophelia to correct Kylie, but apparently she couldn't get her teeth unstuck from each other.

"I'm Tori," I said. "And she's Ophelia. Like you don't know that."

I nodded at Phee and stepped around Kylie. We'd only gone a couple of steps when Riannon said in her pointy voice, "Are you going to the Gingerbread House?"

"Don't answer her," I said to Phee through *my* teeth.

"We know Gingerbread goes there every day after school, so you must live in a Gingerbread House. Maybe your names are really Hansel and Gretel."

"And maybe you're the Wicked Witch," I said without turning around.

I curled my fingers around Ophelia's sleeve and pulled her with me to the stairs and down. Neither one of us said anything until we were at the front door. Ophelia was first.

"Now do you *see*? Tori, it's already too late. They know everything about us!

"They must have overheard Winnie say—"

"They're everywhere!"

I didn't realize until then that Phee was pinching my arm right through my jacket sleeve. I was pretty sure she didn't even know she was doing it. Her eyes were looking kind of wild.

"We just have to act like it doesn't bother us," I said. "They probably won't say anything else to us since I told them they were witches."

"That was like the *worst* thing you could do *ever*!" Ophelia stomped her foot, exactly the way Hero did pre-tantrum. "I told you this was gonna happen, and you just went right on acting like you're friends with Ginger."

"What am I supposed to do, just tell her to go away?"

"Yes!"

Over her shoulder, I could see other kids starting to stare at us. Any minute they'd be whispering, and by tomorrow it would be all over the school that Phee and I had WWE going on right by the front door.

When did I start thinking like that?

I lowered my voice to almost a whisper. "That just sounds too mean," I said. "I don't think you could say that to her either."

"Then what *can* we do? I don't want to have to worry about going to my locker. Maybe I already do!" She stomped her foot again. "You promised me, Tori. And best friends keep their promises."

"Best friends don't expect each other to make promises they *can't* keep," that other Me said. "My mom's picking me up. I gotta go."

I started for the door, but Phee caught my jacket sleeve in her fingers again. "I don't know what to do if we can't be friends anymore," she said.

"Who said anything about that?"

"Hey, Tor—you ready?"

It was Mom, poking her curly, sandy head in through the door. Her face was all rosy from the cold, and her green eyes sparkled like she was excited. I wasn't happy with Ophelia for ruining this for me. So I said to her, "*You* decide if we're still best friends."

Then I followed my mom out to our car and hoped I could choke the tears back by the time I got in. Because like I said, I hardly ever cried.

Mom spent the first ten minutes (I timed it) we were sitting at a table at the Briar Patch—our fave Mom and Tori place—apologizing for not being around during the Valentine season. She did that every year and said practically the same thing, but I didn't remind her. It was kind of like she needed to say it more than I needed to hear it.

That was one of the reasons why I didn't pay that much attention as she talked and I poked at the cheese in my Cornish pasty. The other reason was that I couldn't concentrate. Things like *I appreciate you understanding* got all tangled up with *you're dead, best friends keep their promises—I don't know what to do if we can't be friends anymore.* It was like a bowl of spaghetti noodles in my head.

I tried to act focused. I looked straight at Mom while she was talking and popped my eyes really big and nodded a lot.

Yeah, well (A) I'm not that good at acting and (B) Dad might be wrong about mothers being able to automatically tell when the dog has been up on the bed, but Mom did always know when I was faking it.

"What's wrong, Tor?" she said suddenly—right in the middle of "We have a lot to catch up on, and I want to hear everything."

I knew better than to say, "Nothing," or worse, shrug. Besides, I really did want to tell her. I'd been *waiting* to tell her. Except that now that she was here and asking, I didn't even know where to start.

She did.

"You and Ophelia having issues?" she said.

"You picked up on that."

"It was hard not to." Mom's pink fingernails tapped against the cup handle. "Anything I can help with?"

It was exactly what I wanted her to ask. But when I opened my mouth to tell her how she could help, nothing came out. Because I didn't know.

Maybe I should just give her the facts.

"There's this new girl," I said.

"Okay. What's her name?" Mom scooted in a little. She did like a good story. Maybe this wouldn't be so hard.

"Her name's—"

Mom's cell phone rang. She put her hand on it, but she kept her eyes on me. "If this is your father or Granna, I'll answer it. Otherwise, we'll continue. Okay?"

I nodded. That was the reason I loved my mom. She might not let me wear my Einstein sweatshirt three times in one week or use the stove when she wasn't there. She might think being a lady is the most important thing, and she didn't think scientifically the way I did. And she worked too much as far as I was concerned. But she really was the best mom, and I knew even as she answered the phone that she would come right back to me and help me sort this whole thing out.

But then I looked at her face. The light was going out of it like somebody had turned off *all* the bulbs in there, and the hand without the phone in it went to her forehead. She was either suddenly having a major headache or the person on the other end was telling her something terrible.

"Is she conscious?" Mom said.

Long pause.

"They're not doing it *here*, are they?"

Another long pause. Who was doing what to who?

"Are you sure?"

Short pause.

"All right. I'll be there as soon as . . . yes, she's with me . . . Are you sure she won't mind?"

Mom stood up, still nodding and saying, "All right," exactly six times. She pointed to my jacket on the back of the chair, and I put it on. My heart was pounding because my mom's hands never shook the way they were right now as she ended her call.

"Mom?" I said.

She stopped and put her hand under my chin. It was a strange time to realize that she could look straight into my eyes now. That was how tall I'd gotten.

"Tor, it's Granna," she said. "She has an aneurysm, and she has to have emergency surgery. Here. In Grass Valley."

"Is she okay?" I said.

Even Mr. V would have to admit that was a lame question. They didn't do surgery on people who were okay.

"I honestly don't know," Mom said. "I'm going to drop you off at the house, and then I'm going to meet Dad at the hospital."

"I want to come!"

"Lydia's going to stay with you until one of us gets home."

"I don't want to be with Lydia—I want to be with Granna!"

Mom pushed open the door with one hand. She was already making a call with the other one. "*We* won't even be with Granna. They're already prepping her for surgery and she's . . . she's not awake."

The person on the other end of the phone answered, and Mom started giving instructions. As I followed her to the car, it felt like every nerve in my whole body was firing. I knew there were a lot of them. We did that report on it last fall.

Strange things to think—things that kept the thoughts that were too scary from getting in.

I was pouting when Mom dropped me off at the house because I wanted to go to the hospital. I didn't care if, like she said, I'd be sitting around for hours, not having dinner, not getting my homework done. I just wanted to be there when Granna woke up.

My plan on the way home was to go straight to my room, but Mom probably read my mind because when I got out of the car she said, "Check in with Lydia. Make sure Nestlé doesn't have her pinned someplace."

So I went to the kitchen. Lydia was putting a dish of something cheesy smelling into the lower oven. The pot holder mitts came almost up to her elbows.

"Mac and cheese," she said. "Homemade. Comfort food."

"I'm not that hungry," I said.

"Nobody is at a time like this," Lydia said and jerked the ginormous mop of curls toward the table. There was a plate of pita bread triangles and baby carrots and hummus in the center.

"Will you stay here while I have a snack?" she said. "If Nestlé Crunch over there is alone with me for too long, he can't resist the urge to 'protect' me."

Nestlé was lying down near the back door where she had probably told him to stay, but even as I glanced at him, he inched forward. Like we couldn't see him doing it.

"Okay," I said, because (A) I'd seen Nestlé smush Lydia against the wall and (B) suddenly the thought of going to my room even with him made me cold all over. And (C) Lydia wasn't looking at me like I was a loser.

"I hope you like your hummus Greek style," she said. "The recipe's been passed down through the generations in my family."

"Are you Greek?" I said.

"My last name is Kiriakos. That's pretty Greek."

It struck me as strange that my parents left me with a person whose last name I didn't even know. Everything seemed strange right now.

I dragged a point of pita through the hummus and put it in my mouth.

"You continue to impress me, Taylor," Lydia said.

I stared at her while I chewed. (A) Because she called me by *my* last name, which nobody had ever done—and I kind of liked it. And (B) because I had no idea why she would be impressed with me. I'd always acted like I was clueless around her.

"You tried the hummus without asking me what was in it. Most kids your age would want to know every ingredient before they'd even taste it. And they'd probably turn their nose up at all of them."

"These chickpeas are different from the ones my mom uses," I said, helping myself to another dollop.

"Your mom probably doesn't shop at a Greek market."

"She needs to start."

"Olives?"

"Did you get those at the Greek market too?"

Lydia nodded.

"Then yes."

She hopped down from the book on the chair and pulled open the refrigerator door. I noticed that the bottom shelf on the door was lined with stuff I'd never seen before. I also noticed that the kitchen was starting to smell like melted cheese. Maybe I was hungry after all.

And then I thought of Granna.

"Do you know what an aneurysm is?" I said.

Lydia put a bowl of the darkest olive-green olives I'd ever seen on the table and climbed back onto her seat. It was like watching a coordinated toddler.

"I do," Lydia said. "I looked it up online while I was waiting for you."

"Why?" I said.

"Because I had a feeling you were going to ask that. I would."

"Can you explain it to me?"

"Again, impressive. You aren't saying, 'Is she going to die?' You just want the facts."

Yeah. And I didn't want to ask, "Is she going to die?" because I was afraid of the answer.

"It's a weak, bulgy spot in the wall of one of the arteries in the brain," Lydia said. "Kind of like a thin place in a balloon."

"It pops?" I whispered.

"Not always, but in your grandmother's case, it did rupture, and that's why she had to have surgery. But she has a 60 percent chance of making it through."

The oven timer went off. Lydia didn't hop off the chair. It was like she was waiting for me to say something.

"That's a good percentage, isn't it?" I said.

"It's very good, and it's probably better than that since your grandmother is in such great shape otherwise. And she's pretty feisty, I understand."

"Will that help her? Being feisty?" My voice had tears in it.

"Studies show that the will to live plays a huge role in people's recovery," Lydia said. "And with you around, why wouldn't she want to live?"

She did hop down then, which was good, because (A) I didn't know how to say I'd been wrong about her and (B) I really needed to get a handle on the crying situation.

Chapter Twelve

I did my homework at the kitchen table while Lydia cleaned up after mac and cheese. She let me fall asleep on the couch, where I woke up Wednesday morning. Mom was sitting there, stroking my hair.

I could tell from looking at how long her face had become over night that everything wasn't okay.

"Is she . . ." I said.

"She hasn't come out of the anesthesia yet. They say that isn't unusual. She's holding her own."

"Then she's gonna be okay?"

Mom pressed the back of my hand to her lips before she said, "I won't lie to you, Tor. We still don't know. If she makes it through the day, then she's probably home free."

I struggled to sit up, but Mom wouldn't let me off the couch yet.

"Before you say anything, let's talk about what Granna would want you to do today."

In my opinion, Granna would want me to take the day off and

eat ice cream and pray. I didn't pray that much, but she did and today seemed like a good time to start.

That wasn't Mom's opinion, at least not the part about me taking the day off.

I went to school and tried to concentrate. Ophelia didn't say anything about our almost-fight the day before. She was all about hugging me and sharing her mom's cookies at lunch and telling me over and over how her grandfather had an operation and he was better after it than he was before. And so on.

Winnie was nice to me too, and so was Ginger—when Ophelia wasn't wedging herself between us every time Ginger got near me.

"I know you want to help," Ophelia told her in a kind voice I knew she had practiced for a play at some point. "But she's really upset."

Even though I wasn't crying, I *was* upset. If the Pack messed with any of us, I didn't notice. All I could think about was Granna. I'd have given anything to hear another Lola Montez story.

Mom said I should do everything like I always did it, so our group walked to my house after school like usual. Dad wasn't there, but Lydia was and she sat right down with us and a big basket of chips and a bowl of salsa. Ginger dunked a chip up and down in it, and I counted five times before Lydia moved the bowl, just as Ginger was starting to splash on the table.

"What's going on with that little Heidi chick?" Lydia said.

"You remember her name?" Winnie said.

"There's more than one of her," Ginger said.

"What does that mean?" Ophelia said.

"It's like they all act the same, dress the same, talk the same," I said.

"And bully the same," Lydia said. "Who's the Queen Bee?"

"Huh?" Okay, so Mitch did ask a question now and then.

"A woman wrote a book several years ago about girls that bully. She called the girl who's in charge of them the Queen Bee."

"Kylie," I said. "Only we call her the Alpha Wolf."

Lydia nodded. "Let me guess. She gives the orders and her 'friends' carry them out."

"Why did you do this?" Ginger said, forming her fingers into quotation marks the way Lydia had.

"Because they're not really her friends. They're more like her servants."

"More like her slaves," I said.

"And they all have jobs. There's her right-hand girl who passes down the orders."

"Riannon," I said.

"And the next one down, the one who keeps track of everything."

We looked at each other. Finally Winnie said, "Heidi."

"And the messenger?"

"You mean snitch," Mitch said. "Izzy."

"And the one who would absolutely leave the group if she weren't scared to death."

"Shelby," Ophelia said. "But what does this have to do with our project?"

"I think it's the whole point of your project," Lydia said. "This group of girls . . ."

"We call them the Wolf Pack," I put in.

Ophelia kicked my ankle, and this time I turned right on her.

"First of all, ouch. And second of all, I'm glad we're finally telling a grown-up about this. I'm sick of trying to figure it out ourselves."

Ophelia's eyes filled with tears. Could I not say anything that didn't make her cry?

"It's not really *our* problem," she said.

"Oh, honey, it's everybody's problem." Lydia's face was on fire again. "Even mine."

"Why?" Winnie said.

"Because I can't find out about a situation like this and not try to teach you how to handle it so it doesn't go on and on and on the way it's been allowed to for so long. Now it's getting worse."

"Worse than it was for you?" Winnie said.

"I think so. Here's the thing, ladies."

Lydia paused. It was clear she wasn't going to continue until we all looked at her. We had to wait for Ophelia, but she finally did it.

"If this is just going to be a science project, I don't think I can help you any more than I already have. But if you want to actually make a difference, I'm here for you."

"Make a difference how?" Ophelia said.

"Become a tribelet and stand up for everyone's right to live without being afraid."

"I like that *tribelet* word," Winnie said.

I liked it too.

"So that's like a small tribe," Mitch said.

Lydia nodded her mop of curls. "A small part of a big tribe. The Maidu Indians—"

Them again.

"Stretched over a huge territory and all spoke the same language, but they lived in separate little settlements, kind of like villages. Those were called tribelets."

"Why are we a tribelet?" Winnie said.

"I got this one," I said. "The whole school is like the tribe, and our group is kind of like its own 'village.'"

"So far so good." Lydia pushed the salsa back toward Ginger, and this time she dunked a chip in it without slopping tomatoes all over the table. "The thing is, sometimes the tribelets had to stand up for themselves and their neighboring tribelets if somebody got too much power and starting pushing them around."

One of those cartoon lightbulbs went on over my head. That was what Dad was talking about that day: people putting whoever they wanted in charge just because they were popular. It was sounding like "popular" and "powerful" could be the same thing.

Kylie would definitely agree with that.

"What if a tribelet just wanted to mind its own business?"

We all looked at Ophelia, who was talking to the end of the braid she'd been chewing on.

"That would have been pretty selfish," Lydia said. "That—and they wouldn't survive."

As hard as Lydia was looking at Ophelia, I was pretty sure we weren't talking about the Maidu Indians anymore. Maybe we never were.

"Did you all come up with an example of a time when somebody was mean to you?" Lydia said.

Ginger nodded until I thought her head might come off, which was no surprise. Same for Winnie and me. And Ophelia, who dropped her eyes at me like she wanted to make sure I knew I was her example. What did surprise me was that Mitch nodded too. I couldn't help saying, *"You?"*

"People used to say I came from a 'tard family' because my brother has Down syndrome." Mitch picked at a piece of skin near her fingernail. "I finally got sick of it and punched a kid out. I got in trouble, but nobody ever said that to me again."

Lydia pointed her finger straight across the table at Mitch.

"You don't want it to get that far," she said. "It *shouldn't* get that far. That's why as a tribelet, you can't stay neutral and expect this to just go away."

"Does 'neutral' mean not do anything?" Ophelia said.

"Yes."

"No offense, but that was working fine for us before."

"No, it wasn't."

They all looked at me. Ophelia's brows were so pinched together her eyes were about to change places.

"It *wasn't* working," I said. "Kylie started picking on me about my unibrow, and the Pack spread rumors about Winnie before Ginger even got here. And they laughed at everybody's papers in Mrs. Fickus's class. At least, everybody who wasn't one of them."

"Not only that." Lydia shifted her eyes right onto Ophelia. "Maybe it's just the Pack that does the bullying, but everybody is responsible for seeing that it stops."

"That's not fair!" Ophelia's voice went so high I thought I heard it hit the ceiling.

"Mr. V says nobody ever promised us fair," Winnie said.

"He's right." Lydia folded her hands on the table in that tidy way she had. "If you do nothing, you're partly responsible for the consequences. If you want me to, I can teach you what to do."

"I don't get it," Ophelia said, chin stubborn. "I mean, no offense, but why do we have to do all the work when it's mostly directed at one person."

"You don't," Lydia said. "You're only partly responsible." Her eyes went to Ginger, whose own blueberry ones seemed like they were stuck to Lydia's every move. "Don't you think I've been exactly where you are? You have to take back the power to be yourself. You have to focus not on what's 'wrong' with you, but on what's right. These girls can help you, but eventually that will be your job."

Ginger's eyes came unstuck. Suddenly they were all over the place, like she was looking for a way to escape.

"I don't think I can do that," she said, foghorn voice blaring. "I tried before, and I can't."

Then she grabbed her backpack and flung herself out of the chair and went for the back door. Nestlé yelped as she tromped on his foot trying to get it open. When she did, icy air rushed in and Ginger rushed out.

Lydia climbed down from her chair and looked out the window. I did too. Ginger was sitting on the back step. Lydia came back to the table.

"How's she gonna get home?" Winnie said.

Ophelia's chin jutted out. She was doing a lot of talking with that chin. "No offense, but is that our problem too? If she doesn't want our help, why should we risk *us* being bullied?" Her voice cracked. "It's already starting to happen."

"I say we declare war on the Pack," Mitch said. "We can give them worse than they ever gave Ginger."

But Lydia shook her head. It was easy to know what she was about to say because her hair announced it.

"You're both wrong," she said. "First of all, Mitch, it's not about power *over*, it's about power *to*. If you want to declare war, let it be on bullying itself, not on the bullies. You can't turn into wolves yourselves or you won't accomplish anything except to keep the whole thing going."

"No offense," Phee said, "but that doesn't make any sense at all."

Lydia looked at her. "Honey, if you want to question anything I say, feel free. But when you say, 'no offense,' that means to me that you know what you're about to say is going to offend me." She looked around at all of us. "If you're in this, you have to start by saying what you really mean."

Lydia waited. Phee finally mumbled, "Sorry."

I suddenly felt as embarrassed as Phee looked. "I might have already done what Mitch is talking about," I said. I told them about the gingerbread house conversation. "I probably shouldn't have said that about the Wicked Witch."

"Did it make you feel better?" Lydia said.

"For about five seconds. I didn't time it exactly."

"It's really pretty simple, tribelet. And much easier than declaring war. The rule of thumb is to ask yourself what you want people to do for you. Then jump right in there and do it for *them.*"

"Even when they don't ask you to?" Winnie said.

"*Especially* when they don't ask you to," Lydia said.

She pulled her hands in to fold them again, and I realized two things. (A) The reason she did that was probably because her hands shook just a little bit all the time and (B) even though they did, she seemed stronger than just about anybody I had ever known. It made me want to follow her advice.

But it seemed like I might be the only one.

Mitch was still balling and unballing her fists like she'd rather just get in there and take out the whole Pack—the way they'd threatened to take *me* out if we did this project.

Winnie was looking from Lydia to Ophelia and back again, face in pre-whimper. I didn't like to hurt people's feelings, but Winnie was the poster child for trying to make everybody happy. If she agreed to this, Ophelia would think that meant she wasn't her friend. Was it just me or was Phee starting to act like a puppeteer? Sure, she was scared, but . . . jeepers.

"Will you at least think about it?" Lydia said.

Mitch grunted. Lydia grinned. "I'll take that as a yes."

Winnie gave her a tiny "okay."

I said I would too.

That just left Ophelia.

"You just want us to think about it?" she said.

"That's all I ask."

"Then okay. I will."

Still, I was glad Phee left with everybody else. As soon as they were gone and Lydia went outside to talk to Ginger, I put on my jacket and Nestlé and I went up to the Spot. I didn't care that my hands instantly turned red in the raw air and that the tip of my nose lost all feeling. I didn't even ponder the blood vessels that were responsible for that.

I'd read about hypothermia before. I could lose some of my digits if I kept sitting there. But I couldn't go back down to the house either. Without even thinking about it, I just let Nestlé and me into the cabin out of the wind and lay down with my head on him. His breathing made it go up and down, sort of like being rocked.

"How did it all get so hard?" I said to him. "It used to be Phee and I agreed on everything so nobody had to be the boss. I didn't feel like I had to do everything her way. Her way and my way were just always the same. For Winnie too. Now it's like we don't agree on anything. Except Granna. She was great to me about Granna."

A pain went through my chest. I hadn't thought of Granna since we got home from school. None of this even mattered really—did it? Not if Granna . . . didn't make it.

I flung my arm back to feel Nestlé's soft ear. It was cold around the edges.

"I wish I were like Lola Montez, Nes," I said. "Then I could dare to be different from Phee and the Pack and just be a scientist, like before. Know what I mean?"

He answered by sitting up and knocking me sideways. He sniffed toward the cabin door and started thwacking his tail on the dirt floor.

"What is it, boy?" I said.

"It's me," said a low voice.

Dad.

Uh-oh.

"Gee, thanks for the warning," I whispered to Nestlé.

Dad poked his eagle head in and squinted. My eyes had gotten used to the dark, so I'd forgotten how black it actually was in the cabin. I took that opportunity to start making a case in my defense.

"I know you and Mom said don't come up here," I said, "and I wasn't actually gonna come *in* here—I was just gonna sit on a rock out there, but it was windy so I kind of forgot. Well, no, I didn't, I just had all this stuff on my mind, so it just kind of happened. I didn't mean to disobey you."

"Tor," Dad said. "Take a breath."

He lowered himself to sit beside me and let Nestlé greet him with a thorough ear-cleaning before he made him move.

"It does make a good thinking spot, doesn't it?" Dad said.

"How did you know where I was?" I said.

"I have ways."

Dad had left the door open a crack, and in the light, I saw that even though he was kind of joking with me, his face was pinchy and serious.

"It's Granna, isn't it?"

"She's still the same," Dad said and squeezed my knee.

"Is that good?"

"It is for now."

"Are you scared?"

"Concerned. You?"

"Is there a difference between scared and concerned?"

Dad tilted his head. "I think scared means you've lost hope. Concerned—that's when you don't know how it's going to turn out, but you keep hanging in there."

"Then I'm concerned too."

We sat there for a minute. I was glad Nestlé was on the other side of me now, because between the two of them they were keeping me warm, like a Dad-and-dog sandwich. But Dad was still pinching his face like he didn't see a way out of someplace.

"*Are* you scared about something?" I said.

"I'm *worried* about something." He gave me a sideways glance. "That's almost scared, but not completely without hope."

"What is it?" I said.

He paused like he was considering not telling me, which would have scared me even more than I was starting to be right now.

But finally he said, "You remember me talking about the Maidu and how they were mistreated by the government?"

I could not get away from those Indians no matter what.

"Uh-huh," I said.

"It's become clear to Lydia and me as we're working on this film that what happened to the Maidu is part of the story of the Gold Rush and the Empire Mine. But the powers that be—the producers in San Francisco—don't see it that way. They're saying we need to stick with the success of the mine and not focus on how badly the government mistreated the Maidu and what they got away with."

"So you have to convince them," I said.

"If I try, I might lose the contract."

"But that's not fair!" As soon as it was out of my mouth, I put up my hand. "I know. Nobody ever promised us fair, right?"

Dad's eyebrows went straight up. "Right. And if I don't try and do it their way, I'll lose my respect for myself."

"You could always get another contract," I said. "You're the 'leading expert.' I looked it up."

"It's a pretty big contract, Tor. Enough to get you through college."

I didn't remind him that I was only in sixth grade.

"And if word gets out that I was an 'uncooperative client,' that could hurt my chances at getting future work."

"You mean, like this could ruin your reputation?"

"Yes."

"By doing the right thing?"

"Yes."

Something smacked me right in the face, and I stared at Dad in the halfway light. "So it's like you're being bullied!"

"That's exactly what it's like. Only in the grown-up world, Tor, it's called 'business.'"

I sounded like Mitch as I grunted. "In the kid world, it's called being 'popular.'"

Dad nodded like the two of us were grown-ups. "Looks like we both have decisions to make, doesn't it?" He put his arm around my shoulder. "I know one thing. I want to make you proud of me."

If I could have said it without crying, I would have told him the same thing.

So . . . after that, there really wasn't much of a decision to make.

Chapter Thirteen

I don't know why I thought it was going to be easy once I decided to stick up for Ginger. The first person to make it hard was Ginger herself.

That next day, Thursday, I talked to her the first chance I had, which was right before lunch. She was headed for the restroom, brown bag in hand, when I caught up with her. I could smell peanut butter. And pickles. Who ate that?

"Why did you run out during our meeting yesterday?" I said.

Ginger shrugged. My mom was right—that really was the most irritating thing ever.

I got between her and the restroom door. "I know what Lydia said freaked you out, about you having to stand up for yourself eventually. But I've been doing some thinking and I figure that's going to be a while. I don't know exactly how long. I haven't looked up the statistics."

I paused, because at that point in any conversation with me, most kids my age started looking like they had no idea what I was talking about. But Ginger was nodding like she was following me fine. She just didn't like where I was going.

"Wait," I said as she started to edge away. "I want to do what Lydia was saying after you left. I want to help."

"Nobody can help."

The bell rang, which meant we should already be in the cafeteria. With my luck, Mr. Jett would be appearing in the hall with us in exactly six seconds.

"I have to hide," Ginger said, and I was pretty sure I couldn't stop her unless I dragged her to the lunchroom by the leg.

"Okay," I said, "but still be in our group for the project. If you don't, you'll fail and then Kylie and those girls will win."

Ginger's blueberry eyes looked dead.

"They already have," she said.

"Stay in the group."

She shrugged again.

"Does that mean yes?" I said.

"I guess."

"So you're coming to my house after school, right?"

Ginger looked at the floor. "Okay," she finally said.

Then she went into the restroom to eat her peanut butter and pickle, and I snuck my way into the cafeteria. For once, my luck held out. Mr. Jett didn't notice me because he was too busy yelling at somebody in the middle of the room.

Where the Pack always sat.

But Mr. Jett wasn't hollering at one of them. He had his face right in Mitch's and the whole bald part of his head was bright red.

"You know what you are, Michelle?" he was basically screaming at her. "You're a bully—and we don't put up with bullies around here!"

"Yes 'we' do," Mitch said. "'We' do it all the time."

She jabbed her thumb at the Pack, and my eyes followed. Heidi had her head on Kylie's shoulder, and Kylie was stroking her hair while she cried. Riannon and the other two were huddled together like they'd just been released from a hostage situation.

"You watch your tone, young lady," Mr. Jett yelled at Mitch.

Even if he hadn't been screaming, the whole lunchroom would have heard him. It was like a vacuum in there while everybody gawked. I was sure some of it was shock that anybody would look back at Mr. Jett the way Mitch was doing: like he was about the most clueless person who ever walked through a middle school.

"Are you accusing *these* girls of bullying?" he said to her. "Because from what I saw, you were the one attacking them."

"I was just giving them what they give to everybody else," Mitch said. "Only I was doing it better."

"All right, that's it. Let's go."

Mr. Jett looked like he wanted to yank Mitch to the office by the arm, but he didn't because (A) teachers weren't allowed to touch students and (B) Mitch was as big as he was and it wouldn't look good for her to take him down. At least, that was how I saw it.

He jerked his head toward the door, and Mitch went ahead of him like she'd expected this outcome all along. I ducked into our table.

"What was Mitch thinking?" Ophelia said to me. "She's gonna get suspended."

"What happened?"

Even though it was just the kind of story Ophelia told really well, she just poked at her pizza slice. I looked at Winnie.

She peeked around me to check out the Pack table, but they were all stretched across it trying to get close enough to each other to review. They'd never hear Winnie anyway. Her voice was like a cobweb as she started in.

"They sat down to eat their lunch," she said. "And they all had the burritos because Kylie got one so they all had to have the same thing, I guess."

"So . . . " I said.

"So they were unwrapping them, and all of a sudden there was Mitch, sitting with them. She just knocked all their stuff off that chair and plopped herself down."

"And that's bullying?" I said.

"You haven't heard the whole thing." Winnie inched closer to me, like she wasn't already almost in my lap. "They looked at her like 'What are you doing here?' but nobody said anything. I thought they were just gonna let Mitch sit there, and I thought that was cool of Mitch—you know, like Lydia said. Taking back your rights."

"*Then* what happened?" I loved Winnie, but she was totally dragging this out.

"Oh, for Pete's sake," Ophelia said. "Mitch couldn't leave it alone. Every time one of them started to take a bite she'd go, 'Gross, Heidi. You chew like a cow,' and 'What are you, a cave woman, Kylie? That's disgusting, the way you eat.'" Ophelia pushed aside the piece of pizza she'd destroyed and leaned into the table. "They were totally not even wanting to eat until they saw Mr. Jett come in, and then Kylie gave Heidi this look like, 'Turn it on,' and Heidi started bawlin' like Mitch was killing her. Mitch didn't see Mr. Jett, and she just went, 'Dude, you cry even more disgusting than you eat. You're getting snot in your hot sauce.'" Ophelia's eyes widened. "They should try out for plays. They totally fooled Mr. Jett."

I shook my head. "They don't have to be good actors to make Mr.

Jett think they're the poor little victims. He believes it anyway. All the teachers think they're wonderful."

"Even Mr. V?" Winnie said.

I looked down at my hands. "Especially Mr. V."

"So why even try to do this whole fight-bullying thing?" Ophelia said. "Nobody will ever believe the Pack are the bullies—and now the teachers are gonna think *we* are if we keep hanging out with Mitch."

I started to take out my sandwich, but I tossed it aside.

"What?" Ophelia said.

"First, you don't want us to talk to Ginger. Now we're not supposed to have anything to do with Mitch. You'll hardly talk to me if I don't do absolutely everything your way. You give Winnie the stink eye if she doesn't. What do you *want*?"

"I want it to be like it was before!" Ophelia cried out. "Before we had to be afraid all the time!"

"Please don't start fighting, you guys," Winnie said.

"It's too late for that," Phee said. "It's already happening."

"Only because you won't listen," I said.

"No, because *you* won't! I keep trying to tell you if we do this project and become this 'triblelet' thing, it's going to be worse than you can even imagine."

"Jeepers, Phee, enough with the drama!"

"It's not drama. It's real. You think I'm just saying that to get my own way or something, but I'm not. I'm trying to protect us."

She was talking through her teeth again. I was starting to almost hate that as much as my mother almost hated shrugging.

"If you were really my friend, you wouldn't ask me to go through stuff like yesterday."

"That's *so* not fair," I said.

Ophelia folded her arms and looked at me with her ginormous brown eyes. "And who ever promised you fair, Tori?"

Winnie burst into tears. Phee turned to comfort her. I just got up and left.

Eating in the bathroom didn't seem like such a bad idea after all.

~

Our whole group walked together to my house after school, except for Mitch. I figured she'd probably been kicked out of school for the rest of her life, especially if Kylie's starving mother had been brought in. As we hurried through the cold to Sunrise Lane, Ophelia hung back, so Winnie did too, although she kept begging me with her eyes not to be mad at her. I could feel Ophelia's eyes burning into me as Ginger stuck to my side like Velcro.

It was the longest walk ever.

Lydia had cheese and crackers ready for us and the usual hot chocolate. She looked at the grizzly bear mug Mitch always used and raised an eyebrow at me.

"If you're looking for Mitch," Ophelia said, "she got in trouble at school for bullying."

"That's not exactly what happened," I said.

"Fine. I'm a liar." Ophelia slumped down in her chair and folded her arms and stuck out her chin.

"Does anybody want to bring me up to speed?" Lydia said.

"Not me," Ginger said. "I don't even know what's going on."

The doorbell rang, and Nestlé barked like a wild thing and I went to see who it was while Winnie and Ophelia filled Ginger in. Through the window in the door, I saw a grizzly bear hairdo.

"It's Mitch!" I called toward the kitchen.

"Perfect," Lydia called back.

By the time Mitch made it through Nestlé's greeting and got out of her jacket and took her cocoa from Lydia, Ophelia obviously couldn't stand not knowing any longer.

"What happened?" she said. "Did you get expelled?"

But Lydia wouldn't let Mitch tell that part until she explained what went down in the lunchroom. It was pretty much what Ophelia had described and what I saw with Mr. Jett.

"So he took me to Mrs. Yeats," Mitch said.

"Who's Mrs. Yeats?" Lydia said.

"The principal," Ophelia told her, eyes lit up. She'd obviously forgotten she was pouting. "She is so-o-o strict. She'll suspend you for chewing *gum*."

"Has that ever actually happened?" Ginger said.

Lydia nodded at Mitch. "Moving on . . ."

Mitch, of course, grunted. "She listened to his side of the story and then she asked for mine and I started to tell it and before I was even done he said it wasn't true and I said then there wasn't any point in me even finishing and she told me I had an attitude and I needed to change it."

"That's it?" Ophelia said.

"No. I said I'd change mine when everybody else changed theirs. She said I could only change mine."

"And then you got suspended," Ophelia said.

Jeepers.

"No," Mitch said again. "I told her I would."

"Would what?"

"Change my attitude." Mitch took a sip and wiped the milk off her lip with the side of her hand and looked at Lydia. "I only did all that to see if you were right. And you were."

"Right about what?"

"About not starting a war by doing worse to them than they do to us. It doesn't work. So . . . I'm ready to do it your way."

If (A) I was the hugging kind and (B) Mitch would have put up with me being the hugging kind, I would have hugged her right then. It looked like Lydia wanted to too. Maybe even Winnie and a little bit Ginger.

Ophelia, not so much. She raised her hand.

"Yes, ma'am," Lydia said.

"Are we going to work on our project today?"

"I think that's what we're doing."

"No off—how am I supposed to write up a presentation out of this? Are we figuring out what makes people mean?"

"I think we are," Lydia said.

"I'm in," Mitch said.

"Me too," I said.

Ginger looked across the table at me. "Do I have to do it by myself yet?"

"Good heavens, no," Lydia said.

"Then I'm in."

"What do we have to do?" Win said in a tiny, tiny voice—like she was hoping Phee wouldn't hear her.

"Mitch," Lydia said, "would you turn that board around, the one on the snack bar?"

Mitch flipped a portable dry-erase board I'd seen up in Dad's office before and showed us the side with writing on it. It said:

NOT BYSTANDERS BUT DEFENDERS.

NOT WITNESSES BUT ALLIES.

"The first thing to do is get clear on what your role is as a tribelet," Lydia said. "Are you committed to being the defender and ally of anyone who's bullied?"

Everybody nodded except Ophelia. She was back to pouting.

"The next thing is to realize that this is entirely doable. Here's a statistic for your presentation, Ophelia: 15 percent of girls your age bully, 10 percent are bullied, and 75 percent are in the middle."

"Yes!" I said, loud enough to wake Nestlé up. "Don't anybody go anywhere—I'll be right back."

"More cocoa, anyone?" Lydia said.

I came back in a flash with the chart I'd made of all the girls in the class. I propped it up in front of the dry-erase board.

"Check it out," I said. "It's true. There are way more of us middle people than any other group."

Mitch high-fived me. Winnie almost smiled. Ginger just kept counting the people, over and over.

"This looks like potential for that power *to* I was talking about," Lydia said.

"Except how are you going to get Evelyn and Brittney and the rest of them to do this?" Ophelia said.

"First your tribelet has to do it," Lydia said. "After that, success breeds success. But let's not get ahead of ourselves. Like I said, first you have to do it—and that starts with what you *don't* do."

"Don't do what I did, you mean?" Mitch said.

"Right. And, Ginger, don't let the bullies see you cry or get mad or show any emotion at all. Of course you're going to feel emotion, but you can't let them see it. That's what they want. Don't give them what they want. Save the tears for later."

Ginger looked a little sick. "It's too late. I've already done that like a hundred times."

"Just don't do it anymore."

Mitch sat straight in her chair. "So she does have to get a thick skin."

"Nope, she just has to pretend she has one in front of them."

"You could teach her how to do that, Phee," I said. "You're the best actress."

"You don't have to get an Academy Award, Ginger," Lydia said. "You just have to hide what you feel long enough to get away. That's where the tribelet comes in. Everybody up."

We all followed Lydia into the living room, even Ophelia, only because Winnie took her by the hand.

"Ophelia, you be the Alpha Wolf," Lydia said, "since you have the acting gift. I'll be one of your fellow bullies." She waved the rest of us over to the doorway while she pulled Ophelia to the front of the china cabinet. "This is Ginger's locker. Ginger, you come over here and try to get to it. The rest of you stay there for a minute."

Then Lydia turned to Phee and pretended to be whispering and pointing until Ginger got to them.

"Ask her what she wants," Lydia whispered to Ophelia. "Be the Alpha Wolf."

I held my breath. If Phee couldn't participate in this, then was she even the person I used to know?

"I suppose you want to get into your locker," Ophelia said to Ginger. She smiled meanly.

"Not happenin', loser," Lydia said.

"Why?" Ginger said.

"Because we don't want you here," Lydia said. "Right, 'Kylie'?"

Ophelia shook her head. "Do we have to keep doing this? I don't like it."

"What don't you like?"

"How mean I can be!"

"Don't worry," Lydia said. "We know you're not mean like that in real life. But isn't it scary how mean anyone can be if they're allowed to? Let's do it again, only this time, Mitch, you and Tori and Winnie come with Ginger. Act friendly to her and do *not* say anything to the Pack. Just walk Ginger straight to her locker. Ginger, all you say is, 'Excuse me, but I need to get to my locker.' Got that?"

We all nodded. Lydia looked at Phee. "Just work with me, okay?"

"Okay," Ophelia said.

Lydia and Ophelia went back to pointing and snickering at Ginger. Ginger started toward the "locker," and we all went with her.

"What do you need out of your locker, Ginger?" I said.

"My science book," she said.

"Don't forget your Spanish book too," Winnie said, and then she giggled.

Mitch didn't say anything, but then she probably wouldn't in real life either.

When we got there, Lydia was still looking at Ginger like she was pond scum and I could see Ginger start to wilt. I nudged her in the back.

"Excuse me!" Ginger blurted out. "I need to get my stuff out of here."

She took another step forward, and we stepped with her. Ophelia immediately got out of the way and let her through.

"Why did you do that?" Lydia said to Phee.

"Because there's more of them than there are of us," Phee said.

"Did anybody give you a scary look?"

"No. Well, Mitch kind of did."

"Dude, that's the way I always look," Mitch said.

"So you didn't feel threatened?"

Ophelia shook her head. "I just felt like, 'What's the point in still standing here?'"

"Exactly."

"But is the Pack gonna do that?" Winnie almost whispered it.

"If you stand there long enough, probably. Try it."

We did. Phee and Lydia stood there until our noses were almost touching. Even after Winnie started to giggle, they finally moved.

"That's called safety in a group," Lydia said.

"Let's do another one!" Winnie said.

"That's enough for now," Lydia said, although she looked pretty happy with Winnie. "This is all about taking baby steps. One small thing at a time. Besides, I have one more important thing to tell you. Let's sit down."

While everybody else regrouped in the kitchen, I tugged Ophelia back by her sweater sleeve.

"You did good," I said. "Are you in now?"

She put the end of her braid to her lips. "Maybe."

"I totally am," I said. "And Winnie is. You don't want to be left out, right?"

"Are you ladies joining us?" Lydia called from the kitchen.

Ophelia brushed past me and headed down the hall. The bathroom door slammed behind her.

What did I just say to make that happen? I sighed and joined everybody else in the kitchen.

Lydia didn't ask where Phee was. She just got very serious and told us this:

"You can change a lot of this bullying as a tribelet. But I want you to promise me that if you run into something that you can't change, you will report it to an adult."

"Tattle," Mitch said.

"No. Tattling is when you tell on somebody to get them *into* trouble. Reporting is when you tell something to get somebody *out* of trouble. Tattling is sort of like that whole eye-for-an-eye thing you tried. 'I'm going to tell on them so they'll get what they deserve.'"

"Neener-neener-neener," I said.

Winnie giggled.

"Exactly," Lydia said. "Are we clear on that?"

"So if the Pack is about to beat somebody up and we can't talk 'em out of it, we go get a grown-up?" Mitch said.

"Send somebody for the grown-up first, before you try to talk them out of it," Lydia said. "Mitch, you could stay and try that. Maybe Tori too. But send Winnie for the adult." She put her hand on Winnie's arm. "You're stronger than you think, honey, but not for that role."

Winnie turned into a puddle of relief.

"You all see if you can agree to that promise," Lydia said as she climbed down from her chair. "I'll go see what's up with our friend Ophelia."

As I watched her do her kind of rocking sideways walk out of the kitchen I thought two things: (A) She would probably be a better friend to Ophelia right now than me, and I never thought anybody could be and (B) her walk looked wobblier than it usually did.

"I promise."

I looked at Winnie and said, "Huh?"

"I promise to always report to an adult if there's something we can't handle."

"I will too," I said.

Mitch grunted a *yes* and poked Ginger in the arm. "What about you?"

"I don't know. I've tried telling a grown-up before and all they say is stuff like 'What did you do to her first?' or 'Why can't you girls just get along?'"

I wouldn't have believed that before all this, but I did now.

"Maybe if we didn't report what was happening to us but only what was happening to somebody else," I said. "So like if somebody was threatening to hurt you, I would go get somebody, and if it was happening to me, you would go get somebody."

She seemed to consider that. Mitch nodded at me.

"What?" I said.

"I always thought you were just book smart," she said. "But I think you're pretty smart about a lot of stuff." She held up a hand to high-five me. Then she high-fived Winnie, which was really pretty funny looking. Winnie started giggling again, and she was still at it when Lydia came back in. She stood behind her chair, peeking over the top.

"Where's Phee?" I said.

"She went home."

"Home?"

"She was upset so she called her mom to come get her."

"Why was she upset?" Winnie said, looking suddenly upset herself.

"She wouldn't tell me, but I wouldn't worry too much." Lydia's eyes were on me. "She probably just needs some time to figure things out."

"That means she's decided not to be in the tribelet," Mitch said.

"For now," Lydia said.

I think everything would have crashed in on me right then if my dad hadn't come in the back door wearing a grin almost bigger than his shoulders.

"I have great news!" he said and came right to me and put his face close to mine.

"Granna?" I said.

"She's awake," he said. "Let's go see her."

Chapter Fourteen

Mom and Dad had a different definition of "awake" than I did.

From the way Dad was smiling in the car, in spite of the rain pummeling the windshield like icy little fists, and the way Mom looped her arm through mine as we walked down the hospital hall together, I expected to see Granna sitting up in bed telling everybody she didn't need to be there because she was healthy as a sixteen-year-old.

They could have told me she'd be flat on her back hooked up to all kinds of weird, beeping, light-up machines. They *should* have told me she opened her eyes for only about fifteen seconds out of every minute. And that she wasn't talking.

I stood next to her bed staring down at the person who looked more like an extraterrestrial than Granna and wished she'd say, "Victoria, my pet."

"Talk to her if you want," Mom said. "She can hear us."

"How do you know that?" I said.

"Watch this." Dad put his lips close to Granna's ear. "Mom, Tori's here."

Granna's eyes drifted open about a thirty-second of an inch, to be almost exact, and then closed.

"See?" Dad said.

I wasn't convinced.

If all those machines had been hooked up to a stranger, I could've gotten into studying them. But since it was Granna they were connected to, they were starting to freak me out. Mom obviously saw that because she looped arms with me again and walked me to a family waiting room at the end of the hall.

"You all right?" she said when I'd dropped onto a square-looking couch.

"Kind of," I said. "Are you sure she's gonna be okay?"

Mom sat beside me and brushed the hair out of my face. It dawned on me that while she'd been there taking care of Granna I hadn't been too good about brushing and flossing and matching my clothes. Her eyes were droopy and baggy, so I figured she was too tired to notice that I wasn't being a lady.

"I know it seems like she's still sick, and she is," Mom said. "But she's out of danger. Now she just has to recover."

"Is she always going to have those tubes in her nose?"

Mom lowered her face at me. "Are you serious? Do you really think Granna would put up with that? They're keeping her sleepy so she won't rip everything out and announce that she's going home."

"So she'll be like she was before?"

Mom nodded. But not before I saw a shadow go through her eyes.

"She won't, will she?" I said.

Again, my mother pushed some hair from my forehead. "We can't get anything past you, can we, Tor? They won't know until she's totally conscious and that could take a few days. But she's breathing on her own and her heart is beating strong. Those are good signs."

All of a sudden it felt like my face was collapsing. Mom pulled me into her chest and held on while she petted my head the way I did Nestlé's.

"Go ahead and cry," she said. "You honor Granna with your tears. God love you, sweetie."

As I've said before, my family didn't talk a lot about God. If his name was coming up now, we must really need help. I wasn't sure how to pray right then. All I could think of was "Our Father who art in heaven," so I said that in my head.

I wished somebody could tell me exactly how that could work to fix this.

Mom took me home so she could shower and go back to the hospital to relieve Dad. Lydia was still there at the house, making a pot of what she told me was cream of potato soup. Ginger was buttering bread, and Winnie was setting the table. Mitch stood at the stove stirring while Lydia sprinkled things into the pot.

I could feel my face starting to collapse again.

"I thought you might need your friends around you," Lydia said. "Nothing like your tribelet in times like these."

Ophelia should be there.

I had to shove that thought away, or there would be no putting my face back together, ever.

Mom took some soup with her to share with Dad, and our tribelet gathered at the kitchen table. Nestlé lay with his head smothering my feet. He knew I'd be letting him lick my bowl when I was done, but I also decided he knew I was feeling like pieces of me might fall off and he was holding them on.

"I'm going upstairs to catch up on some work," Lydia said. "You all holler if you need anything."

I wondered how it was okay with my dad that she was spending so much time with us. But I pushed that away too. I was just glad she was.

Who'd have thought I'd ever feel that way?

"Do you want to talk about your grandmother?" Ginger said.

"Not really," I said.

"That's cool then. I hate when people make you talk about stuff you didn't even get a chance to think about yet."

I was surprised, until I remembered about her mom dying. She must know from experience.

"Then can we talk about what Lydia told us?" Winnie said. "I'm getting it all confused."

Mitch half grunted, half slurped. "What's to be confused about? You got 'Baby Steps'—that's 'start small' and don't try to save the whole entire world all at once. Then you got that whole 'Golden Rule' thing."

"What 'Golden Rule Thing'?" I said.

Ginger waved her spoon, launching a piece of drippy potato across the table. "Like 'do unto others,' that one."

Mitch nodded. "She said that was our rule of thumb."

"We could call it the gold thumb."

"You mean like a code?" Ginger said to me.

"Yeah," Mitch said. "And then you've got 'Save the Tears.'"

"Don't cry in front of the Pack when they're mean to you." Now it was Winnie who had the cartoon lightbulb over her head. "I get it. So we have a code name for each of the rules."

"Don't forget about, 'We have to tell an adult if what they do gets out of control,'" I said.

Winnie gave me a little frown. "I think it's always out of control."

"Report Alert," Ginger said.

Mitch held up her hand, and for a minute Ginger just blinked at it. It took her that long to figure out Mitch wanted to high-five her.

Strange about Ginger: (A) she was way smarter than you thought at first about a lot of things, but (B) she knew hardly anything about stuff friends did. Probably because she'd never had any.

Jeepers.

~

The next day, Friday, started off with waffles that were hot so the butter collected in golden pools in the squares. Mom even warmed up the maple syrup and told me to pour on as much as I wanted. Too bad I didn't feel like eating.

"I think Granna's going to get stronger every day," Mom said as she kissed me good-bye on the forehead. "You keep thinking that too."

I tried. But that wasn't the only thing killing my appetite.

I wanted to talk to Phee. I *needed* to talk to her, or I was going to turn into pieces of confetti. But she wasn't at our usual place on the second floor by the big window when I got to school. It was the first time that whole year.

Winnie was there, though. And so was Mitch. They both sat on the floor with their backs to the wall looking at something together.

Then Winnie saw me and her eyes lit up like a couple of birthday candles. I hadn't seen that in a long time, so they must be looking at something so cool it took her mind off Phee.

"She made these," Mitch said when I joined them and handed me a stack of cards.

They were the size of the kind you play Uno or Go Fish with. They were even covered in clear contact paper to make them stiff like real cards. On the front of each one was a picture and some words, which she'd obviously made on the computer.

The one with "Baby Steps" on it had a pair of baby's shoes.

For the "Gold Thumb," there was a big yellow, well, thumb.

"Save the Tears": a huge smiley face.

"Safe in a Group": a bunch of hands joined.

But my favorite one was "Report Alert." That one showed a person running like she was totally on a mission. It actually looked a little bit like Winnie.

"She made them," Mitch said again, jerking her head toward Win.

"Did you high-five her?" I said.

Winnie giggled. "About twelve times."

"Only five," Mitch said. "One for each card."

Mitch got kind of a goofy smile on her face, and it occurred to me that she probably hadn't had too many friends in her life either before now.

"This is way cool, Win," I said.

I started to hand the cards back to her, but she shook her head. "Those are yours. I made a set for each of us. Ginger too. And Ophelia. Just in case."

"She'll totally dig these," I said. "And maybe it'll make her change her mind."

"I already tried." The shine in Winnie's eyes faded. "She said no."

I didn't know how I could sit next to Ophelia in first period and not say something, but she wasn't there, and she didn't show up for any of our other morning classes either. By the time we got to fourth period, I really was turning to confetti.

"Is she sick or something?" Mitch said, pointing to Phee's chair when we got together for our fifteen-minute group time.

"I don't know," I said.

"I thought you guys were best friends," Ginger said.

I felt a couple of pieces of myself fall off.

"Are we meeting at your house today?" Winnie said, voice wee.

"Got to," Mitch said. "We're reporting our research."

"What about Ophelia?" From Ginger's face, I knew *she* understood the definition of *concerned*. I wasn't sure why. Phee just wasn't that nice to her.

"I guess we'll have to start without her," I said.

I was grateful to Mr. V right then for telling us the dates for our presentations were on the board and we should write them down. Like Ginger said, sometimes you can't talk about stuff you haven't had a chance to think about yet.

It was just Winnie and me at lunch, until Mitch joined us. I could tell she had news.

She pulled a piece of paper out of her sweatshirt pocket and flattened it on the table. "That Kylie chick was passing this around and I got it."

"How?"

"I just grabbed it from Douglas. He barely even noticed. Those boys are about two puppies short of a pet store."

Winnie giggled. I didn't. I was reading the paper on the table, and it was *so* not funny.

"Did you read this, Mitch?" I said.

"Yeah. That's why I brought it over here."

I glanced at the Pack table, where Kylie had obviously broken a nail because they were all hovering over her fingers with files and a bottle of polish that smelled worse than the corn dogs.

"Don't let them know you have this," I whispered.

"Why?" Winnie said. "What does it say?"

I pushed it toward her and read it again silently while she ran her eyes down the page.

We Hate Gingerbread Lovers Club

If you hate Gingerbread or people who love Gingerbread tell why and you will be a member. You have to make a new reason. You can't copy somebody else's.

That part was typed. Below it were a bunch of lines with numbers beside them, like a test where you had to fill in the answers. A couple of people had.

1. Gingerbread smells gross. I can't stand to be near it.
2. Anybody who likes gingerbread has to be blind. Or stupid.
3. ONE of the Gingerbread People thinks she's smarter than everybody else and she's so not. She's just conseeded.

"That's not even how you spell *conceited*," Mitch said.

"This is about Ginger, huh?" Winnie said.

"Not just her. Us," Mitch said before I could stop her.

Winnie practically dissolved beside me, just like I knew she would.

"We're 'Gingerbread People'?" she squeaked out. "Just because we're in a group with her?"

If my heart had been attached to one of Granna's machines, it would have been beeping all over the place and nurses would have come running. But it was time to tell them.

"They're trying to make everybody hate us so nobody will believe our report."

Mitch scowled at the paper and said, "Huh?"

"How do you know that, Tori?" Winnie said.

"Because. One of them told me if we did our project on mean people, I was 'dead.'"

Winnie gasped so loud the soccer girls at the other end of the table all looked at us.

"Don't have a heart attack," I said to Winnie. "They're not really going to *kill* me."

"No," Mitch said. "You'll just wish you were dead."

"What do you *mean*?"

For somebody whose voice you could hardly hear half the time, Winnie was making enough noise to get everybody in the whole cafeteria stretching their necks toward us. I shoved the paper under my lunch tray.

"It's just an expression." I gave Mitch a really hard look. "Right?"

Mitch just grunted as usual. Winnie covered her face with her little hands. Why did Ophelia have to pick today to be absent? She always took care of Winnie when she started to melt down. I was no good at it.

But neither was Mitch, and somebody had to do it. Wasn't that what Lydia was trying to teach us? To be a tribelet who was there for each other?

I dug into the pocket of my jean jacket and pulled out the cards. I put "Save the Tears" on the table and then poked Winnie.

She peeked out between her fingers. Slowly she nodded and took a bunch of deep breaths.

"Way to suck it up," Mitch said. "Good job."

Then I put "Baby Steps" on the table.

"We have to do something," I said. "Nothing big."

"Like go shove that club thing in their face," Mitch said.

"Right. We should just . . . just throw it away so nobody else sees it."

"They're gonna wonder where it went."

"And they'll know it was us." Winnie's hands were about to go over her face again, so I grabbed one and pressed the "Save the Tears" card into it.

"I don't know if I can do this," she said.

"You don't have to *do* anything," Mitch said. "Just quit cryin'."

Winnie nodded, and I saw her swallow. At least she was trying.

"Is it time for a 'Report Alert'?" she said.

Mitch shook her head. "There's no names on there. And no teacher's gonna believe I saw Kylie passing it around. Besides, it's not like they're saying they're gonna do anything."

"Okay then," I said. "I'll just dump my tray and put this in the trash with it. Meet me at the lockers. We're gonna make sure Ginger can get her stuff for English, right?"

Winnie looked like I'd just asked her to throw herself in front of a train, but she nodded. Like I said, she was totally trying.

I left the table and stood by the trash trying to decide the best way to totally destroy the stupid paper.

"Are you actually going to *dump* that tray, Vic*tor*ia?" said a voice behind me. "Or do you like standing there looking at the garbage?"

Kylie.

I closed my eyes. Which card should I go with?

"Well, it figures you'd want to hang out with whatever smells disgusting."

A faint howling began. The whole pack was there, behind me. "Safe in a Group" definitely wasn't an option.

"Save the Tears" . . . "Baby Steps" . . . "Gold Thumb."

I whirled around. Kylie was still standing there, head tilted so her splashy haircut fell across her cheek like a model in a kids' clothes catalog.

"Put your stuff on my tray," I said. "I'll dump it for you."

Her blue and gold eyes got bigger. "Excuse me?"

"As long as I'm hanging out here I might as well throw your garbage away too. Put it on my tray."

Okay, so I wasn't actually following the golden rule. Not totally. I really just wanted her and her Pack out of there.

I could almost see the possibilities flipping through Kylie's brain. I could be tricking her. Setting her up for a prank. Trying to make her think I wanted to be nice to her so I could surprise her with food in her face.

Oh, wait, her eyes seemed to say. I wasn't smart enough for that. That was *her* specialty.

"Okay," she said. "Here."

She took a step forward and tilted her tray. An open carton of milk slid toward me and slipped past my balled up lunch bag and right into the front of my jacket. It was followed by two mustard-covered burger buns and a paper container full of ketchup. I was covered in the remains of Kylie's picky-eater lunch.

"Oops," she said. "Here. Take my tray too, why don'tcha?"

She shoved her tray under mine, which meant I had to open my fingers to grab it. When I did, the paper I'd been protecting under there got loose and made a lazy descent to the floor. It landed right side up.

The smirk vanished from Kylie's face, and she swooped down to pick it up. My brain finally kicked into gear, and I whipped around and dumped the contents of both trays into the garbage. Just let me get rid of the trays too and then I could escape to the restroom to clean the milk and mustard off myself.

"Where did you get this?" Kylie was close to the side of my face and her mint-gum breath was hot in my ear. Just like it was before. I was about to be told I was going to be "dead" again, and I was sick of it.

"You mean your I Hate Gingerbread Club Membership form?" I said and dropped the trays into the holder.

Kylie pulled back, although the paper still hung about an inch from my nose. "You were going to throw it out, weren't you?"

"That was my plan."

She snatched it away, nostrils flaring like little trumpets. "I don't know why you're even trying because you can't stop us."

"Stop you from what? Being mean to people?"

That obviously wasn't what she expected me to say. It wasn't what I expected me to say either. So we both just stood there while people worked around us with their trays.

"Tori Taylor!"

Mr. Jett. Again. For once I was glad he was there because Kylie ducked through the crowd and disappeared.

But I stopped being glad when he said, "This is your third and last chance to decide you're going to go with the flow around here. Next time: automatic lunch detention."

"Kylie too?" I said. Stupidly.

Mr. Jett adjusted his glasses, nose and all. "What is it with you girls picking on Kylie?"

I wanted to say, "Are you serious?" But I wasn't that stupid.

"Sorry," I said instead. "Can I go now?"

"Go. You have five minutes before the bell rings."

As soon as Mr. Jett was too busy yelling at someone else to watch me, I broke into a run. I had to get to the lockers or "Safe in a Group" was going to be a total bust.

Although I didn't clock it, I got to the top of the stairs in record time, mostly because everybody got out of my way when they saw Kylie's lunch plastered all over the front of me. Ginger, Winnie, and Mitch were waiting for me at the end of the lockers and just like they always were, the Pack was lounged against Ginger's.

"Where you been?" Mitch grunted at me.

"Long story."

"What's that all over you?" Ginger said.

"I'll tell you later. You ready?"

Ginger peeled her gaze from my jacket and drew herself up taller. "You're gonna stay with me, right?"

"Right," I said.

Mitch gave Ginger's back a little poke, and she stumbled forward. The Pack looked up, all except Kylie who apparently couldn't be bothered to move her eyes from her new manicure.

"What do you need from your locker, Ginger?" I said, just like we'd rehearsed it.

She didn't say anything. That *wasn't* how we rehearsed it.

"Say you need your literature book," Winnie whispered to her.

"Lit book!"

"And Spanish?"

"Spanish!"

"Is somebody deaf?" Riannon said from her position next to Kylie. "Heidi, do you think someone's deaf? Is that why she doesn't hear when we say to get lost?"

"Don't answer," I muttered to Ginger.

She didn't. She just kept walking, and we kept walking with her. It was like watching a movie where the car is about to hit a wall and you're in it.

We continued moving forward, shoulders touching, until Riannon narrowed her eyes at us and said, "Hello, we're standing here."

"Excuse me," Ginger said, foghorn going full blast. "I just need to get some stuff out of my locker." It had never dawned on me until then that she only talked like that when she was really nervous.

Heidi took a tiny step sideways, and then she sort of jumped like somebody had pinched her. Probably because Kylie had.

"You don't need to go to your locker, Gingerbread," Heidi said. "You just think you do."

Mitch opened her mouth, but she was on the other side of Winnie so I couldn't stop her. Ginger beat her to it anyway.

"I'm getting my stuff out of my locker. So please move."

We moved, two steps more. Any closer and I was going to be looking up Kylie's nostrils again. Fortunately, she didn't have any food to dump on me this time . . .

Wait . . . why hadn't I thought of it sooner?

I squeezed myself between Winnie and Ginger so I was at the front of our little crowd. It was actually fun to watch five pairs of eyes pop, one by one. I took another step, and the Pack split right in half. Seriously. Who wanted to have Kylie's lunch all over *them* too?

Ginger slipped through to her locker, and Mitch stood on one side of her, Winnie and I on the other, while she got her books out. When we turned to head for Mrs. Fickus's class, the Pack had disappeared.

"Good job, tribelet," I said. "We better get to class."

I peeled my jacket off along the way and stuffed it, inside out, into my backpack. We got to the room with thirty seconds to spare.

As we slid into our seats, I couldn't remember ever feeling that . . . satisfied. Yeah, that was the word.

I sure wanted to share it with Phee.

Chapter Fifteen

When Mitch, Winnie, Ginger and I rounded the bend on Sunrise Lane where we could see my house that afternoon, I stopped right in the middle of the road. Ophelia's mom's van was there, and Ophelia was getting out.

"I guess she got better," Mitch said as the van pulled away.

I went into high gear up the hill with Winnie right on my heels so I could catch Phee before she went inside, but she waited for me on the porch. She and Winnie hugged, and then Phee said, "Win, could you go on in? I need to talk to Tori for a minute."

Winnie did it, but not before I saw her face turn a shade paler.

"You're better!" Ginger bellowed out when she and Mitch got to the porch. "That's so cool!"

"I'm a *little* better," Ophelia said. "I just came to give my part of the research because my mom said I have to." Then she added, "I'm not contagious."

I looked at her closer. She didn't look even a little bit sick to me. Phee never did. Even when her whole family got the flu last Thanksgiving, she could still eat turkey and pumpkin pie.

My stomach churned like I'd had the tacos at lunch. Which I hadn't.

When the door closed behind Mitch and Ginger, Ophelia said, "I can only be here as long as we're talking about the project. My mom says I'm not required to stay when we start talking about the Indian tribe thing because it doesn't have anything to do with our project. I'm supposed to call her when that happens, and she'll come get me."

I would have argued with her if it hadn't sounded like she was reciting lines she'd rehearsed—and not even with that much expression.

"It's not an 'Indian tribe thing,'" I said. "It's the 'tribelet.'"

"Whatever." Her face was still all blank, like she wasn't feeling anything. But I knew she was because (A) she was my best friend and (B) she wouldn't look at me.

"Jeepers, Phee," I said.

"I'm not supposed to say anything else," she said.

And then she turned away and went into the house.

By the time I got there, Ophelia was already giving the same rehearsed speech to Lydia and the girls.

"Fine with me," Mitch said.

It wasn't fine with me, and I knew it wasn't with Winnie either. Even Ginger looked like she could cry any second, although I still couldn't figure out why. I almost didn't want Phee there if she was going to act like this.

Lydia said we should give our reports then, so Ophelia could get back to bed.

We each told what we'd looked up and Winnie wrote it all down.

Mitch informed us that there was no gene for being mean. "No mean gene!" Ginger said. I had to admit that was kind of funny. Mitch also said there was this childhood development thing that every normal kid went through, and being hateful to other people wasn't on it.

Ginger said she found out that since being mean was a "learned behavior," it could also be unlearned.

Winnie gave us a list of the ways boy-mean and girl-mean were different. Boys mostly just stuffed other boys into trash cans and stole their lunches and stuff like that. Not like what the Pack did.

Ophelia leaned sideways in her chair and looked at what Winnie had written down. "Is that enough then? Are we done? We answered our question, right?"

"Which one of those three things do you want me to answer first?" Lydia said. She'd been listening really quietly through all our presentations, like she respected what we were saying. Now she was smiling at Ophelia.

But Phee didn't smile back. "I just want to know if we have to talk about this anymore."

"That's up to the group," Lydia said. "You've definitely answered the question about whether meanness is inborn or learned. But wasn't the whole study supposed to be about *why* people become mean?"

"Yes," I said.

"But why do we have to do that?" Ophelia said.

"Because!" Ginger wasn't using the foghorn voice, unless a foghorn can sound desperate, like there's no other way to get through the mist. "I want to know why they have to pick on me! I know I'm not the prettiest girl ever and I don't have good clothes. I don't have a mom to teach me all that stuff. But why can't they just leave me alone? I try and try and they just keep . . . bullying me. I know you're all trying to help, but is it ever gonna stop? I don't know who else to be!"

Ginger was crying so hard I didn't think any amount of Kleenex would help, but I got her the box anyway. Lydia climbed from her chair and went to stand beside Ginger, who had to look down at her.

"That Kylie person doesn't bully you because there's anything wrong with *you*. She does it because there's something wrong with *her*. And what's wrong with her is that she's a bully. You've all learned that's not normal and it's not okay. And I'm teaching you how to stop it *because* it's not okay. Not because *you're* not okay."

By then Winnie was crying too. "I like you, Ginger," she said. Well, blubbered. "You're smart and you never make fun of anybody and I wish I was as brave as you about speaking up."

"You are, though," Ginger said, also blubbering. "You should have seen her today, Lydia."

"I think you're awesome," Mitch said, punching Ginger in the arm. "Who needs clothes and all that stuff anyway? Okay, so you could wash your hair more often, but that's no reason to not let you go to your own locker. I don't get that."

I kind of wanted to remove Mitch's tongue, but Ginger was grinning at her like she'd just told her she was Miss Universe material.

There was so much crying going on, I decided to get us back on track. I also didn't want Ophelia to leave yet, and she was looking like she wanted to. She was going to have to have her stomach pumped if she consumed any more of her hair.

"So it's scientific," I said. "If you have a problem, first you have to find out why it's happening and then you can fix it. So we're not done with our project."

Ophelia let out a sigh big enough to blow the George Washington place mats right off the table. "How are we supposed to find *that* out?"

"I think it's time to do a little field study," Lydia said. "You've learned all you can from the books and the Internet. Now you need to observe what's going on in your own environment."

"I don't get it," Mitch, Phee, and Ginger all said at the same time. Winnie would have probably said it too, but she was busy writing stuff.

"While you're taking your Baby Steps," Lydia said, "and keeping Safe in a Group and all the rest of the things on Winnie's wonderful cards, observe how people respond. That will tell you some of the whys."

"You're going to keep showing us how to do that, right?" Winnie said.

"If you want me to."

The whole tribelet said yes. Except for Ophelia. She slipped out of her chair and headed with her jacket for the living room, where I knew she was going to call her mom.

I followed her. Nestlé came with me. It was like he knew what was about to happen because he flopped himself down right in front of the door and gave me a worried look. Not concerned. Worried.

Ophelia was already poking buttons on the phone by Dad's chair.

"Don't go yet, okay?" I said.

"Mom?" she said into the receiver. "It's happening again."

"What's happening?" I whispered.

"Yes, come now."

She put the phone back on the table and turned to look out the window, like her mom was going to be teleported or something.

"Did your mom really say you can't be in the tribelet?" I said.

"She says it's silly. She said there were always bullies and there always will be, and it'll go away if we don't make a big deal out of it. And that's what we're doing."

"I don't get it," I said. "You're the one who keeps saying it *is* a big deal."

"Unless we just leave it alone!" Ophelia still had her back to me, but I could see her reflection in the mirror. She was done trying not to look like she felt something. Now she was feeling everything. "I didn't tell her you were forcing me to make a choice though. She'd be mad at you."

"*Me?* When did *I*—?"

Ophelia whirled around so fast she hit her own self in the face with her braid. "You said if I didn't join in, I'd be left out!"

"That's not what I meant!"

"Yes, it is. That's why I was so sick I couldn't go to school. My mom doesn't know that either."

"You don't have to choose," I said. "Because it's working. Ginger got to go to her locker today because we went with her. And Winnie was so brave!"

"Well, I'm not brave! I can't do this, Tori!"

"Even if it's no big deal?"

"It *is* a big deal. Okay? It is! I want to believe my mom, but I don't."

"So faking being sick is just an excuse not to help?"

"Why do you keep hurting my feelings?"

"I don't mean to."

Ophelia turned back to the window. "That's my mom. I'm going."

"Wait," I said. "What's gonna happen now?"

She stopped halfway to the door, but she still didn't look at me. "I'll give you my part of the report. I'm not gonna be in the tribe. And if you want me to be your best friend again, that'll be when you're not in it either."

"Now who's making somebody choose?" I said.

She didn't answer. She just stepped over Nestlé and flew out the front door. I ran to the window and peered between the curtains to watch her. She would be back. She wouldn't even get to the car before she ran to the porch again, threw her arms around me, and said, "I'm so sorry, Tori! I take it all back."

But she just got into the front seat of her mom's van and didn't even look my way as they drove down Sunrise Lane.

Something heavy pressed my leg, and I looked down to see Nestlé leaning against me. His eyes were droopy and sad. I was sure I looked just like him.

Chapter Sixteen

After Mitch and Ginger left with Winnie's mom, I couldn't even move from my kitchen chair. Lydia came and sat next to me.

"You want to talk about it?" she said.

"Do I hurt people's feelings?" that other Me said.

"I've never seen you do that. Did someone say you did?"

"Ophelia. All I said was that she was faking being sick as an excuse not to help and that her mom is helping her get out of it by telling her she didn't have to be part of the tribelet to do the project."

Lydia gave a soft, husky laugh. "You really are a smart girl, Taylor. That's very perceptive."

"I shouldn't have said it to her though."

"Why not? She needed to hear it. I told you girls in the beginning to say what you meant, or this isn't going to work."

"Yeah, but she's scared. I should've been nicer."

Lydia curled a piece of her hair around her finger. "Are *you* scared?"

"Sometimes. Some stuff those girls say is just dumb. But then

Kylie gets this look in her eye, and it's like, my palms start to sweat. Then I feel like a loser."

"You are most definitely not a loser. Look . . ."

She waited until I actually looked at her.

"Nobody feels safe in the presence of exclusion and victimization."

She paused again, like she wanted to make sure I knew those words.

"Really?" I said. "Even when you get the power *to* like you have?"

"Just because I'm brave doesn't mean I don't get scared. But I keep going, doing what's right, because that's what God wants me to do."

She said God so naturally I almost didn't notice it. What I did notice was how much more she was limping as she climbed from the chair and rocked her way over to the refrigerator.

"How about a grilled cheese sandwich?"

"Does it hurt to be a little person?"

Lydia stopped with her fingers around the fridge handle. "You're far more compassionate than you give yourself credit for, Tori Taylor. That's why you're the leader of the tribelet."

"I am?"

"You are." She pulled open the door. "And yes, sometimes it does hurt. And then I pray."

~

Later, Nestlé and I went upstairs to say good night to Dad.

"I was just getting ready to come down, Tor," he said. "Everything feels kind of disconnected these days, doesn't it?"

I nodded as I curled up in my chair. He got his pipe and sat with me. Even with Granna getting better, his face was still pinchy.

"Do you get to keep your contract?" I said.

"Don't know yet. I have to go to San Francisco to talk to the producers this weekend."

It felt kind of selfish to think it, but I said, "Is Lydia going with you?"

Dad chuckled. "No. I think you need her more than I do."

"Is it okay with you that she's been helping us?"

He did a curious Nestlé-head-tilt. "Of course it's okay. She's getting her work done up here." He motioned his pipe toward the wall in front of us. "Did you see what she did for me?"

I looked up at a map that had all colors of pushpins in it, with drawings of buildings and streets, and things written in printing so good I at first thought it was done on a computer.

"That's Grass Valley the way it looked in the Gold Rush days," Dad said. "Best one I've ever seen." He got up and pointed with the pipe. "You can see where all the wealthy mine owners and investors lived—here along Church—and then down here where all the people who made the money for them lived. I've never seen the difference between the big people and the little people made so clear."

I stared at it. But I wasn't seeing the mansions and the shacks. I was seeing Gold Country Middle School.

"You just gave me a great idea, Dad," I said. "Thanks!"

"Don't thank me. Thank Lydia. That young woman is a gold mine in herself."

"I know, right?" I wriggled out of the chair. "I need to go do something, okay?"

"You go. But don't stay up too late."

"When's Mom going to start sleeping at home again?" I said.

"As soon as Granna's awake enough to give everybody a bad time. Won't be long now."

"For real?"

"For real."

"Then I need to go do something while it's still fresh in my mind."

"Do it," Dad said and kissed me on the top of the head.

I almost cried then. I wouldn't really be happy until Granna was doing that. And saying, "Victoria, my pet."

I stopped at the top of the steps so fast Nestlé ran into me. When Granna said it, maybe it would drive out the memory of Kylie saying it to make fun of me.

Yeah, I really needed to make a map. And not just for Ginger.

~

Dad didn't say anything about me staying up until midnight doing it, even though we had breakfast together at the diner the next morning. Mom joined us. Maybe that was why.

"I want you to sleep all day," Dad said to her.

"For a few hours maybe. Then I need to check in at the shop. Make sure it's still there." She squeezed my hand. "How you doing, sweetie?"

"I'm okay," I said.

"She's amazing, is what she is," Dad said.

That seemed like a good time to ask . . .

"Is it okay if the tribelet comes over after your nap? We're working on a project."

"Did you say 'tribelet'?" Dad said. "Like the Maidu?"

I nodded. "Lydia taught us that."

"I really am out of the loop," Mom said.

It occurred to me that she really was. She didn't know anything about, well, anything, because my whole world had changed since January 26. To be exact.

"Absolutely they can come over," Mom said. "It's the least I can do for you being amazing."

As soon as I got home I called Winnie and asked her to get Ginger and Mitch and come over. It was a good thing she was efficient and got everybody's phone numbers at the start of the project. I never thought about stuff like that. We really did each have a job we were good at.

It made me miss Phee again. The old Phee.

By the time they all got there, Mom had gotten up from her nap and gone to the shop. The four of us tried to cram into my room, but with Nestlé in there too, it was way crowded. I asked Dad if we could go up to the cabin.

"As long as you don't get too cold up there," he said.

Nobody was even thinking about the cold once they saw the cabin.

After everybody finished telling me how lucky I was to have a "hideout," as Mitch put it, I passed out flashlights and pointed to the map I'd tacked to the wall.

"These are the places the Pack won't let you go, Ginger," I said, running the light over the restrooms, the cafeteria, and the lockers.

"You forgot in front of the office where they always go before school," she said. "And the library after school."

"Jeepers," I said.

"They think they own the whole place," Mitch said, "which is a joke because they don't ever go in the seventh- and eighth-grade wings. They might be all that in our wing, but they'd be toast over there."

"We're not even allowed in that part," Ginger said. "I tried going to the restroom in the seventh-grade wing, but Mrs. Yeats told me I couldn't be there."

"It doesn't matter," I said. "You won't need to go over there because we're gonna make all these areas"—I shined the flashlight again—"safe for everybody."

"How?" Winnie said.

"First, we reroute our moves from class to class so we don't even have to deal with the Pack if we don't want to."

"That's runnin' scared," Mitch said. Even in the almost dark I could see her hair standing up.

"No," I said, "it's just saving our energy for when we need it. Seriously, do you want them in your face everywhere you go?"

Winnie said no before Ginger did.

I pointed out the new routes I'd figured out. We went over them until I was sure we all had them down.

"Now, see these yellow areas?" I said. "These are the places where we always need to be when Ginger needs to go there."

"Okay, but there's five of them and only four of us now," Winnie said.

"It worked yesterday, didn't it?" I said. Although I was a little nervous too. I wouldn't have Kylie's lunch on my clothes every day to make them move.

Still, no one argued.

"So we need to come up with a schedule. Ginger, when do you usually need to go to the bathroom?"

"Between first and second, between third and fourth, and between fifth and sixth."

"You sure pee a lot," Mitch said.

"Okay," I said quickly. "Does the whole Pack stop you from going in, or just one or two?"

"They take turns."

"They have a schedule too?" Winnie said.

Yeah. The Pack was even more on-purpose mean than I thought.

"Then you only need one of us with you each time," Mitch said. "I'll take between fifth and sixth. I have to go then too."

We got that all divided up. I took between third and fourth.

Then we moved on to lockers. Ginger said she didn't mind carrying all her books around, but she'd like to go before and after school. We decided we could all be there at those times, since the whole Pack usually was.

"Don't they have anything else to do?" Winnie said.

"They need to get a life," Mitch said.

"I still don't get why they gotta do this to me," Ginger said.

"That's what we're trying to find out," I said. "Lydia said to observe how they react when we foil their plans."

Ginger gave her foghorn laugh—which made Nestlé lift his head and shake his ears. "I love the way you talk. 'Foil their plans.' That's so cool."

I didn't say that was really from Ophelia. I did better if I just didn't think about her too much.

We spent the whole afternoon acting out our various plans until it started to get dark and cold in the cabin. The one we had down best we called "Walk It, Girl," where we just surrounded Ginger and went straight down the hall no matter who tried to stop us or what they said—including Nestlé, who was the whole Pack for rehearsal purposes. Winnie said she'd make us each a new card for "Walk It, Girl."

"I think we're ready," I said.

They answered with "yes!" and "sweet!" and "yo!" Nestlé even barked that high-pitched happy-sounding yelp he used when Dad told him he was getting a soup bone.

Then it got quiet. I wondered if maybe we should pray, like Lydia said she did. But I wasn't sure how and I didn't know if anybody else would want to.

So I just said, "God love you, tribelet."

That felt kind of like it could have been a prayer.

Chapter Seventeen

I couldn't believe how awesomely our plan worked Monday morning.

We were all at Ginger's locker with her before anybody from the Pack even showed up. Mitch looked disappointed that we didn't get to do our "Safe in a Group" thing, but we made up for it when we all "Walked It Girl" down the hall to first period by the gym. We kept our heads up and our eyes forward, and only Winnie whimpered a little when Kylie, Riannon, Heidi, Izzy, and Shelby all came into view, in their usual knot outside Mrs. Zabriski's door.

"Just keep walkin'," I whispered to her.

We did, and in my peripheral vision, I saw Izzy's round mouth drop open like she was about to get checked for tonsillitis. Riannon's eyes popped. Any minute she'd be looking for one of her green contact lenses.

"Awesome," Mitch muttered to me when we were safely inside the classroom.

That replaced her high five. We decided Saturday that it wasn't a good idea to celebrate in front of the Pack. They were going to be mad enough as it was.

I didn't notice whether they were ticked off or not during health class. The only thing I *was* aware of was Ophelia sitting beside me. I guess I'd still hoped she'd forget what she said Friday. Two days was a lot of time for her to be BFF-less, especially since the same rule applied to Winnie. Winnie and I were busy with the plan, but Phee . . . she obviously didn't have anything else to think about. Her fingernails were chewed way past the usual sawed-off looking place, and she was wearing her braid in a circle around her head, probably because her mom saw how much she'd been biting on the end of it.

But mostly it was the way she was trying not to make it look like she knew I was there—that was my real clue. Every time I glanced at her during first period, which was a lot because we were watching a video about lice and Mrs. Zabriski was busy shouting down all the squealing, Ophelia's head twitched because I caught her looking at me.

My other clue . . . well, I guess you would call it evidence . . . was when she dropped a note on purple paper on my desk before she practically ran out of the room at the end of class. My hands went into immediate sweat mode as I unfolded it and read her curlicue handwriting.

How come you'll do all this stuff for somebody you hardly even like and you won't do one thing for the person who was supposed to be your best friend? Forever?

"Hey," Mitch said from the doorway. "You comin' or what? We gotta meet Ginger and Winnie when they come out of the bathroom."

I stuffed Ophelia's note into my backpack and hurried after Mitch. I didn't know how to answer that question anyway.

"Maybe we shouldn't have given Winnie the first bathroom shift," I said as Mitch and I took the new route to the girls' restroom on the second floor.

"Nah, it's okay. Those girls haven't figured out what we're doin' yet." Mitch gave me her halfway grin. "They're not as smart as us."

I had to admit that was probably true, because when we got there, Winnie and Ginger were just coming out, and Izzy was up against the wall outside the bathroom, talking really fast to Heidi and Riannon and Kylie. They might as well have been Mrs. Yeats and Mr. Jett, as scared as Izzy looked.

Winnie, on the other, didn't look frightened at all. Her face was all pink, and I could tell she had a hard time holding back a giggle until we got inside Mr. Jett's class.

"It was so easy!" she whispered to me.

"What did you say to Izzy?" I whispered back.

"'We need to go into the restroom. If you need to go, there's plenty of stalls.'"

Just like we'd practiced it. Now *I* wanted to give her a high five. But I didn't, because I could hear the hissing from the den part of the social studies room. Izzy got the pass from Mr. Jett and left crying. I almost felt sorry for her.

The move from there to the third-period math room was tricky because we were taking one of our alternative routes, and it was going to be hard to go all the way down to the first floor, down the main hall, and up the other set of stairs and then book it ten doors down . . . and get there on time. Mrs. C-C kept close track of people's tardies. Of course. She was a math person.

I was a math person too, though, and I had it all calculated. We could move faster because we wouldn't have to deal with the Pack at all on that route, and there weren't usually any teachers on the stairs between classes so we could run there. If my calculations were correct, we should get there with exactly fifteen seconds to spare.

The key was to be the first people out of the room, which wouldn't be easy because Ginger had to get her social studies book back into a pack already stuffed with everything she owned. Mr. Jett got all over people who started getting their stuff together before the bell rang.

We had a plan for that too. As soon as class ended, Mitch grabbed Ginger's book and took off for the door. Winnie picked up her jacket and followed. I did a quick check for debris around Ginger's desk and herded her to the door.

Perfect.

We were in our seats five seconds before the bell rang. It would have been sooner, but Mrs. C-C stopped us outside the door to ask us why we were all out of breath.

"You weren't running in the halls, were you?" she said. She wasn't smiling, but her gray eyes were.

"No," I said. "We weren't. We just hurried so we wouldn't be late for your class."

She looked at me like she was trying to see through my cracks, but then she did smile and sent the lines in her face all spreading out and said, "I'm not going to argue with eagerness."

Winnie squeezed my arm when we got inside. "Tori, you lied!" she whispered.

"No, I didn't. We weren't running in the halls. We were running on the stairs. And we did do it so we wouldn't be late for class."

Winnie giggled. The Pack didn't.

I could practically feel an Arctic breeze coming from their part of the room. The Pack knew we were up to something, that was clear. But so far they hadn't figured out what, and Ginger was sitting tall in her desk and waving her hand to do the first problem on the board. Lydia was going to love hearing about this.

I was up for bathroom escort at the end of math. Shelby was the one standing guard at the door. She was the weakest wolf in the Pack.

But then it occurred to me that she had to try harder because she was also the one most likely to be kicked out if she messed up.

I didn't tell Ginger that, though. We just headed for the bathroom door, and Ciara and Josie opened it to go in right then so Ginger and I slipped in before Shelby could jump back in the way. It was almost like cheating.

"Go ahead," I told Ginger, and she went into a stall.

I pretended to be washing my hands, but I watched for Shelby in the mirror. She came in, looked around, and let her shoulders drop almost to the floor. Actually, everything on her dropped. She was like a wet puppy, only with freckles.

"Is she in there?" Shelby said, waving a floppy hand toward the row of stalls.

I really, really wanted to say something like, "That's where people usually end up when they go in the bathroom." But we weren't supposed to lower ourselves to their tactics, so I just nodded and went back to rinsing my hands.

"Which one?" she said.

"I don't know," I said. And then before I could stop myself, I added, "It's not my day to watch her."

"It sure looks like it is," Shelby said, letting her hair fall across her cheek just the way Kylie did. "You guys have been all over her all day."

The toilet flushed, and I stuck my hands under the dryer. Shelby's mouth moved, but I couldn't hear what she was saying.

"What?" I said as Ginger came out of the stall and went straight for the sink. "Did you say something?"

"I said," Shelby yelled. The dryer stopped but she was still yelling. "'What do you guys think you're doing, anyway?'"

Man, I really wanted to say, "Is someone deaf?"

But I just nodded Ginger toward the door.

"We're using the restroom," I said. "And now we're going to class. You?"

I didn't wait for an answer. Ginger and I bolted out the door. And straight into Heidi and Riannon.

"Excuse us," I said.

Ginger and I stood there, just like we were supposed to. Any second they would have to move.

Yeah, so why was my heart slamming in my chest like ten hammers? And why weren't they moving?

I counted. One Mississippi. Two Mississippi. Three . . .

I got to ten, which was the point where we needed to go around either side of them. I gave Heidi one more blank stare—

And she stepped aside.

"What are you *doing*?" Riannon said to her.

We didn't hear the answer. Ginger and I walked right between them and straight into the science room.

When we got to our desks, which Mitch had already pulled into a circle, Winnie looked like *she* needed to go to the restroom.

"What took you so long?" she said. "I was starting to get scared."

"We got past Shelby, but Heidi and Riannon were waiting outside."

"They're onto us," Mitch said.

Winnie whimpered.

"Yeah, but I think it's okay," I said. "It takes them exactly ten seconds to give up. I timed it."

"Could we please work on our project?"

Ophelia's voice was small and dry, like little flakes of Grass Valley snow. I actually saw Winnie shiver.

"I've been thinking about this," Phee said.

I gripped the side of my desk. Should I hope?

"And since I'm not putting together the presentation, I should do some of the writing. I am one of the best writers."

"You are!" Winnie said. "We could work on it together!"

"No. Just give me half and I'll do it by myself."

I thought Winnie was going to slide right out of her desk. It was one thing to be all snippy with me. I could take it. But not Winnie. I really, really wanted to tell Ophelia that was one of the meanest things I'd seen somebody do, and I'd seen a lot of mean stuff lately.

Everybody went silent. I started counting. One Mississippi. Two Mississippi.

Once again I got to ten. Then Ophelia said, "Okay. We can do it together. But it has to be here at school."

"Not after school," Mitch said. "That's when we meet at Tori's."

"At lunch then," Ophelia said.

Winnie started to nod, and then she looked at me.

"Go for it," I said.

The prickles all seemed to lie down like porcupine quills. We handed our research to Winnie, and she tucked it into her folder. Then we just sat there and waited for the fifteen minutes to be up.

It was the longest fifteen minutes in the history of tween-hood.

~

Mitch knew what she was talking about when she said the Pack was onto us. When fourth period ended and we gathered to walk Ginger to the cafeteria, the Alpha Wolf and her Pack were nowhere in sight. The BBAs, however, were stationed six feet in front of the door. They were hanging out all casual, doing the usual burping and shoving, but as we approached like four people all sharing the same umbrella, they formed a line, shoulder to shoulder. The Pack couldn't even do all their own dirty work?

"Keep walking," I whispered. "Safe in a group."

"But it's boys," Winnie whispered back.

"I can take 'em," Mitch muttered to me.

"No," I said.

"Then *what*?" Ginger was obviously trying to muffle the foghorn, but any minute she was going to be blaring.

"Gold thumb," I said.

"Huh?" Mitch said.

I stepped out in front of the tribelet. "Hey, guys?"

Andrew turned his shaggy head. "You talkin' to *me*?"

"Yeah. Just a heads-up: Mr. Jett always comes around that corner exactly seven seconds from now. If he catches you hanging out here, he starts counting up for lunch detention."

"How do *you* know?" Douglas said. He had the most-likely-to-head-off-into-the-stratosphere voice of all adolescent boys.

"Because one more and I get mine," I said. "So if you'll excuse us."

Andrew got on his toes and looked over Mitch's shoulder down the hall. Douglas and Patrick jockeyed around us on the other side, peering with their mouths hanging open. Among the three of them, they seemed to have lost exactly twenty-one IQ points.

Which was fine with us, because we simply walked between them and into the lunchroom. Behind us, I heard Mr. Jett yell, "What are you boys doing hanging around out here?"

Like I said, perfect.

Until the four of us got to our table. Ophelia was already there. She smiled at first, and hope flickered up somewhere inside me.

And then her eyes went from large brown circles to lines so thin I could hardly see the brown at all. They were slanted right at Ginger.

Mitch and Winnie obviously didn't see that because they both slid into place across from Phee. Beside me, Ginger took two little sidesteps.

"I'll just go sit . . . in the bathroom," she said.

"No." I sucked in enough air to get my heart to stop slamming. "You're in the tribelet. You should eat with the tribelet."

Ginger searched my face with her blueberry eyes. It was a strange moment to notice that her hair looked like it had been washed just that morning, and that she smelled like laundry detergent. She didn't look exactly pretty, but she was definitely prettier than Ophelia right then. Nobody looked pretty with their face all flattened like that.

I sat down next to her.

"Could you slide down so Ginger can sit here?" I said.

It didn't take ten seconds for Ophelia to respond. She stood right up and said, "No, I won't. If she's going to sit here, I'm sitting someplace else."

For the first time that day, Ginger gave in to a blurt. "Why do you hate me, Ophelia?!"

Mitch yanked Ginger's arm, and she dropped to the seat beside her.

"Save the Tears," Mitch muttered.

"But she's not a bully," Ginger said. "Can't I tell her how I feel?"

I had to bite my lip to keep from pointing out that Phee was sure acting like one. Ginger bit hers too and lowered her voice maybe a tenth of a decibel.

"Why do you hate me?" she said again.

Ophelia had her tray in her hands. "I don't hate you. I just hate that you came in here and changed everything."

"I didn't mean—"

"She didn't change things, Phee," I said. "The Pack did. And we can't stand around and let them get away with it."

Ophelia's knuckles went white on her tray. She was blinking hard, trying not to cry, I knew. Hope . . .

One Mississippi. Two Mississippi. Three . . .

"You know what?" She flipped the braid she'd loosened from around her head. "Don't call me 'Phee' anymore. In fact, don't call me anything. I'm so done."

She slipped behind me with her tray over my head. I wouldn't have been surprised if she had dropped it on me. But she held on to it until she got to the end of the table and then she leaned to look past Mitch at Winnie, who was huddled in her seat and trembling like the small, scared rabbit she suddenly was again.

"Meet me before school tomorrow if you want to work on this," she said. "Or we can just divide it up."

With another flip of her braid, Ophelia turned to go.

"It's okay, Win," I said. "We can get Ginger to her locker without you."

"No," said the wee voice. "Ophelia?"

Ophelia looked over her shoulder.

"I'm helping Ginger before school," Winnie said. "So I guess we should just divide up the writing."

I expected another braid flip. What we got was Ophelia's face twisting like it hurt.

"See?" she said to me. "You even turned Winnie against me! We are never . . . *ever* going to be friends again."

Chapter Eighteen

At first I thought I really would end up a pile of confetti. When Mitch escorted Ginger to the restroom after lunch, I told Winnie to go ahead to her locker. I needed some time to think. At least I remembered not to linger in the cafeteria. I so didn't need lunch detention right now.

I walked really slowly to Mrs. Fickus's room and did what I did best. I argued. With myself.

Ophelia was the only best friend I ever had.

Until now.

I should be loyal to her, right?

Or wrong? What if we didn't believe the same things anymore like we always did? Like that boys were absurd little creeps and science projects were cool and she was the writer and I was the mathematician and we were the smartest ones in the class . . .

"You're like a gang now," someone said.

I smelled strawberry shampoo and new clothes and peppermint gum.

I was only one door away from Mrs. Fickus's room. I could just go straight there and not say anything. I could "Walk It, Girl."

But Kylie was suddenly in front of me, walking backward. One glance over my shoulder with that peripheral vision and I saw Heidi and Riannon. Shelby and Izzy must have been sent away in shame.

"You *are* a gang," Kylie said.

"I'm a gang all by myself?" I said.

"No," she said, like I was an idiot.

Why, I wondered, *did everybody think Kylie was so pretty?* Her lip was halfway up her trumpet nostrils so that her gums showed. What was cute about that?

"You and Mitch the Witch and Winnie the Ninny and *Gingerbread*."

I stopped walking. So did Kylie. Either Heidi or Riannon, I couldn't tell which, stepped on the back of my sneaker but I didn't flinch. I was too busy deciding whether it was worth it to smack Kylie right there. She had names—ugly names—for my friends. Was I supposed to just let her get away with that? Was there a card for that?

I sucked in air and started walking again. Kylie fell into step beside me, except just enough ahead to make it awkward.

"Yeah, you're a gang," she said. "Mitch the Witch, Winnie the Ninny, Gingerbread and . . . Vic*tor*ia, my pet."

"Don't."

I came to a halt, and this time Riannon plowed right into me.

"Stop right in front of me, why don'tcha?" she said.

"Why can't I call you that, Vic*tor*ia?"

Because only Granna calls me that, and it sounds dirty coming out of your mouth just like everything else you say because you're an Alpha Wolf.

All of that crowded into my brain, ready to bust out. I jammed my hand in my jean jacket pocket and felt the cards. I wasn't with my group. I couldn't think of a thing I wanted that these people would want too. I wasn't going to cry.

Baby Step. Take a baby step. Toward what?

"Since you're a gang, maybe you want to fight us," Kylie was saying. She shook her hair back, and it splashed all over and settled right back to where it was, like she'd trained it to do that. "Not like beat-you-up kind of fight. We don't do that."

By then the hall was filling up. I saw Mrs. Fickus step out of her door. She was looking the other way. Why did the teachers always seem to be looking the other way?

Kylie got right up beside me, and before I knew it, I was being moved to the side of the hall. "If you want war, we'll give you war," she whispered in my ear, her breath like a heater. "You declare it, and we'll fight you." My back pressed the wall. "But you won't win."

Baby Step? I could only think of one. It was like Lydia was right there in front of me, coaxing me forward.

"We're not declaring war on *you*," I said. "We're declaring war on bullying itself."

Kylie took a baby step too, backward. For exactly three seconds, she looked surprised. I took that opportunity to slide away from her and head for the door. Three bodies were suddenly around me. Mitch, Winnie, and Ginger. They sure didn't feel like a witch and a ninny and a moldy piece of Gingerbread to me.

"Did you just call me a *bully*?" Kylie said.

The tribelet just kept Walkin' It, Girl. When we got to the door, Mrs. Fickus was looking right at us. Of course.

She tilted her sprayed-in-place head. "Is everything all right, y'all?"

It was my turn to be surprised. So surprised that I didn't say what I probably should have said, which was, *No, it's not all right.*

There's bullying going on right under your nose, and you won't even see it because you think Kylie Steppe is perfect.

"It's okay," I said.

"No, it's not," Mitch said to me when we got to our seats. "Something happened, didn't it?."

"I'll tell you about it later," I said.

I pretended to read the short story Mrs. Fickus assigned us and tried to get my heart to stop pounding so hard it hurt my chest. I had just declared war on bullying.

And there was no turning back now.

~

I waited until the tribelet was at my house—eating blackberry cobbler with our cocoa because Mom was actually home—before I told them what happened in the hall with Kylie. I wanted Lydia to hear it.

"Did I do it right?" I said.

"More than."

Lydia folded her tidy hands, which still shook a little. "You did great. But it sounds like you can't overestimate the power these girls think they have over you."

"*Think* they have," Mitch said.

"I want you to be very careful, Mitch." Lydia's eyes were like drills. "It would be so easy for you to turn this into a war on them, not on what they're doing."

"How do we know the difference?" Mitch said.

Lydia got that look like she was flipping answers through her head the way Mom flipped through the folders in her file cabinet. We all waited. I guess we'd figured out by then that anything that came out of Lydia's mouth was worth waiting for.

"You think of them as the Pack, right?" she said at last.

We all nodded.

"Why is that?"

"Because they're always skulking around, watching for something to attack," I said.

Ginger bellowed a laugh. "Did you just say *skulking*? What a cool word!"

She sure was in a good mood. I felt like I was carrying everybody's backpack in the sixth grade on my shoulders, and she was laughing.

"Do you want to be like that, attacking back?" Lydia said.

"I do when I'm doing it," Mitch said. "Then later I feel like I'm not any better than they are."

Lydia pulled one of her square little hands out of the tidy fold and held it up to Mitch. Now *she* was high-fiving.

"That's exactly it," Lydia said. "What do you want to do instead? What will you feel good about later?"

"Stop the attack!" Ginger said.

"Right. And if you do that like wolves, it's just going to end up in a big old nasty thing with teeth tearing and fur flying . . ."

"No!" Winnie looked like somebody was about to put their teeth into her right then.

Lydia rubbed her arm. "Sorry. But you get my point, right?"

"So what animal are we supposed to be?" Ginger said.

Mrs. Fickus would be loving this conversation.

"Sheep," Lydia said.

Mitch grunted. I hadn't heard her do that all day.

"Just hear me out. Sheep never attack, and they never fight back. They just go where they're supposed to go and they stay pure. B[illegible] also have to be sharp."

"Um, sheep are stupid," I said. "No offense to the sheep but, they kind of are."

"They're smart enough to follow when they're led right," Lydia said. Her eyes glowed at me.

You're the leader of the tribelet, she'd told me.

And I was the one who had declared war on bullying.

"Okay, Win," I said. "We need a new card."

Winnie poised her pen over her notebook.

"Think Sharp. Stay Pure."

"I like it," Mitch said.

"I do too." Lydia looked at each of us, so that we knew we were being looked at one person at a time. "Don't be pulled into playing the game like they do. But don't be bluffed into silence either."

Winnie raised her hand.

"Yes, Win?" Lydia said.

"Should Tori have told Mrs. Fickus what happened in the hall? Wasn't that a 'Report Alert'?"

"Can I answer that? Because I've been thinking about it," I said.

Lydia nodded.

"Kylie said they don't *fight* fight, like hitting and stuff. So it's not like anybody's in trouble."

"Yet," Lydia said. "Just remember there's more than one way to be hurt."

"I know," Ginger said.

"You're protecting everyone's right to be exactly who they are."

Everybody smiled at Lydia.

"Tori."

I looked up to see Mom in the kitchen doorway. She crooked her finger at me. She only did that when she was about to do a very mother thing.

"Go ahead," Lydia said. "We're almost through anyway. I have to leave for an appointment in a minute."

I left the table and followed Mom. When she led me all the way to my bedroom, I knew this was going to be more than a "Why didn't you pick up your dirty clothes?" kind of chat. We hadn't had one of these since I let Nestlé eat my brussels sprouts when I thought she wasn't looking. Back in December.

Then she closed the door. Not good.

"I didn't want to embarrass you in front of your friends," she said.

She leaned against my closet door and motioned for me to sit on the bed. I guessed that was because I was getting so tall and she needed to be able to look down at me. That was not good either.

"What did I do?" I said.

"I'm not exactly sure. I just got a call from Ophelia's mom. She says Ophelia's so upset she's making herself sick because you won't be friends with her anymore. Something about an Indian tribe?"

Mom's face was one big question mark—so big I didn't even know where to start.

"She's the one who doesn't want to be friends with me," I said, trying not to let my voice go all high like Douglas. "Or at least she won't unless I drop out of the tribelet."

Mom pressed her fingers against her temples. "What *is* that, Tori? Is it some kind of clique?"

"No!" I lost the battle with the screechy voice. "It started out as our science project and then—"

"Mrs. Smith also said you've cut Ophelia out of the project."

"That's not true! She's doing her part. She just doesn't want to meet with us. Her mom won't even let her!"

I stopped before I could say, "Why is that *my* fault?"

Mom rubbed her lips. I wished Nestlé was there. It would have been good to have somebody to hang onto so I didn't blurt out things that were going to get me grounded until eighth grade.

"All right," Mom said. "Ophelia *and* her mother both have a strong sense of the dramatic, I'll give you that. And I'm not one to interfere with your friendships. You girls have to learn to work out your own drama. But it's not very nice to treat your friends like that."

Drama? Why did that not sound like the right word?

"I just want to make sure that you're not excluding Ophelia. I like that you're making new friends, but you and she have been together a long time. It's not okay to cut her out just because other people want to be around you too."

I could feel my eyes glazing over. I had to let them, or I really was going to say something punishment-producing. Prickles stood up on the back of my neck. Mom hadn't been there since exactly January 26 when this all started. Suddenly she was home and telling me what to do, when she didn't even know anything about it—

She reached over and drummed her fingers on the top of my hand. "I have to get back to Granna. We can talk about this later."

Whatever.

"Okay?"

"Okay," I said.

"I'm going to trust you on this," she said. But as those words hung in the air after she left, I didn't hear trust coming out of them. I heard, "I really don't have time for this."

I waited until the car started and then I headed for the kitchen. Mom might not have time, but Lydia always did.

When I got there, though, she was gone, and so were Winnie, Ginger, and Mitch.

Even with Nestlé nosing at my hand, I'd never felt so alone.

Chapter Nineteen

The next day, Tuesday, our tribelet stayed with our new routine, and it worked without a hitch. Ginger was practically doing the Happy Dance by the end of the day, and Winnie was smiling like she was her own little sunshine. Mitch had apparently been saving up her high fives all day because she did them with each of us until my hands were stinging. We were going to have to think up a different celebration ritual for Mitch or nobody was going to have any palms left.

But I couldn't help being suspicious. The Pack got out of our way when we "Walked It Girl" down the hall. They didn't figure out our alternate routes. And even though they "guarded" the restrooms in twos now, we caught onto that before third period and we went in pairs too. Still, they weren't stepping things up the way I thought they would.

From the way they had their heads touching every chance they got, I deduced they were planning. During science and in the lunchroom and in English class when Mrs. Fickus took us all to the library and they got the table behind the biography section, they all leaned together and once in a while a head would pop up and swivel around and go back down. It was like watching a bunch of meerkats.

I did watch them. Think Sharp. That was my job.

So how did I miss what they were planning until it was too late?

~

During science class Tuesday, Mr. V told us to start bringing in our work on our projects so he could check our progress. After school at my house, Lydia wasn't there—Dad said she had another appointment—so we made our charts showing the statistics, the child development line, and the differences between girl-mean and boy-mean and the reasons people bully, each one in a different color. That last one was Ginger's idea. Winnie already had the written part in a binder, and while we made charts, she punched holes in the pages Ophelia had given her.

It really did feel like a tribelet and I was liking that, when all of a sudden Winnie said in a jittery voice, "Um, guys? Look what Ophelia wrote."

Winnie passed the paper to me and everybody leaned on the table.

"Some psychologists," I read out loud, "say that it's normal for children to exhibit aggressive social behavior starting as early as age six. Usually it peaks at age eleven or twelve and fades out completely in the middle of high school."

"That is *not* in her own words," Winnie said.

"Not only that, it's not even true," Mitch said.

"It says *some* psychologists," I said. "We're supposed to give all sides."

Winnie pointed at the paper. "Look what else it says."

"After interviewing teachers," Ophelia had written, "I can conclude that students blow drama out of proportion, because teachers rarely see it and when they do, they ignore it and it almost always disappears in time."

"When did she interview teachers?" I said.

We all looked at each other, except Ginger, who was staring a hole into the table.

"What, Ginger?" I said. "C'mon, we have to be honest with each other."

"I saw her talking to Mrs. Fickus in the library today. And Mr. Jett at lunch."

Why hadn't I seen her? I felt a pang. It used to be I saw everything Phee did. Phee, who I wasn't allowed to call that anymore.

"What are we gonna do, Tori?" Winnie said.

"Okay," I said. "We have to include both sides, but we have more stuff on the other side, so we can still come to the same conclusion."

Winnie flipped through her own pages. "'Bullying is learned behavior, and it can and should be unlearned,'" she read.

"So we're gonna stand up and say Mrs. Fickus and Mr. Jett are wrong?" Ginger's face was going blotchy.

"Don't use their names," Mitch said.

"And talk to some other teachers who do get it."

I stared at Winnie. "And who would that be?"

"Mr. V. Right?"

"No!" I wanted to scream. "He's in on it with them!"

I must have shaken my head pretty hard because Mitch said, "Why not?"

"Because he's our teacher for the project," Ginger said. "That wouldn't be right."

I looked at her in surprise. When she looked back at me with her blueberry eyes, I knew she knew about Mr. V too. Why not? He was the one who set her up for the moldy gingerbread prank.

"We should just leave it like it is," I said. "Scientists include all the information they gather."

We got busy spreading everything out in the kitchen and stepped back to look at all of it.

The rest of the group decided that Mr. V would be impressed. I wasn't so sure—not after the gingerbread incident. But we couldn't let him bluff us into silence either. And since I was the leader, I was going to make sure of that.

~

Winnie was in charge of bringing everything Wednesday morning, rolled up into wrapping paper tubes, because her mom always dropped her off at school on her way to work. Besides, Winnie was the best at keeping things neat. We excused her from locker duty before school so she could take it directly to Mr. V's room.

My imaginary antennae should have gone up when the Pack didn't leave their den before school and come up to the lockers to harass Ginger.

And when they all came in almost late to Mrs. Zabriski's class.

And when Shelby didn't guard the bathroom door before fourth period because she and Izzy and Heidi were in there scrubbing marker off their hands like they were preparing for surgery.

Even though Kylie hardly stopped staring at me all morning, looking like she'd already won the war and I didn't know it, I still didn't find out what was going on until the tribelet followed Mr. V into the lab to give him our progress report.

My first clue was when the whole classroom, the room that always buzzed like a hive of bees, got totally quiet when Mr. V told us it was our turn. Of course, Kylie would want to hear what we were saying. She'd already told me I was dead if we did our presentation.

Don't let them bluff you into silence.

I kept repeating that to myself as we lined up in front of Mr. V with our backs to the class. I didn't like *that* arrangement, but there was nothing I could do about it.

Just as we'd planned, each of us held a chart or list that we'd done on big paper and when it was our turn to speak, we would step forward. Ophelia didn't have a chart, so we asked her to hold the binder and tell Mr. V what she found out. That was only fair. She pouted like she didn't think so, but I was starting not to care *what* she thought.

I was first. I stepped forward and unrolled my chart on bullying statistics, to first show that meanness/bullying was a problem to begin with. I stepped to the side of it so I could see it at the same time Mr. V did.

The quiet-as-a-bank classroom erupted into a unanimous snicker. I tried to ignore it and continued down the graph of what I thought were pretty impressive statistics. I sure didn't see anything funny about them. Mr. V didn't seem to see *anything* about them. He kept looking up at the class, because as I stood there the noise evolved from snickers to guffaws to a full-out roar.

Finally Mr. V put his hand up for me to stop and then moved around us toward the classroom.

Mitch poked me in the back. When I turned around to look, all I saw was Ginger with her hand smothering her mouth. She was *not* "Saving the Tears." They ran down her face like two little rivers.

"What is going *on*?" Ophelia said between her teeth.

Nobody answered. Winnie just pointed to the back of the graph I was still holding.

I looked. And then all I could think was, "*No! Nonononono! No!*"

On the back of the graph I'd worked so hard on, someone had reproduced the I Hate Gingerbread Club sign-up sheet in thick marker—about six times the size of the original. The lines were all filled up this time, but I didn't read them. I was feeling throw-up sick enough already.

"Tori, look!" Winnie whispered.

The back of her chart had more "I Hate Gingerbread" comments on it. So did Mitch's. Ginger's was different. Hers had a drawing that looked almost exactly like her, only the cheeks were all puffed up like someone had pumped them with a bicycle pump. Something brown was drawn coming out of the mouth.

"I have to get out of here," Ginger said.

"No," I said. "You can't let them win."

"They already have," she said.

The foghorn was dead. And I couldn't blame it.

But Mitch held onto Ginger's arm and Winnie whispered in her ear. I moved so I could hear what Mr. V was saying to the class.

Actually he wasn't talking. Kylie was.

"I'm sorry we laughed, Mr. V," she said, eyes all round and serious. "It really isn't funny. Why would they do that to a member of their own group?"

Big throw-ups. *Big*.

"I don't know, Kylie," Mr. V said. "Why would they?"

Heidi raised her hand. "Because some people are just *immaCHUR*?"

"Let me at her just one time," Mitch muttered behind me.

Mr. V turned to us. I'd never seen him look so . . . old. "Did you ladies do this?" he said.

"No," I said. "We. Did. Not."

"Of course they're going to say that," Riannon said.

Mr. V whipped his head toward her. "How about if you let me be the teacher?"

The whole Pack looked like they'd been slapped.

"All right, everybody take a seat."

We started to roll up our charts, but Mr. V said, "Leave that. Sit down."

We did. Mitch was still holding on to Ginger's arm so she wouldn't fly out of the room. And I handed Winnie a wad of Kleenex out of my backpack. I didn't even look at Ophelia. I didn't want to see I-*told*-you on her face.

"I have had enough of this Gingerbread deal, people," Mr. V said. His elastic mouth was like a drawstring pulled really tight. "I don't know who started it or why or who's still involved, but it ends right here, right now. Am I clear?"

"Yeah, I can see right through you," Andrew said.

"I'm not joking, Andrew."

I never saw a kid wipe a grin off his face so fast. Meanwhile, the Pack all had Miss Innocence expressions on theirs. Kylie was doing everything but saying, "This *so* does not apply to me."

"I should have put a stop to it sooner," Mr. V said. "And, Ginger, I apologize to you. That's my share of the responsibility." He leaned on his high stool with both straight arms. Jeepers. He was almost scary. "And I will get to the bottom of this and make sure whoever else is responsible is brought to justice."

Heidi had the nerve to giggle. "It's not like . . . somebody broke the law or something."

"Something doesn't have to be illegal to be wrong," he said. "And in my class, this is wrong."

The bell rang, and the class erupted like a mini-volcano to get out of there. We were going to have to wait if we didn't want to get trampled.

"Kylie, stay," Mr. V said. "Heidi, Riannon, you too. I want to talk to you."

"We'll get in trouble with Mr. Jett!" Heidi said.

"You're about to be in trouble with me if you don't stop arguing and do what I ask you to do."

I knew I was the only one in our tribelet except Ginger who was confused. We were the only ones who knew he was in on this whole thing. No wonder he felt "responsible."

I didn't share any of that with the tribelet. I just let them quietly celebrate through lunch, especially since the three Pack members never did show up and Izzy and Shelby sat at their table looking like they didn't even know how to eat without Kylie to show them how to do it the cool way.

They did come to English class. I couldn't read anything on their faces, but when Izzy whispered something to Kylie, she shut her up with a "Leave me alone!" that actually got her name on the board. I thought Mitch was going to do a somersault.

Me? I knew all of this was just making Kylie angrier. This war was about to get ugly.

I found out I was right, from the last person I ever expected.

Chapter Twenty

That night I had dinner with Mom and Dad, and they told me I could see Granna on Sunday, and I'd gotten to talk to Lydia long enough to tell her what happened, so I was feeling a little better. I was even starting to hope that Mr. V was going to take over and fix this whole thing, maybe because he felt guilty.

And then the phone rang when I was getting ready for bed and Mom hollered for me to answer it because it was the Smiths' number. I took the phone in my room before I said hello.

Ophelia just said, "I need to talk to you, Tori."

I closed my door. "I'm alone, except for Nestlé, and he won't tell anybody anything."

"I'm not alone. Meet me by the library before school."

I started to say I had to be at the lockers before school, but I changed my mind. Ophelia's voice sounded like a thread. One wrong thing out of me and it would probably break, and I'd never have a chance to hear what she wanted to tell me.

"Okay," I said. "I'll try to get there early."

~

Phee was there before me, pulling her braid out of the coil thing. A couple of her fingers had Band-Aids on them. The places under her eyes looked like dark crescent moons.

"You don't look so good," I said.

"Thank you *so* much!"

"I didn't mean it that way," I said. As far as good starts went, this one was about a minus one. "You just look like you're sick."

"I am. I'm going to ask the nurse to send me home when first period starts. I just wanted to tell you something."

I nodded.

Ophelia looked over her shoulder and pulled me into the corner by the trash can. She really didn't have to do that. Nobody else was in the halls. The library wasn't even open yet.

"You have to find a way to do the presentation of our project without the whole class seeing it."

My heart took a total nosedive. "Jeepers, we already went through this a hundred times."

"No! Listen to me! I heard Kylie and them talking. I'm invisible to them again, like we used to be, because I'm not . . . with you anymore."

I bit into my lip and waited while she blinked back a bunch of tears.

"They don't even realize I'm around when they're talking and that's why I know they're planning a big plot."

"What kind of plot?"

"Against you. Because you're the leader like Kylie's the leader and she hates that, and she doesn't want you getting bigger than her and more popular."

"That is the stupidest thing!"

"I *know* that. They're going to do something right after the presentation . . . I don't know what it is. If I find out, I'll tell you. "

"How are you going to find out if you're not at school?"

"I will be after this," she said. "I have to go home today because I didn't go to sleep the whole night because I was so scared about this."

"You don't have to do the presentation with us," I said. "I promise we'll say what you found out, even though—"

"I don't even *care* about that!" Ophelia was digging her fingers-without-nails into my arm. "I'm scared for *you.* It's *you* they're after."

Keys jingled from someplace down the hall. That meant the librarian was on her way. Ophelia gave me one last look with her big eyes that had grown to twice their size.

"Find a way, Tori," she said. "They can't hear that presentation."

"We can't let them bluff us into silence. Besides, what are we supposed to do, take an F?"

"I don't know. Maybe it would be better—"

"You're not *serious*!"

No. Nonononono. She was not asking me to fail. If I did that, I'd be failing the tribelet too.

Ophelia shook her head. "Then I don't know what to do anymore," she said.

~

I counted the minutes until I could get home and talk to Lydia. The tribelet wasn't coming that day because we had to see what Mr. V gave us on our progress report before we could go any further. Mom said she was going to be at the shop. Dad was with Granna today. It would just be Lydia and me.

Only it wasn't how I expected it to be.

She had a snack ready like always in the kitchen. Her hummus and pita bread, my favorite. And Greek olives. But that was the only thing that was like always.

"Tor," she said when she had folded her shaky little hands, "I have to go into the hospital for surgery."

Did someone just run over me with a truck? A *big* truck?

"Surgery?" I said. "What kind of surgery?"

She kind of smiled, although she didn't seem like she was in the mood to. "I knew you'd want to know that right off. I have spinal stenosis. It's a common complication of dwarfism."

"That's what hurts."

"Yes. That's what hurts. I've known I was going to have to have a laminectomy and we planned it for this summer when the movie's done, but the symptoms have gotten worse and they want to do it right away."

"What happens if you don't?"

"I might lose the ability to walk."

I couldn't say any of the things screaming in my head. *You won't die, will you? You won't stay asleep for weeks like Granna, right? You won't be different? You'll come back—you'll be here . . .*

"I'll be okay, Taylor," she said.

"Do you promise?"

She paused. "No, I guess I can't promise that. Nobody knows what can possibly happen during an operation on your spine, but statistics are in my favor. You like statistics, right?"

Until now. Now I just wanted a promise.

"Besides, even if I'm not physically okay, I'll be okay here." She pressed her hand against her stomach. "I've got God, and that means I'll have the strength to get through whatever lies ahead." She moved her hand to my arm. "You will too. I know you're worried about the tribelet carrying on, but you know how to do it. And I'm not the only adult in the world. You're going to need more grown-up support anyway."

"There isn't anybody else!" I said. "You're the only one who can help us!" I waved my hands in front of my face, like I could erase what I'd just said. "That sounds really selfish. I'm scared for you, and I want you to get better. We can just wait 'til you come back."

"I don't know when I'm coming back here. I could have a long recovery ahead. I'll be working from the rehab center for your dad, but I won't be here until I'm really ready." She made little fists and rested her face on them. "Then I'll be back to at least visit. We *are* friends, right?"

"Yeah," I said.

But you're leaving me. You're leaving me. Just when I need you the most.

"I know this is the worst possible time for me to go."

I actually put my hand on my forehead to make sure my brain hadn't opened up for her to see inside.

"But you can do this, you and the tribelet. You have all the tools. Do you want to go over them?"

What I wanted to do was tell her about the plot and ask her whether to trust Mr. V. But Dad opened the back door and fended Nestlé off and said, "You ready to go?"

Lydia looked at the cell phone I hadn't even noticed on the table. "Is it that time already?"

"Where are you going?" I said.

"To the hospital in Auburn," she said. "Just pre-surgery tests. The operation's tomorrow."

"Tomorrow?"

"You can come with us now if you want, Tor," Dad said. "We'll get burgers on the way back."

But I shook my head. I knew if I went I'd want to talk about all my stuff, and I didn't want to with Dad there. And it just felt wrong to be thinking about that when Lydia . . .

"I'll stay here with Nestlé," I said.

She climbed down from her chair and I stood up and she hugged me around the waist. Her head came to my chest, and I could look down into the top of her curls.

"There's mac and cheese in the fridge," she said. "Comfort food."

When they were gone, I pulled it out. As I placed the dish in the microwave, I started to cry.

~

When I got to school Friday morning I knew I looked baggy-eyed and sick like Ophelia did the day before. But I couldn't abandon Mitch and Winnie and especially Ginger. After yesterday when she said, "I can never, ever do this without you," I couldn't be absent. Not until this "war" was over.

Only, what war?

The Pack had totally backed off. Mr. V was still waiting for somebody to come forward and, as I heard Patrick put it in the lunch line, "spill their guts."

Boys were so gross. But at least you knew what was going on with them. Kylie and the others were walking around with faces like in those old-fashioned photographs where everybody looks like they died and don't know it.

Ophelia still wasn't talking to me in class, and she always disappeared the rest of the time. I had no idea where she went, and I didn't have time to look. We were still going everywhere with Ginger, just in case.

Things were so quiet I started thinking Ophelia had heard it wrong about the so-called plot. Or maybe it had gotten all blown up in her mind. Even my mom said she had a "strong sense of the dramatic."

But my invisible antennae went up again after school.

Mitch, Winnie, and I went to Ginger's locker with her as usual. Ginger had her whole head in there, searching for who knew what. She had as much stuff in her locker as she did in her backpack.

"Do you have anything left in your house?" Mitch said.

Winnie giggled as she slid our project binder into her way-neat backpack on the floor. I bet everything in there was in alphabetical order. That was just our Winnie.

"Winnie the Ninny," Kylie had called her. It was so hard for me not to call her Kylie the Wiley. Like the coyote in those old Road Runner cartoons.

"Excuse me?"

I jumped at least an inch and found myself looking right into the blue eyes with the gold specks. Jeepers . . . I hadn't said any of that out *loud*, had I?

None of the Pack looked like I'd just called their leader a coyote to her face. In fact, they were all wearing that Miss Innocence look they gave teachers all the time.

"Gold Thumb," Winnie whispered.

The perfect card for this.

"Did you need something?" I said to Kylie.

"Yes." She bumped her shoulder into Riannon's.

"We wanted to say that we're declaring a truce," Riannon said.

She was still smiling, but I guessed there was nothing she could do about her eyes being so close together. That sort of canceled out the grin.

"Define *truce*," I said.

This time Kylie shouldered Heidi. They had obviously divided up the parts before they came.

"We don't want to fight you guys anymore," Heidi said.

Mitch grunted. "Who said we were fighting?"

Heidi opened her mouth, but Kylie waved her off like she was suddenly annoying her.

"Whatever. We just don't want a war. We'll stay out of your way, and you'll stay out of ours. Okay?"

"For real?"

That came from Ginger, who had finally pulled her head out of her locker. Her red hair was full of static so some of it flew out from her head like it was trying to get away. Izzy snickered, until Kylie glared at Heidi, who delivered the glare to Izzy.

"How long?" Mitch said.

"How long what?" Riannon said.

"A truce has a time limit."

They all looked the way people do onstage when everybody forgets their lines. I saw it happen once in a play Ophelia was in. Phee had saved the day. I could do that.

"How about forever?" I said.

"Fine," Kylie said. "Because really, this just isn't worth it. Know what I mean?"

"Oh, yeah," I said. "I definitely know what you mean."

The gold and blue eyes locked onto mine, and I could almost hear Ophelia's voice in my head. *I know they're planning a plot.* But I heard Lydia's too. *Stay pure. Think sharp.* Kylie might say, "I want a truce," with those glossy lips, but her eyes were telling me, "Bring it."

And then her lips said, "All right, everybody shake on it."

"Huh?" Mitch said.

"To make it official." Riannon stepped up to Mitch and stuck out her hand.

Mitch looked at it like she thought it might have lice.

"Baby Steps," I muttered to her.

I put my hand out to Kylie, and she squeezed it for exactly one tenth of a second. I didn't watch to see if she wiped it on her jeans after. The three-foot space in front of Ginger's locker looked like one of those scenes on the news when a candidate for something comes through and everybody's pumping each other's arms up and down when they don't even know each other. Kylie insisted that every single person shake every other single person's hand—although there was a nanosecond pause before she let Ginger touch her. That time she *did* wipe her palm on her jeans.

Then she turned to Shelby. "Are we done?"

What was Shelby, the handshake monitor?

"Uh-huh," Shelby said.

Kylie splashed her hair along the side of her face. "All right then," she said and led the Pack away from the lockers. I waited until I heard their pricey Uggs pad down the stairs before I turned to the tribelet and said, "That was weird."

"Do you think it was for real?" Winnie said.

She looked so hopeful, with her little black eyebrows reaching for her bangs. Ginger was smiling so big I could see most of her teeth. They didn't look so buttery anymore.

"I think we should trust it until they give us a reason not to," I said.

"Huh."

"What *huh*?" I said to Mitch.

"You sound like Lydia."

I smiled myself then. But I wished Lydia were there. I kind of knew the war wasn't over. The Pack was just going to fight it in a different way.

I wished I knew what that was.

Chapter Twenty-One

Saturday started off as a circle-it-on-the-calendar-in-red day. In a good way.

Mom had pancakes going when I got up. Dad had left for San Francisco to meet with his producers, and she said it was going to be a Mom-and-Tori Day, except for the two hours in the afternoon when she was going to visit Granna and then check in at her shop.

"Can you take all that time off?" I said.

Mom paused with the whipped cream can in her hand and licked at her lips for a minute. "I'm sorry, sweetie."

"For what?"

"For not being here for you at all these last few weeks. I know you've been going through some things, with Ophelia and all, and I haven't been much help."

I felt like I had a hair ball in my throat. "It's okay."

"No. No, it's not. That's why I'm making today all about you. So eat up, and then we'll do whatever you want."

"Whatever I wanted" was to tell her everything that was going on with the Pack. But I knew she wouldn't really get it. She thought it was just "drama." Besides, how often did these kinds of days happen? I didn't want to drag the entire Wolf Pack into my time with my mom.

"Bookstore?" I said.

"Yes. What else?"

"Um, lunch at Cirino's?"

Mom laughed. "You're not going to be a cheap date, are you?"

She sprayed some whipped cream on my nose, and I was pretty sure I'd made the right choice.

~

It was a great morning. We went to the bookstore next to the Lazy Dog, and I got another biography of Einstein (I'd already read one). I was ready to get back to real science.

After meatball subs at Cirino's, we got ice cream at the Lazy Dog and walked around licking our cones. It reminded me of the last time Granna and I did that. The day she told me Lola Montez dared to be different. I didn't even know that day that *I* was going to have to take that dare, not just Winnie. It suddenly struck me that I wasn't the same as I was then. *I* was different. I couldn't measure it. I just knew.

When we got home, Mom asked me if I wanted to go with her to the hospital and then to her shop, but I told her I needed to stay home and work on the paper Mrs. Fickus had assigned us.

"Is Ophelia going to help you?" Mom said.

She was already standing in the doorway, car keys in hand, so I just shook my head.

"You two still having trouble?"

"It'll be okay," I said.

"Maybe tonight I can help. We'll talk about it over dinner. Pizza?"

"Really?" I said.

"I'll get the good kind at the Briar Patch. Keep the phone with you."

From the window of my room, I watched her go. She must really feel bad about not being there for me. She never suggested pizza for supper, even the organic gourmet kind. It *was* a red letter day.

But as soon as I sat down to write my paper for English, it was like things started falling on me.

The topic was "The Person You Admire the Most." At least we didn't have to compare that person to an animal or a tree or a model of car. Mrs. Fickus did say to try to use a metaphor that we could carry through our five paragraphs.

It was like she was in the room with me. "In your first paragraph, tell what your three points are. Give each point its own paragraph. In your last paragraph, remind us what you've just told us."

I could do that, even without Ophelia, if I could decide who I admired the most. The list I made was pretty impressive. Dad. Mom. Granna. Lydia. Nestlé. No, he wasn't a person, at least not to Mrs. Fickus. Albert Einstein. Stephen Hawking . . . but she said it had to be somebody we knew.

I had just decided to approach it scientifically when the phone rang. It was Winnie. The minute I heard her voice, I knew she was freaking out.

"To-*ri*!" was my first clue.

"What's wrong?" I said.

"It's gone!"

"What's gone?"

"The binder for our project!"

"It's in your backpack, Win. I saw you put it in there."

"It's not there anymore!"

I stopped counting exclamation points.

"Are you *sure*?" I said.

She didn't even answer me, probably because it was the lamest question ever. Winnie always knew where all her stuff was all the time. That was why she was the one holding on to it for us.

"Maybe it fell out in your mom's car," I said.

"No, Tori! It's not anywhere!"

I didn't tell her it had to be somewhere. She was starting to cry in big gulps.

"What are we going to *do*? We don't have time to do the whole thing over!"

"Okay," I said. And then I said "okay," again. I had to say something while my brain flipped through its files. Why didn't we have cards for this kind of stuff too?

"Okay, first of all, save the tears," I said.

"I can't!"

"Okay, forget that. Baby steps. That's what we need. We'll get everybody to find their notes again while you keep looking. You call Ginger, and I'll call Mitch. What's her number?"

"I don't know," Winnie said.

"What about the list?"

"It was in the binder."

"Oh. Well . . . then we just wait 'til we get to school Monday. Maybe somebody found it and turned it in."

"They *found* it in my backpack?"

I felt like something was crawling on my skin.

"I don't know," I said. "But it's not like the end of the world, okay?" Jeepers, what would Ophelia say right now? "Hey, Win?"

"Yeah?"

"I love you. It's gonna be okay."

"Okay . . ."

It came out all wobbly and wet, but at least she didn't sound as bad. Ophelia would've done that better, though. I missed her.

I missed everybody. When Winnie hung up, I felt so alone, like the house was too big for me to be in it.

"Come on, Nestlé," I said. "We're going up to the Spot."

It was the last day of February. Some Grass Valley days in almost-March were (A) so cold you just wanted to wrap up in a blanket and read about Einstein with your dog. Or at least I did. Or they were (B) hurt-your-eyes bright and only cool enough for your favorite long-sleeved T-shirt.

That day was type B, so even though it was three thirty in the afternoon, it wasn't cold inside the cabin. I left the door partly open to let some sun in, and Nestlé laid right in the light-shaft on the floor and started snoring in exactly sixteen seconds. I counted.

It used to be that everything was that exact. There was a cause for everything. If A happened, then you knew B was going to happen. Now it seemed like almost nothing was the way you expected it.

I hadn't said it to Winnie, but I knew what happened to the report. The reason for the whole truce thing and all the handshaking was to distract us so one of those Wolves—probably Shelby—could take the binder out of Winnie's backpack without anybody noticing. I never saw Winnie zip it up after she put it in there because the Pack arrived right then.

But I couldn't prove it. The Pack was always so careful to make sure we didn't have evidence. Even the "vandalism" on our charts couldn't be definitely linked to them. They were smart. Scary smart. And when it came to this stuff, they were smarter than me.

Nestlé did a twist thing, the way he did when something woke him up out of a doggie dream. One of his brown ears flopped the wrong way as he lifted his head and sniffed. His nose was like a vacuum cleaner hose.

And then he barked, so loud and deep I went, "Jeepers! What, Nes'?"

But he was already out the cabin door, barking and crouching like he was going to jump off the rock ledge.

"Use the path, Nut Bar," I said.

He backed up and headed for it. I watched from the cabin door as he disappeared in the bushes and then came into sight again at the bottom. The barking turned to a happy yip. That was his "Oh boy, a treat. You have a treat for me. Oh boy" voice. I was going to have to ask our neighbor not to give him so many or he was going to turn into a wide-load Lab.

While Nestlé was scoring down there, I went back into the cabin and sat with my back against the wall. Now I really felt lonely. I wondered what Lydia was doing. She was probably pretty lonely herself, waking up from her surgery. I shivered, even though the sun was still sneaking through the doorway. What if nobody was with her? She never said anything about her family. *Dad* took her for her blood tests. Where was *her* dad?

Then I just kind of knew: Lydia would be praying. She said that was what she always did. She was never alone because she had God. Maybe that was what I should do. What did she say to God, though? Why hadn't I ever asked her?

Nestlé's nose came through the door. I waited for him to push it all the way open before I said, "Come here. I want to smell what you got. Bacon strips? Is that it?"

Nestlé came to me, tail smacking the wall beside me. I pulled his face up to mine so I could sniff his breath. It was sweet. What was that smell? I put my nose close to his fur, and then I gasped so hard some of his hair went up my nose.

He smelled like strawberry shampoo.

I grabbed Nestlé around the neck and really took a long whiff. Something crisp poked me. Nestlé shook himself away and a rolled-up paper came loose from his collar and landed in my lap.

I held my breath.

Maybe I shouldn't open it. The paper wasn't purple, but it smelled like Kylie too. She should never try to be a spy. The CIA would be able to follow her scent without even using bloodhounds.

So . . . if she was being that obvious, maybe it was just another part of the truce. It would make sense for them to put it in writing so nobody could say they didn't "try."

Only, why deliver it to my house, through my dog? Why not give it to me at school?

I realized at that point that I was still holding my breath. I let it out and unrolled the paper.

"If it's really awful, I'll stop reading," I said to Nestlé.

Yeah, well . . . it was. And I didn't.

"The Person We Admire Least," it said at the top in computer-typed letters.

Then came paragraph one.

"The person we don't admire is Victoria-My-Pet. She really is like a pet. Like your pet dog. She is smelly and shaggy, and she runs around with a pack of other dogs who think they're special and they're not."

Paragraph two.

"First of all, V-M-P stinks. That's because she hangs out with a pug dog named Gingerbread, who makes everyone around her smell like no-deodorant and gross, dirty clothes."

It was written in perfect Mrs. Fickus form. I dragged my eyes down to paragraph three.

"Victoria-My-Pet looks like a dog too. She doesn't brush her hair, and she always wears the same clothes over and over. That's because a dog can't change its coat. She shouldn't be allowed to come to school looking like that, but she gets away with it because the teachers think she's a very smart dog. She got all As in obedience school."

I tried not to read paragraph four, but I couldn't make myself stop.

"But the teachers are wrong because Victoria-My-Pet is not that smart. First, she wrote a stupid paper about being like a bird when everybody knows she's a mutt. And when we had to find a question for our science project, it took her and her kennel two weeks to think of something. And when they did, it was about why people are mean. We can already answer that question because she thinks it's about us. We aren't mean. We're just honest. If somebody is weird and not cool, we just say it. We don't pretend we like pug dogs like Gingerbread and pit bulls like Mitch the Witch and chihuahuas like Winnie the Ninny, because they're the only ones who will hang around with her. All they do is try to hide from us or make us look stupid, but everybody laughs because they're dogs trying to act like humans. Victoria-My-Pet once had a pretty golden retriever friend named Phee-Phee, but she got smart and she won't be in their dog pack anymore. She knows we're going to win, and she doesn't want to be a loser. We might even adopt her as a pet."

The last paragraph was a conclusion, just like Mrs. Fickus taught us. I finally stopped reading there. I could only think of two things: (A) Mrs. Fickus would probably give that paper an A, and (B) at that moment, I wished I *was* a dog. Then I could just go to sleep like Nestlé and forget I ever read that.

~

I went back into the house and put the paper inside my literature book, flattened out. That night I had so many bad dreams about turning into a dog, I woke Nestlé up. That's when I let him get in bed with me, and Mom didn't even say anything about it when she came in to get me up.

"Hey, sleepyhead," she said as she pulled my curtains open and let the sun blind me.

If it was that bright through my window, that meant it was already over the tops of the pine trees.

"What time is it?" I said.

"Time to get dressed. Did you forget you're going to see Granna today? Nestlé, down!"

I had forgotten. How could that have happened? I felt myself scowling as I climbed out of bed. Did the Pack have to ruin absolutely everything?

"It's going to be okay, Tori." Mom was looking at me closely, a perfect curly tendril hanging just right beside each eye. "Granna is doing great. She wanted to wait this long so you wouldn't think she was never going to be the same." Mom rolled her eyes. She actually did. "Trust me, she's just as ornery as ever. So don't worry. This is going to be great for you."

After that, I made a superhuman effort to wipe the worry off my face. It *was* going to be great. I missed Granna so much it hurt, and nobody was going to ruin seeing her.

Save the Tears. Gold Thumb. Baby Steps. Walk It, Girl.

~

The minute I saw Granna sitting up in bed wearing earrings with five shamrocks hanging down to her shoulders, I knew it *was* going to be great.

"It's about time you showed up!" she said.

"You two have a lot to catch up on," Mom said. "I'm going to go grab some coffee. You want hot chocolate, Tor?"

"Bring me some," Granna said. "And a meatball sandwich. The food up here is for sick people."

"I told you she was ornery as ever," Mom said to me.

I grinned all the way to my earlobes.

"Come over here," Granna said.

I went to the bed, and she motioned for me to bow my head so she could kiss the top of it, just like I wanted her to.

"Victoria, my pet," she said.

Yeah. That's when I lost it.

Chapter Twenty-Two

Granna let me cry until the front of that funky gown thing they made her wear was soaking wet like Nestlé had slobbered all over it. Then I sat up on the bed beside her and told her everything. Everything. Even things I didn't know myself until they came out of my mouth.

Like when I told her about Ophelia, I said, "Why *did* I do all this stuff for Ginger when sometimes it's hard to even like her, but I couldn't do what Ophelia wanted even though I love her?"

"Why *do* you think you did that?" Granna said.

I wiped some remaining stuff from under my nose. "Because it was the right thing to do."

"Then there you have it. Do you remember the last time you and I sat in church together?"

"Um . . ."

"Jake was preaching about the Good Samaritan, and I told you that was your solution."

"Oh, yeah. And I thought Lola Montez was supposed to be my solution."

Granna nudged me with her elbow. "Lola can't hold a candle to you when it comes to being daring. The whole time I've been lying in this bed, you've been out there being the Good Samaritan. I'm proud of you."

"But, Granna . . ." I felt myself starting to cave again. "What do I do now? They're just laughing at me for even trying. That paper they wrote . . ."

"Is a pack of lies and you know it." She gave me another elbow nudge. "Are you being who you are?"

"I think so."

"If anyone criticizes you for being exactly who you are, she's wrong. No matter who she is."

Granna rested her head back on the bed, but she kept watching me with her eyes like Dad's. And mine. Smart eyes.

"This looks like a heavy conversation." Mom crossed the room from the doorway and handed me a Styrofoam cup with a lid on it. Then she looked at me. "What's going on?"

"She'll tell you," Granna said. "And I strongly suggest you listen. But you both need to go because I need a nap. They don't let you sleep at night around here."

I let her kiss me on the top of the head again.

"Will you please say it, Granna?" I said.

"You mean, 'Victoria, my pet'?"

"Yes."

She whispered it, and I smiled. It was ours again.

~

Mom took me home and made me some real hot chocolate. We sat by the fireplace the whole afternoon, and now that I'd talked to Granna,

I told Mom everything too. Only I wasn't crying, so I gave her more detail. We had to turn on lights and feed Nestlé when I was done, that was how late it was.

We ate our leftover pizza, and then it was Mom's turn to talk.

"First of all, I'm so sorry. I didn't know it had gotten this far because I didn't listen to you. You've told me everything now, right?"

I nodded.

"You know I can't just let this go." Her eyes were wide and serious, and they flickered with the fire in them. "When your dad gets home tomorrow, I want us to go talk to Mrs. Yeats."

"It's not a 'Report Alert' yet!"

I was bordering on arguing. But Mom just paused like she was trying to remember which one 'Report Alert' was.

"Nobody's really in trouble," I said. "They don't hit or—"

"I call someone coming to our house and putting a note on our dog's collar 'trouble.' That's trespassing, for one thing."

"But if you and Dad go to the principal, then it's like we failed."

She tapped her lips. "How do you figure that?"

"Because we couldn't stop it ourselves!"

"Sweetie . . ." Mom cupped my chin in her hand. "You've done so much by yourselves already. Sometimes you have to let the grown-ups take over."

"Just give us two more days. Please? We'll do our presentation, and then they'll know we aren't going to chicken out. Then you can back us up. Please?"

Mom paused a minute before she said, "I'll talk to your dad when he gets home. You have at least until then." She lowered her face like she did when she needed me to really look at her. "But you have to promise me that if anything happens at school that makes you or the other girls scared, you'll call it a 'Report Alert.' Okay?"

I nodded and hugged her. The hug was because she was using our words. And like I said, I wasn't the hugging kind.

~

When I got to the lockers Monday morning, Winnie was standing there alone, and she was holding something to her chest and crying.

My antennae went up so far they almost popped out of my head.

"What's wrong, Win?" I said.

"Look."

She held out what she was holding.

"Is that our report binder?" I said.

Winnie nodded. She was crying so hard, she couldn't even talk.

"Where was it?"

She pointed to the floor in front of her locker.

"It was just sitting there?"

"Uh-huh."

"When you got here?"

"Uh-huh."

I looked around. The halls were still quiet except for a locker door slamming someplace else.

"So somebody just dropped it there?" I said.

"I guess *I* did."

"When?"

"Friday?"

I squirmed under the straps of my backpack. "You didn't drop it. I saw you put it in your backpack."

"I don't care! It's here!"

Winnie hugged the binder again, and I shut up. For a minute. Then I said, "So how come you're still crying?"

"Because . . ." And then she really, really started crying. In huge sobs that sounded like she was going to stop breathing.

I got her by the arm and took her over to our spot under the window and made her sit down on the floor with me. Then I found a wadded up, but clean Kleenex in the bottom of my backpack and handed it to her. Although, that clearly wasn't going to be enough. She had it soaked before I could even get her to talk.

"You gotta tell me what's going on. Lydia says we have to be honest with each other. We're a tribelet."

"No, we're not." She stared down at her hands, clenched together in her lap in a little pink ball. "I got three prank phone calls this weekend."

"The Pack?"

"Uh-huh. The last time my grandmother took the phone from me, and she heard one of them say something really awful."

"What was it?"

"I don't know. Gramma wouldn't tell me. But she made me tell her what was going on and she wouldn't even let me finish. She just said—" Winnie choked, but I couldn't let her stop yet.

"What?" I said.

"I'm not allowed to be in the tribelet anymore."

Winnie broke all the way down then and cried and cried against my shoulder. Mitch found us like that, and she stared down four or five kids who thought they were going to stop and gape. Then she sat down on the other side of Winnie, and I told her what happened.

"I got calls too," Mitch said. "We have an unlisted phone number, so that's weird."

"It's all my fault!" Winnie said.

"Huh?"

"Never mind," I said to Mitch. "Did your mom find out?"

She nodded her grizzly head. "She told me to call them back and say worse stuff. She said I shouldn't let them get the best of me. I told her I wasn't into an eye for an eye and then she left me alone." Mitch looked like something was itching her. "I sure want to though."

"Want to what?" I said.

"Get back at them. Look at Win. She's a mess. I'm sick of them doing this to her and you and Ginger. I could take them all out, you know."

"No."

All three of us looked up to see Ginger standing over us. She was wearing a striped top and brand-new red tennis shoes and her hair looked kind of silky.

"We can't give up," she said. "We have to take back the power."

"I'm not allowed to anymore," Winnie said. "I'm not even supposed to be talking to you."

She scrambled up and took off down the stairs. It felt like the air was shrinking. Now we were down to three.

"Okay," I said. "Who's still in?"

"Me," Ginger said.

"Me," I said.

Mitch grunted, naturally, and stood up and put her hand down to pull me to my feet.

"Me," she said.

"And you won't punch anybody?"

"No. It's stupid anyway to fight like that."

"Okay," I said. "So, Baby Steps."

"Save the Tears," Mitch said. "And Gold Thumb."

Ginger shifted her gigantic backpack. "Then, Walk It, Girl."

~

The first three periods of the day went smooth, even with only two of us to shield Ginger. I would have felt safe loosening up on that some if the Pack hadn't barked every time we passed them. They weren't loud barks; the Pack was too smart for that. Personally, I didn't even think they sounded like dogs. I just focused on keeping Mitch from growling at them and Ginger from running away with her tail between her legs. I mean, like, if she had one.

Right before fourth period, that was when things got strange.

I escorted Ginger to the restroom without anybody harassing us. I did my usual hand washing while Ginger looked for an empty stall. She tugged on one door, and it wouldn't open.

"There must be somebody in there," I said, trying not to sound impatient. She still drove me nuts sometimes.

"There's no feet under it," Ginger said.

She was right about that.

"It's probably just stuck. Try that one."

Ginger disappeared into another stall, and I went back to rinsing. I wouldn't put it past the Pack to lock the doors from the inside and then climb out underneath.

I shook my head at myself in the mirror. Was I serious? None of the Wolves would ever crawl around on the bathroom floor.

"Oh!"

I turned around and said, "Ginger?" but I knew that little noise hadn't come from her.

"I'm hurrying," Ginger said.

I didn't answer her. I was looking at the stall with the stuck door. A foot was just being pulled up, and some fingers hooked into the top of the door for a second. Just long enough for me to see the nails bitten halfway down.

"Phee?" I said.

"Yeah?" she said. Her voice sounded almost as tiny as Winnie's.

The door opened, and Ophelia stepped out. Her face was so white I could almost see through it.

"Were you standing on the toilet seat?" I said.

"Me?" Ginger said from inside the stall. "No!"

"I'm talking to Ophelia," I said.

Only I wasn't. When I looked back, the bathroom door was swinging shut behind her.

Ginger emerged, face bewildered. "What was she doing?"

"I don't know," I said.

And I didn't *want* to know. Because every reason I could think of hurt way too much.

~

Fourth period was our last time to meet to plan our presentation. The Pack was in the lab, practicing with pom-poms, so we could talk more freely. That is, if anybody had had anything to say.

Ophelia just played with her braid. I noticed it was cut close to the band at the end so there was nothing left to chew on.

Winnie sat there hugging the binder like she was afraid somebody was going to snatch it right out of her arms.

Mitch didn't talk because, well, Mitch was just Mitch.

Ginger looked across the awkward circle at me and said, "So how are we going to do this?"

"I guess we should just divide up the parts and read them," I said.

"That's boring," Ginger said.

"We have the charts."

"Just so you know . . ."

We all looked at Ophelia.

"I'm not holding up one of those things. Not with that stuff on the back."

"We could do them over," Ginger said.

Mitch grunted.

It was like all the energy had been sucked out of us. And that made me mad. Granna, Lydia, my mom—they all believed in us. I couldn't let them down.

I couldn't let the Tribelet down.

I couldn't let me down.

"Okay," I said. "I'll divide up the parts and hand them out to you after lunch. Everybody read it over so you can at least do it with expression."

Another grunt from Mitch.

"Jeepers . . . come on, guys!"

Nobody could even look at me. Except Ginger, and I knew what she was thinking. *I can't do this without you ever.*

The Pack came back in with their pom-poms, which meant the bell was about to ring.

"Give me the binder, okay, Win?" I said.

"Will you be sure nobody takes it?"

Perfect timing. Kylie stopped right next to Winnie's desk and squatted down. If I had been new, I would have thought they were best friends.

"Did somebody take your binder?" she said. "For your project?"

"I wonder who?" Mitch said.

I kicked her under the table.

"She just lost it for a while," I said. "You have to be careful where you leave your stuff, y'know?"

I was Gold Thumbing all over the place. Everybody else might be giving up, but I couldn't.

"I *know.*" Kylie pressed her hand to her chest. "Do you have an idea for your presentation? Like you usually do—all acting it out and everything?"

"We're workin' on it," I said. The rest of my group was on mute.

"I have an idea."

Kylie perched herself on the arm of Winnie's desk. Win froze.

"Since you're doing such a serious subject, I think you should just read your report. You're all good readers, so that would work."

"Thanks," I said. "We'll keep that in mind."

"We're still keeping the truce, right?" Kylie said.

Ophelia's chin came up. Oh, yeah, she didn't know about the so-called truce. Speaking of which . . .

"So, Kylie," I said.

"Uh-huh?"

"Is barking allowed under the rules of the truce? Just asking, because I kept hearing sounds like dogs when we were walking down the hall."

Kylie's eyes flinched, but she smiled. Jeepers. Did she have her *teeth* whitened? She was *eleven.*

"I'll talk to my people and see if they heard it," she said, voice all chummy.

"Anything else?"

How was it that she could talk like the teller at the bank and still be so—how did Riannon say it? *ImmaCHUR.*

"That's it," I said. "Thanks."

Kylie stayed there for a few seconds, like she wanted to make sure we knew it was her idea to leave. But when she did, she had that "bring it" look in her eyes.

The bell rang, and Ophelia jumped from her desk and practically ran for the door.

"I think I'm gonna be sick," Winnie said, and I believed her. Her face looked like a bowl of mashed potatoes.

"I'll walk you to the nurse," Ginger said.

"No!" Winnie said, and then she shriveled.

So did Ginger.

I told them all to go ahead, that I'd catch up later. Then I took the binder to Mr. V.

"Could you make a copy of our report?" I said.

He gave me one of his elastic smiles. "Sure. Any particular reason?"

Because I'm not taking any chances.

"We need it for our presentation," I said, which was true.

"You got it."

"And would you keep an eye on it? Like, really close?"

His smile snapped into a concerned line. "Anything you want to tell me, Tori?"

"No," I said. "I'm good."

That part, I thought as I hurried toward the cafeteria, that part was a lie. I was far from good. Our whole tribelet was coming apart, and the project we'd worked so hard on was going to bomb in front of the exact people it was about. And tomorrow my parents were going to go to Mrs. Yeats, who would probably say we were all being overdramatic.

"Tori Taylor, what's it going to take?"

I stopped just before running straight into Mr. Jett. Like, so close I could see the individual hairs on his mustache. No, I was clearly not "good."

"The bell rang for lunch a whole minute ago." He held up four fingers. "Fourth time. You're out of chances."

I didn't say it, but right now, being late for lunch didn't seem like the worst thing that could happen to a person.

"You know what that means," he said.

"Lunch detention."

"Right. Do you have a lunch with you?"

"I'm not hungry," I said, which was the absolute truth.

"If you're sure." For a minute there, Mr. Jett actually looked like he cared. But I'd been wrong about teachers before.

"I'm sure," I said.

"Follow me then."

"Where are we going?" I said, although I was pretty sure I knew we were headed for Mrs. Fickus. That was the kind of day I was having.

"We're going to your science room. Mr. Vasiliev has lunch detention duty today."

Okay, so maybe it was the worst thing that could happen to a person. The only teacher who even halfway liked me anymore was now going to know that I was such a flake I couldn't even get to the lunchroom on time.

I was SO not okay.

Chapter Twenty-Three

Just like I thought, when Mr. Jett deposited me in the lab, Mr. V's mouth went into an upside-down *U*. If that wasn't disappointment, I didn't know what was.

"Didn't you tell him you were late because you were talking to me?"

"There was no point," I said. "It was my fourth time."

The *U* got longer. "I'm actually glad you're here. I want to talk to you about something."

He motioned for me to sit down at one of the lab tables and then went into his office and came out with our binder. My heart was doing that double-action hammer thing again as I watched him put it on the table and sit backward on the chair across from me.

"I was looking this over while I was making copies—or starting to." Mr. V flipped the front cover open. "Something seems a little off to me. See what you think."

He was talking like we were two scientists about to review somebody's research results. I would have gotten into that, if I hadn't felt like I was going to die of a heart attack any minute.

Mr. V ran his finger down the first page. "I quote: 'Boys bully, too, but they do physical things like punch each other.'" He looked up at me. "That sounds like . . . Winnie?"

"Yes."

"That was what I expected. Then I get to the bottom of the page." He pulled at his lower lip as he looked down. "Here. 'But scientists and psychologists don't know anything about what goes on in a middle school. If they did, they wouldn't call what we do bullying. There's always been groups, and some of them are popular and some of them aren't. Scientists probably weren't when they were in school, so how would they know?"

"Mr. V."

He looked up again.

"None of us wrote that."

Mr. V closed the binder and pushed it away. His forearms rested on the back of the chair. "So how do you think that got into your report?"

I wanted to tell him so bad I could taste it. Only what I was really tasting was the memory of moldy gingerbread.

"Tori, I want you to trust me."

"I can't!"

"What have I ever done to make you think that?"

"Because you were in on it!"

It was too late to bite my tongue off.

"I was in on what?"

"Valentine's Day."

"You're going to have to give me more information."

He was half smiling and that made me want to, well, do exactly what I did.

"You called Ginger over to talk to you when she opened her locker door so they could put that stuff in there."

"Who? What stuff?"

"The Pa . . . Kylie and Riannon . . . "

None of that turned on any lightbulbs over his head, until I got to Izzy saying, "I could ask Mr. V again."

"They said they wanted to put a treat in her locker because she was new and probably didn't get any valentines."

"They didn't put a treat in there. It was moldy gingerbread, and it smelled disgusting."

"You're not serious."

"I'm telling you the truth."

He nodded at me, but I still studied his face. I didn't see any doubt there. What I saw was him getting a mental whiff of that nasty stuff. Then he shook his head.

"All this time you thought I was part of that, Tori?"

My facial temperature increased by about twenty degrees. "Yeah. I mean, you always joke around with them, and it's like you never see it happening . . . or you don't want to—none of the teachers see it—so I thought . . . I guess I was stupid."

"Uh, no, that's not a word I would use to describe you. So this whole gingerbread thing, this was 'them.'"

I didn't answer for a second. I was right in the middle of a "Report Alert," and I wasn't sure how I got there.

"Yes," I said.

"And who are 'they'? And, hey, this isn't tattling."

"I know. It's reporting. To get Ginger out of trouble."

His forehead went up. Jeepers, his whole face was elastic. "You're even smarter than I thought you were."

"That's not me," I said. "It comes from our . . . the person who helped us with our report."

Before I knew it I was telling him about Lydia and the tribelet and showing him our cards. I would have felt bad doing it without them there, except I wasn't sure it mattered anymore. I ended up telling him about that part too.

"You've been through a lot," he said. "Here's the deal. I'm not going to make you redo your report. I know what's your group and what isn't. In fact, you don't even have to do the oral presentation if you don't want to."

"Really?" I said.

"Why don't you talk to the group? You can come in here after school if you want."

That was way too much to think about all at once. I needed to get something clear first anyway.

"Mr. V?" I said. "What are you going to do, I mean, about the gingerbread situation? They're going to know I told, which is fine, but I just need to know so we . . . I can be prepared."

"Let me think about that, because we still don't have real evidence. But I won't do anything until after the presentations. Fair enough?"

"Nobody ever promised us fair," I said. "But I'll take that."

∾

We went to Mr. V's room after school—Mitch, Ginger, Winnie, and I. I had to fight not to cry, because it felt like it was the last time we would meet as the tribelet. I wished we were in my kitchen eating chips and salsa. With Lydia.

On the way to the science room, Mitch walked beside me and I could tell she was working up to say something.

"Problem," she said finally.

"What?"

"Ophelia."

"What about her?"

"She ate lunch with the Pack today."

I stopped so fast my sneakers squealed on the floor.

"No way."

"Way."

"Did they invite her?"

"I guess. They were all talking to her. Y'know, like holding her hands and all that stuff I'm glad we never do."

My eyes blurred.

"Mitch?" I said.

"Yeah?"

"Are we still a 'we'?"

"Huh?"

"Will you still be my friend after the project is over?"

"Well, yeah," she said. "I mean, duh."

I waited for the proof. I got it. She high-fived me.

That made me feel exactly 20 percent better. I added another 20 percent when we got to the science lab and Mr. V had done all the corrections on our report so the Pack's stuff was all out of there. But the best 20 percent was when he showed us our charts and graphs. He had stapled white paper to the backs of them so nobody could see the I Hate Gingerbread stuff.

"Just in case you decide to do the presentation," he said.

He gave us the copy he'd made, and we divided them up among us. Ophelia wasn't there, so Mr. V said he'd keep hers for tomorrow.

~

I was feeling a total of 60 percent better when I got home just as it was turning dark. I went up to seventy when Dad greeted me at the door. The whole house smelled like popcorn. That was worth at least another five.

"We're celebrating, Tor. What are you drinking?"

"Orange juice," I said. "What are we celebrating? Is Granna going home?"

"Granna is coming *here*. But that's not why we're celebrating." He handed me the popcorn bowl and told me to sit by the fire.

He came back with two tall glasses of OJ and clinked his against mine. "Here's to standing up for the underdog," he said.

"Mom told you."

"No. I already knew."

"Um, huh?"

"Lydia kept me apprised. I hope that's okay with you."

"She *told* you?"

"Actually I told her."

"Dad, *what* are you talking about?"

Dad jiggled some popcorn in his palm. The eagle face went serious. "The first time you came to me about the problems you were having, I knew I was totally out of my area of expertise. I mean, what did I do—tell you some story about the Maidu?"

"Yeah . . ."

"When I saw how much Lydia liked you—"

"Wait. Lydia *liked* me?"

"From the first. She didn't feel like she made the best first impression but . . . I don't know. Anyway, I saw you were floundering and your mom couldn't be there for you, so I asked Lydia if she could help." Dad grinned even as he chewed. "I didn't expect her to get as involved as she did, but it seemed to be working."

I started to sag. Dad shook his head at me.

"Don't go there, Tor," he said. "Lydia helped you because (A) she likes you, (B) she doesn't want to you see any of you suffer the way she did, and (C) she saw the leader in you. That's something your mother and I haven't necessarily brought out in you. It's time we did."

If I wasn't mistaken, there was a sheen over Dad's eyes. If he cried, I was going to lose it again.

But he just kept chewing until I finally said, "Thanks for celebrating that with me, Dad."

"Actually, that's not all. I have news too."

I sat up straight. "Lydia?"

"Ah, yes. The operation was a success, and she's headed for rehab day after tomorrow."

"Can I go see her?"

"She asked me to bring you down. I can do that."

But my little surge of excitement fizzled out. She was going to be so disappointed that the tribelet was splitting up. Mitch said she'd still be my friend, and Ginger would probably stick to me until she moved again. But that didn't feel like the tribelet we worked so hard on.

"But you haven't heard all of it."

I tried to smile at Dad. "There's more?"

"There is. " His face got eagle-solemn again. "I spent two whole afternoons with my producers in San Francisco. It took some convincing, but this morning they finally told me that I should include the plight of the Maidu in the movie."

"Yay, Dad!" I said.

"It was a big risk. A couple of times, I thought I was losing. But I hung in there, and you know why?"

"Because it was the right thing to do?"

He smiled. "Yeah. And because my daughter inspired me to do it."

"*I* did? How did I do that?"

"By doing it yourself." Dad clinked my glass again. "I hope I've made you proud, Tor, because I'm proud of *you. And* your mom and I have decided to wait until after your presentation tomorrow to approach Mrs. Yeats. You've come this far, and we think you deserve the chance to take it all the way in."

I didn't tell him we probably weren't doing the presentation. I didn't want to see that sheen go away from his eyes.

"I almost forgot. I brought you a present from Lydia."

"You saw her?" Why did men tell you things in pieces instead of the whole story at once like girls did?

"Stopped by on my way home. Come up to my office."

Nestlé followed us both up the stairs after he cleaned out the popcorn bowl. Everybody was getting away with a lot today.

Dad told me to sit in my curl-up chair and then he unrolled a big piece of paper, the kind we'd made our charts and graphs on.

"Lydia made this for you before she left. She asked me to give it to you the night before your presentation."

I felt kind of a chill as he turned it around. The kind when you see something that makes it all come together.

Lydia had done the whole thing in calligraphy, that perfect fancy writing you do with a special pen and real ink. She'd even used different colors to draw designs.

But it wasn't just that it looked like it should be framed like art. What it had on it took me straight back to our kitchen table. I could taste hummus and smell Ginger's sort of stale odor getting fresher and hear Winnie giggling and Mitch grunting and all of us calling out answers that Lydia said were right. And they were all on that paper.

"Code for Respecting the Dignity of Every Human Being," she'd written in large letters across the top.

Below that was a list. Our list.

"If everyone in the world followed this code, Tor," Dad said. "All of our problems would disappear."

"Do you really think that will ever happen?"

"I don't know. What I do know is that it definitely won't if no one tries." He grinned. "How about Cirino's tonight, you and me? I don't think we're finished celebrating."

"Okay," I said.

"Don't forget your code."

Dad handed me the rolled-up paper. I couldn't wait to get to my room and unroll it again and really look at it.

"Don't get your slobber on it," I told Nestlé when we were safely behind my closed door.

He pouted in the corner, and I opened up the roll. When I did, a slip of paper floated down like a feather.

I put the code on my desk and picked up the paper. It was only a little thicker than a Kleenex, and on the inside was a note, written just the way the code was.

Only it wasn't a note, exactly.

Dear Tori, Lydia had written.

It will be hard to maintain the code without this:

"Dear God, You've made me the leader of the tribelet, and you've given me a big job to do. Sometimes I feel like I'm alone, even when Winnie and Mitch and Ginger are with me. Please help me find the right grown-ups to back us up. Please give me the courage to uphold the code, even when I have to lose friends to do the right thing. And please, help me know that you're always here, God. Because after all, this was all your idea in the first place. Love, Tori."

"Nestlé," I said through that tear-clog in my throat. "I know what to do now."

And then I bowed my head and read the prayer again.

Chapter Twenty-Four

I was the one with a plan when I got to school the next morning, Tuesday.

The first part of it was to get the tribelet together so I could talk to them. That was tricky since Winnie wasn't supposed to hang out with us, but I got around that by asking Mr. V to request her presence in the science lab.

He also sent Mitch to get Ophelia, but she couldn't find her. I was maybe okay with that.

When we all gathered there, I said, "I'm going to do the presentation today. You don't have to if you don't want to, but I do."

"But, Tori, you hate standing up in front of people," Winnie said.

"I know," I said.

"Are you scared?" Ginger said.

"Nah," Mitch said. "She's not scared. She's the toughest chick I know."

I didn't know about that. Mitch probably didn't know that many chicks. Still, that added a couple of percentage points. I'd lost track, but I must be getting pretty close to one hundred by now.

"One more thing," I said. "Ophelia told me the Pack has a plot that's going to go into effect if I do this presentation."

Mitch gave me a dark look. "I don't believe anything she says anymore."

"I'm just saying you should all not be around me for the rest of the day except in class so you don't get caught up in it."

Then before anybody could say anything, I went to the restroom. I was pretty sure I was going to throw up the French toast Mom had made special for me that morning.

∾

I didn't throw up, but as soon as I got to the science classroom fourth period, I asked Mr. V if I could go first. I wasn't sure how much longer I could handle the sweaty palms and the churned-up stomach and the mouth that felt like the Mojave.

Mr. V shushed everybody as I stood up with the binder, but he didn't really have to. It was so weirdly quiet in there I was pretty sure nobody was even breathing. They'd been building up to this all day. The BBAs. The other boys you barely noticed. The soccer girls and Evelyn. Ophelia. My tribelet.

And the Pack. They all sat back in their den section with their arms folded and their faces like masks. The only expression I saw was the glint of "bring it on," in a pair of blue and gold eyes.

So I did bring it on. I felt like I might faint at first, but once I got past the first page and all the statistics about bullying and the examples of meanness and the research methods we used to find out why it happened, my knees stopped hitting each other and I found some saliva. When I saw Josie in the second row letting her eyes go round and Evelyn stop looking around to see what the Pack was doing, I pushed the binder aside and went from memory.

I told them everything we'd learned about why people are mean in middle school and what it looked like. Once I saw Izzy get squirmy until Kylie gave her a look that was meant to drop her to the floor. I couldn't help it if Izzy heard herself in what I was talking about.

Then I remembered the charts. Only . . . Mitch was already standing behind me holding one up when I turned around. Ciara and Brittney scooted to the fronts of their seats. Mitch held each one up while I explained it, and then she handed it to Mr. V so he could hang it from the hooks on the dry-erase board. Pretty soon the room was full of everything we knew about bullying.

Almost.

When I was done, a couple of people clapped. And then a foghorn voice said, "That's not all."

Kylie groaned out loud, but Mr. V went straight down the aisle and just stood there looking at her until she had to stare down at her desk.

"Isn't their time up?" she said.

Even Heidi winced. And Mitch thought *I* was a tough chick.

"Their time will be up when they've had a chance to say everything that needs to be said."

Mr. V tapped her desk, and Kylie raised only her eyes.

"Are we clear?" he said.

"Yes," she said.

Mr. V turned back to the front of the room where Ginger was now standing beside me.

"Did you have something to add to the report, Ginger?"

"I think it would be wrong to just tell why kids bully and not tell what to do to help stop it. Or what to do if it happens to you."

"I'd have to agree," Mr. V said.

He nodded at Ginger. She took a deep breath and started to talk. The foghorn began loud. Okay, so loud I was sure they heard it over in the eighth-grade wing. She was that nervous. But as she talked, it got softer. By the time she pulled her set of our cards out of her jeans pocket, she was speaking like a normal person.

"This is what we use to help us," she said.

She held up the one with the smiley face on it. "First, you don't show the bully any emotion."

"I can't see," Shelby said.

Kylie slapped her hands on the top of her desk, but Shelby kept craning her neck.

"I'll show mine," said a wee voice.

Winnie started down the first aisle, showing her cards while Ginger talked. After about five seconds, Mitch took hers down the far aisle. I got mine out and went down the center, straight toward the Pack.

Kylie, of course, turned her head when I went by. So did Riannon. Heidi snuck a glance and then looked away. Izzy too. But Shelby was all about it. I had to stand there and show her all of them twice.

"So I guess I'm done," Ginger said.

"Finally," Kylie growled under her breath.

But I was probably the only one who heard her, since I was standing right there. The rest of the class, except Izzy, Riannon, and Heidi, all stood up and clapped. Even the BBAs, although it was probably just an excuse for them to whistle through their teeth the way nobody ever let them do.

"A +, ladies," Mr. V said. "All of you." He looked around. "Where is Ophelia?"

I looked too. Phee was gone. And she'd taken her backpack with her.

~

There was only time for one more report. Except, nobody wanted to be next, so Mr. V said that was probably enough for today and we could take a study hall. Nobody studied, of course, although the room was quieter than usual. A couple of people walked around. I myself went out for water. When I came back, there was a note on my desk.

It wasn't purple. And when I sniffed at it, I didn't smell mint gum.

Why was I even worried about that anymore? With everybody aware of what was going on now, the plot thing had probably already fizzled out.

Besides, the note wasn't from Kylie. It was in handwriting I didn't recognize. *You should make a pledge like the I Hate Gingerbread one,* it said, *only a good one, like what you were up there talking about. And we should all have to sign it.*

I looked around to see if I could figure out who wrote it, but nobody was watching me. Except Kylie. When our eyes locked together in that way they always did now, she mouthed three words. I had no trouble seeing them.

You. Are. Dead.

Really? I mouthed back.

Then I turned away. Mr. V was standing at my desk.

"Do you have any idea where Ophelia went?" he said.

I shook my head.

"Would you please go check—" He stopped and looked at Winnie. "Winnie, would you please go check the restroom? See if you can find her?"

Winnie didn't move for a second, until Mitch said, "I'll go with her."

When they were both gone, I sat next to Ginger.

"You did great," I said.

"So did you."

I expected her to be practically doing cartwheels, but she wouldn't even look at me.

"Is it over now?" she said.

"The bullying? Yeah, I think so. Kylie still hates me, but that's between me and her."

"No. I mean is the tribelet over?"

I felt myself sag, just like she was doing.

"I guess you and Mitch and I could hold it together. Yeah, we can do that."

She did look at me then, with her blueberry eyes. "But are we friends?"

I shouldn't have been surprised. That was so Ginger to just ask right out. Kind of like Lydia said we should.

The bell rang and almost jolted me out of the seat. It was time to get ready for Kylie.

"We can talk about this later," I said. "You need to stay far away from me for now, remember? And *then* it'll really be over."

"What are you gonna do?" she said.

"I've got it handled," I said.

Then with my hand on the cards in my pocket, I went out to be a tribelet of one.

I headed straight for the cafeteria. Mr. Jett would think someone else had taken over my body, because I was going to be one of the first ones there. I wanted to get to the Pack's table at the same time they did.

That was my plan. If I sat down with them, right there in their private den in the middle of the lunchroom, how could they unfold their plot?

But the closer I got, the less sure I felt. It was the first time since

Kylie declared war that I'd gone down a hall without the whole tribelet around me.

Huh. And the whole time I thought it was just Ginger we were protecting.

I straightened my shoulders. There was nothing to be protected *from.* All I had to do was Think Sharp and use the cards if I needed them.

I was almost to the cafeteria door. Mr. Jett had his back to me. And he was talking to Izzy and Shelby. Izzy was bouncing on her toes, like any minute she was going to burst into one of her cheers. And Shelby . . .

I slowed down because Shelby was looking past Mr. Jett, right at me. She bugged her eyes like she wanted me to look where she was looking. Then she jerked her attention back to Mr. Jett.

That's when everything went into slo-mo. I turned my head where Shelby had pointed with her eyes. Three splashy-haired heads rose from behind a cart full of extra chairs. Three perky bodies surrounded me and walked me down the hall the way I'd just come from. Just the way we walked Ginger.

As people floated by us going the other way, Kylie's voice came out in extended words. "Come with u-u-us, Vic-to-o-o-ria. We have a surprise for yo-o-o-ou!"

We were at the corner where the hallway split when I finally snapped into real time.

"No thanks," I said, "I don't like surprises."

I tried to pull away, but it felt like all thirty of their fingers were digging into me at the same time—along my arms, into my shoulders, on the back of my neck.

"Seriously," I said. "Let go."

They didn't. Just as if they'd rehearsed it, they turned me around the corner, away from the sixth-grade hall, and past their den and past the office.

"Let. Go!"

But I was sure no one heard me. The secretaries were inside the office, and there wasn't anybody out in the hallway—because we were headed for the seventh-grade wing, and it wasn't time for them to go to lunch yet.

All I could think of as the three of them carried me toward the double doors that separated our side of the school from the upper grades was that Lydia was right. I was a sheep in a wolf pack.

And I was about to get eaten alive.

"If they go over to the seventh- and eighth-grade wings, they're toast," Mitch had said.

One of the wolves let go of me and rushed ahead. It was Kylie. She leaned against the door and watched as Heidi and Riannon dragged me those final steps.

"Surprise!" Kylie hissed.

She pushed open the door, and ahead I saw freedom. As soon as they flung me through, I would take the first set of stairs I found and get back to our wing. I'd drawn a map of the whole school. I knew how to do that.

But Heidi and Riannon didn't let go. They stayed on either side of me like the identical bookends they were, and just barely over the sound of my own breathing, I heard Kylie whisper, "Wait. Let me go ahead."

As she darted past us and fast-walked down the hall, I thought about screaming. But (A) I wasn't sure anything would come out because no one had ever handled me like this my whole life and I was freaking out and (B) we were in the seventh-grade wing where nobody knew they were bullies . . . where nobody would believe these pretty girls were doing anything wrong. All they had to do was smile.

"Okay," Kylie whispered from the end of the hall.

All the doors we passed were closed. The lights through their windows flicked past as Heidi and Riannon pulled me toward Kylie. I tried to get away again, but they were stronger than they looked.

Must be all that cheerleading, I thought crazily.

Wait. I could still think. I was smarter than they were. I could Think Sharp. Even if I *was* a sheep.

Kylie pushed through another set of doors. Now we were in a space at the bottom of the steps where some tall lockers lined the walls. There was a door that led outside.

Think Sharp.

"Please don't throw me outside," I said. "It's cold."

"What am I, stupid?" Kylie said. "You *want* us to throw you out there."

That was true. I was the worst actress ever, so I tried not to even look at the steps, which was the next best escape. I could probably get away from them going—

A bell rang in the distance. The warning bell for the end of sixth-grade lunch.

"Hurry," Kylie said. "We only have five minutes."

She pulled open one of the long lockers. For the first time, I realized they were tall enough to stand up in.

"In you go," Kylie said. "I told you—you're dead."

I fought, and I fought hard. I even yelled. But they were too strong. They shoved me into the locker and clanged the door shut on me.

"Night night, Victoria, my pet," Kylie said.

And then they didn't make a sound, except for the sighing shut of the double doors.

I wasn't dead. Of course I wasn't dead. But I felt like I was. It was absolutely dark. I couldn't turn around to try to get the door open. How long was I going to be able to breathe?

Panic clawed its way up my throat, and I yelled. At least, I thought I yelled. The sound didn't seem to go any farther than my lips. I pushed my back against the door, but I could hardly move so it didn't budge.

"Help! Somebody help!" I yelled again. And then I started to cry. I shouldn't have gotten involved. I should have listened to Ophelia, and none of this ever would have happened. My crying got so loud I almost didn't hear the voice that whispered, "Tori! Which one are you in?"

I must be hallucinating already. Didn't you do that just before you died?

If I was, I was hearing other locker doors opening, and I was hearing a voice that said, "Don't worry. I'll get you out."

"Phee?" I said.

"Oh my gosh, Tori!"

The locker vibrated. Then I heard some banging.

"Phee, get me out of here!" I cried.

"I can't! The door won't open! I have to go get help!"

"Go, Phee! I'm scared in here!"

"Don't worry—"

"Phee!"

"What?"

"Hurry!"

I heard the double doors to the hallway sigh shut again. There was no point in yelling now. She'd bring somebody back.

But that didn't mean I wasn't panicking again. Think. I didn't need to freak out. I just needed to think—because that's what I did the best. Right?

Think. The Pack must have been planning this for a while,

because it was as if they'd practiced it. Only, how did Phee know? Was that why she ate lunch with them? And hid in the bathroom? So she could find out what they were planning? But why would they talk in front of her when she wasn't one of them? When she was my friend?

Or used to be.

I went cold all over. Was she in on it? Was saying she would get somebody to help me to keep me from yelling?

No. Nonononono. I couldn't think that.

But what else *could* I think? Maybe I wasn't that good at it after all.

I took a deep breath. Did it really feel like there wasn't enough air? No, this locker had those vent things, didn't it? But those were meant for keeping gym sneakers from growing fungus. They weren't made for keeping people alive. Why would they be? Who stuffed a person in a locker?

And who left her there?

The fear surged into my brain again. No. Think. Think of another question.

How did Kylie figure the Pack was going to get away with this? Didn't she know as soon as I got out of here I was going to tell the first teacher I saw? If there was ever a "Report Alert" situation, this was it.

A bell rang, so close I jerked my whole body. But I was crammed in so tight, I didn't actually move. Now it wasn't just my brain that was in a panic. My stomach roiled like there was a hurricane going on down there. What would happen if I threw up right now?

That was it. I screamed.

Then I sucked in my breath and listened so hard I could almost hear my own pulse. There was nothing but my heartbeat . . .

And then suddenly there was so much noise I would have covered my ears if my arms hadn't been plastered to my sides. People were thundering down the steps and through the locker space and slamming through the doors. It sounded like herds of them, but obviously none of them could hear me. Or else they didn't care. Maybe nobody cared if you were locked in a locker or stuffed into a trash can or had your head stuck in a toilet. Maybe no matter what you did, people were going to bully. Maybe my dad was wrong. Maybe it didn't even matter if you tried.

I'd stopped yelling by then and started, yes, crying. Me. Slowly the storm of feet and seventh-grade voices and barking teachers faded, yet even the last of them didn't seem to hear me sobbing.

Another bell rang.

English class had started long ago. Mrs. Fickus would be tapping those seashell fingernails, wondering where I was. So would Mitch. And Ginger. And Winnie. But none of them would even think to look for me here. The only person who knew where I was besides the Pack was Ophelia.

She *was* one of them now. So then maybe it was okay to go ahead and die in here. If I couldn't trust her, then who—

"Stop it," I said out loud for myself. "Just stop it."

"Did you hear that?" someone whispered.

I held my breath. Was that somebody to help me? Or was it one of the Pack? Or was I losing my mind as my life slowly ebbed away?

"It was coming from in there."

I knew that voice. That wonderful foghorn voice.

"Ginger?" I said. "Ginger—is that you?"

"Tori? Are you in a *locker*?"

That was Winnie's voice. Tiny and scared and wonderful.

"Yes!" I said. "This one!"

I got my foot to move some and nudged it against the door. That made me press my forehead hard into the metal in the back of the locker, and I yelped like Nestlé.

"She's hurt!" said the foghorn. "Are you hurt, Tori?"

"Just get me out of here!"

Again the locker vibrated. And again there was banging, and then Winnie saying, "Can't you open it?" And Ginger saying, "It's stuck!"

"Keep trying!" I said.

"No, we gotta get help," Ginger said.

"Don't leave me! Phee left me!" It hurt as much to say it as it did to move.

"You go, Ginger," Winnie said. "I'll stay here."

Wildly I thought, *That's not the way it's supposed to go! Winnie's supposed to go for help!*

But the double hall doors sighed again before I could get that out.

"Winnie?" I said.

"Yeah?"

"Talk to me, okay? Then I won't be so scared."

"Okay."

Silence.

"Win?"

"Yeah?"

"Say something. Where's Ophelia?"

"I don't know. I haven't seen her since fourth period."

"Did she go to fifth?"

"I don't know. We haven't been there yet."

"You're cutting class?"

"We were looking for you."

Winnie's voice wobbled.

"Okay, you can't cry, Win, because then I'll start crying, and there's not enough room in here to cry. I already tried it."

"Okay."

"What happened? Did you go to the cafeteria?"

"No. Mitch and I went to the bathroom to look for Ophelia, and she wasn't there and then we went back to science to get our stuff and that's when we found your note."

"What note?"

"The one you wrote."

"I didn't write a note!" Jeepers. I *must* be hallucinating.

"It was in your handwriting. I know your handwriting."

"What did it say?"

"It said, 'Don't pay any attention to anything they say.' So we didn't. Only I don't get it."

"Wait. I wrote that note forever ago. For Ginger. I never gave it to her . . . it was in my Spanish notebook."

"It was on my desk, and it said 'For Winnie and Mitch.' Only, that part wasn't your writing."

"What did they say?"

"What?"

"What did the Pack say that you didn't pay any attention to?"

"They said . . ." Winnie's words wavered.

"Don't cry, Win. Tell me."

"They said . . ."

"Wait. Which ones said it?"

"It was just Izzy. She said you were in trouble in the seventh-grade wing. Only we knew you would never come down here, and she was just trying to get us in trouble, so we didn't come. I'm sorry, Tori!"

"It's okay." At least calming Winnie down was keeping me from going nuts. "Shouldn't Ginger be back by now?"

"She's not coming," someone else answered.

No. Nonononono. Not Riannon. Pointy, scary Riannon out there with our Winnie? That couldn't be.

But it was. Nobody else could say, "You all made a mess out of everything," the way she was saying it right now.

I could almost see her fake-green eyes poking holes in Winnie. I wouldn't blame Win now if she had a total nervous breakdown.

"It was just supposed to be you in the locker and nobody else involved," Riannon said.

"You talking to me?" I said.

"Well, like, who else would I be talking to?"

"Winnie, are you still there?" I said.

"Uh-huh."

Run, Winnie, I wanted to say. *I don't care if you get help. Just run away from her.*

"You don't have to do everything Kylie tells you to, you know," said a wee voice. "You can take back the power to be your own self."

Winnie? Winnie said that?

"What does *that* mean?" Riannon said. "I already am my own self."

"No," Winnie said, in a little bit louder-than-wee voice, "you just do whatever Kylie wants you to, so you won't be by yourself. I kind of used to do that, but—"

"I do not."

"You look really scared, though."

I wasn't sure that was the best way to go. "Hey, Riannon?" I said.

"What?"

"Are you cutting class?"

"No, I got a hall pass. Kylie told me to come make sure . . ."

"Kylie told you to," I said.

I heard Winnie's soft giggle. "Yeah. It's like I just said."

"So where's Ginger, Riannon?" I said. "Did you put her in a locker too?"

"No," she said, her voice going all high and defensive. "Izzy's with her."

"Where?"

"I don't have to tell you."

"Let me guess: all four of your friends have her cornered in the bathroom."

"We're taking turns," she said. And then I was sure I heard her use a cuss word under her breath.

"You're gonna keep her in there forever?"

"No! We're just keeping her there until we find Mr. Jett."

Mr. Jett? Why him? And then it hit me. "Because he's the only who'll believe *I* tried to do *this* to Heidi so you had to lock me in here."

A pause fell.

"How did you know that?" Riannon said finally.

"Now you *really* look scared," Winnie said. "You want us to help you?"

Winnie was playing every card in the stack. "Save the Tears." "Gold Thumb." I just wished we could "Walk It, Girl." My whole body was starting to ache.

"I don't need your help," Riannon snapped at her. Those eyes were reptilian by then, I was sure.

"So what are you gonna do?" Winnie said, voice all concerned.

"I don't *know*!"

"Maybe you should go get help," Winnie said. "Then you won't get in so much trouble."

"You guys are the ones who are gonna get in trouble."

"I guarantee you somebody is," said a deep voice.

All the hope that had been calming me down went out through the air vent. That was Mr. Jett's voice.

"I am so glad you're here!" Riannon said. Miss Innocence kicked in. "Did Kylie tell you what they tried to do to Heidi?"

So I was right. And Mr. Jett was never going to believe me over the Pack.

"Tori, are you in there?" he said.

I considered not answering, but I said, "Yeah."

"Mr. Jett?" Winnie said.

But there was another locker vibration, followed by more banging. I could have told him that wasn't going to work, but he probably wouldn't have believed that either.

"How long has she been in there?"

More banging.

"Since the beginning of sixth-grade lunch," Winnie said.

"Why didn't somebody get me sooner?"

"We sent two people and nobody came back!" I said. I hoped that didn't count as arguing, but could we please stop talking about it and get me out of here?

One more bang. I fell backward, into Mr. Jett. I didn't hit the floor because he picked me up. I was pretty sure the teachers not touching students rule didn't apply in this situation.

"Are you hurt?" he said, putting his glasses back on his nose. They weren't connected after all.

"I don't think so," I said.

"Can you stand up?"

"I don't mean to argue, but I've kind of *been* standing up."

When he set me down, though, my legs buckled. I didn't fall, but I was shaking all over.

He stared at my forehead. "What happened there?"

"I hit it when I was trying to—"

"You should see Heidi's arm where Tori tried to shove *her* in there," Riannon said.

Winnie's mouth opened, but Mr. Jett motioned with a sharp jab of his hand for her to hold me up. That would have been funny if Mr.

Jett wasn't looking at me like I'd tried to stuff my entire sixth-grade section into their respective lockers.

"This whole vendetta thing has gone way too far," he said. "I've got Mitch telling me there's some plot afoot to go after you because of some report you gave in science."

"That is such a lie, Mr. Jett!" Riannon said.

"She refused to go to class until I came down here."

I was surprised Mitch didn't walk him down the hall herself, until Mr. Jett added, "I sent her to the office."

He turned to Riannon. "What are you doing down here?"

"I came to make sure Tori had gotten out. When she didn't come to class, we got worried about her."

Riannon's contacts were in danger of floating out of her eyes.

Tears? Really? She was an even better actress than Phee.

That thought stabbed me so hard I didn't even try to argue with Mr. Jett. What was the point? Popular really did mean powerful. I could be myself until I graduated and that fact wasn't going to change.

If I graduated. From the look on Mr. Jett's face, I might be suspended for so long I would never catch up.

Chapter Twenty-Five

All right, let's go," Mr. Jett said.

"I just want to get to English," Riannon said. "I can't fall behind in Mrs. Fickus's class."

The only thing worse than the total fakeness of that was the way Mr. Jett seemed to believe her.

"I know," he said, running his hand over the shiny part of his head. "But we're going to get this sorted out once and for all."

He held open the double doors and nodded us through.

"Tori, you go straight to the nurse."

I started to argue, but I bit it back.

"The rest of us are going to the office. We'll have everyone else called down from there." He counted up as he herded us down the hall. "Who do we need? Ophelia. Ginger."

I took in a sharp breath. How could I have forgotten Ginger? I felt my first spark of hope.

"Ginger's being held hostage in the bathroom," I said.

Mr. Jett stopped at the second set of double doors and blinked at me. "And all this time I thought this was a school. Now I find out it's a reality show."

He pushed the doors open with his back and nodded Riannon and Winnie into the office. Then he watched me go up the stairs until I turned on the first landing.

Fortunately, the nurse's office was on the second floor, so he wouldn't know, at least for now, that I didn't go there. I would probably get into even more trouble for that, but I didn't care. I had to do one thing, and it was not "rescue Ginger from the Pack watch in the restroom." I wanted somebody in the office to see that scene. Besides, it didn't make sense that Mrs. Fickus would let one person after another go to the bathroom during class. Especially with so many of us missing already.

What I had to do was find Mr. V. He would tell Mr. Jett and Mrs. Yeats what he knew and then at least we wouldn't be in trouble. Although . . . I couldn't shake off the way Mr. Jett looked at me.

So I clung to the way *Mr. V* always looked at me and half ran down the other set of stairs just like we'd done when we were protecting Ginger and up the hall to the science room. But as soon as his door came in sight, everything in me collapsed on itself. No light shafted through the door's window into the hallway, and when I tried the knob, it was locked. The other door to the lab was too.

No. He had to be here.

I leaned against the door, and I could hear my heartbeat pounding in my ears. Think. *Think!*

"Are you looking for Mr. Vasiliev, señorita?"

The day was getting worse by the minute. I looked up at Mrs. Bernstein. There was no lying to those dark eyes.

"Sí," I said.

She gave me her halfway smile. "This is his prep period. I think he went out to do some errands."

"Is he coming back?"

"I should hope so. He has a sixth-period class." Mrs. Bernstein tilted her head so her ponytail swung. "Are you okay?"

I did lie then. "Yes," I said. "I should go."

"Shall I tell him you were looking for him?"

But I only shook my head as I fast-walked down the hall toward the stairs, before she could ask to see my hall pass. If I couldn't get Mr. V to the office, then I had to go to Ginger.

I risked running up the steps and only barely slowed down when I got to the top. The restroom was just on the left, so I could probably get in there without any more teachers seeing me.

And then I heard Mr. Jett's voice in the hall. Heart pounding again, I took a step back down and planted myself in the shadow.

"You don't know the half of it, Mrs. Fickus," he said.

Like I said, 100 percent worse by the minute.

"I swear, we have completely lost control," Mrs. Fickus said. "I haven't sent Kylie down to you because she's in the restroom and has been for the last fifteen minutes. I sent Heidi after her, and I haven't seen her either."

"What about Ophelia?"

I didn't wait to hear the answer to that. If Ginger was in the bathroom with both Heidi and Kylie, they'd probably destroyed every bit of the be-yourself power Ginger had just started to get. I edged my way along the wall and slipped into the restroom and into the corner at the end of the stalls where I could see three pairs of feet. The two whose heels pressed into the wall wore Uggs. The other pair, facing them, had on brand-new red tennis shoes.

"I told you," Ginger said, "I'm just standing here until somebody comes."

"You're threatening us." That was Heidi's voice.

"No, I'm not. You were the ones threatening me. You can leave any time you want. I'm not stopping you."

That was a relief. And Ginger's voice sounded strong. Not foghorn strong. Just—for real.

"Good," Heidi said. "Then I'm going."

I tried to become one with the corner tiles, but Heidi's Uggs stopped abruptly when Kylie said, "No. Let them find us. Who are they going to believe? Her or us?"

"Me," Ginger said.

Okay, her voice was rising. "Save the tears, Ginger," I wanted to say. But then I heard her take in a deep breath.

"Are you having an asthma attack or something?" Kylie said.

"Mr. V will believe me," Ginger said. "We told him everything."

"No, you did not!" Heidi said.

She made a little hiccup sound. The result of a Kylie poke, for sure.

"Doesn't matter," Kylie said. "There's no evidence, or he would already have reported us."

If that wasn't an example of neener-neener-neener, I didn't know what was. It was time for me to step out and help Ginger before she blew her foghorn.

But before I could, the bathroom door flung open and Mrs. Fickus stepped inside. The place suddenly seemed dingier and smellier than it ever had.

"Miss Hollingberry!" she said. "Step back!"

"Oh, Mrs. Fickus, thank you!" Kylie cried. "She was threatening us!"

It was like déjà vu, only this time I wasn't letting it go.

I stepped out of my corner and said, "No, she wasn't."

Mrs. Fickus startled. Outside the door, she was still holding open, Mr. Jett said, "Is that Tori? I sent her to the nurse."

Kylie got a triumphant gleam in her eye. I saw her nudge Heidi.

"Tori's been threatening us too!" Heidi said. "She's been telling Ginger what to say."

"Really?" I said. "*Really?* I heard the whole thing!"

Mr. Jett was now all the way in the restroom. He was breaking all kinds of rules today, right along with the rest of us.

"I'm not sure you're a credible witness," he said to me.

"But I am."

We all whipped our heads toward the stall where Ophelia made her entrance. Her voice was husky and thick and her eyes were so puffy I could hardly see the brown.

"I'm sorry I didn't go to the nurse like you told me to, Mrs. Fickus," she said. "But you wouldn't listen to me and I didn't know what else to do so I came in here because I knew they were going to take turns holding Ginger in here."

"That is such a lie!" Heidi said.

Mr. Jett looked at her like he was experiencing déjà vu too. Then he said to Mrs. Fickus, "I don't want to discuss this standing in the girls' bathroom."

"Well, no," she said.

"I'm taking this whole crew down to the office."

"I hope you get it sorted out."

She backed the door open wider, and Ginger, Heidi, Kylie, and Ophelia all filed out behind Mr. Jett. I tried to follow, but Mrs. Fickus stopped me in the doorway.

"I've been watching you blossom, Tori," she said. "And I am so sad to see you involved in this." She broke the no-touching rule too and patted my arm. "You just tell the truth down there in the office. That's the only thing you can do."

I didn't say I'd been telling the truth for weeks now. My mother was right. It was pointless to argue. I might never try again.

~

The inside of Mrs. Yeats's office was so crowded I practically had to be shoehorned in.

Mitch stood against the bookcases with her fists balled, glaring at the floor. A paler-than-ever Winnie leaned into Mitch's arm. The chairs were taken up with Riannon and Izzy, who looked a little dazed, like they couldn't believe they were actually in the office for something other than an award for being perfect, and Shelby, who was crying without making any sound. Riannon and Izzy brightened up considerably when Kylie and Heidi walked in and swished themselves into the other two chairs. Talk about "Safe in Numbers."

I wasn't sure where Ginger and I were supposed to go, what with Mr. Jett taking up most of the room, but Mrs. Yeats told him to get more chairs and made the Pack scoot theirs over so when the chairs arrived we didn't have to sit behind them. Kylie rolled her eyes. Of course Mrs. Yeats didn't catch her.

"It seems we have a situation," Mrs. Yeats said, folding her arms across that gold vest she always wore, the one with the Gold Country Middle School insignia on it. At least she didn't reach for those evil detention slips that lived in the pockets. Although, if we walked out of there with only detention, I would probably kiss her loafers.

Kylie raised her arm halfway.

"You'll have your turn in a moment," Mrs. Yeats said.

"But I just want to say that Shelby probably needs to go to the nurse. When she starts crying like this, she needs her inhaler."

"I don't recommend sending anybody to the nurse, Mrs. Yeats," Mr. Jett said. "They never seem to get there."

"Do you need your inhaler, Shelby?" Mrs. Yeats said.

Shelby shook her head. Kylie put her hand on Shelby's arm and squeezed until her knuckles turned white.

Mrs. Yeats leaned, half sitting, on the front of her desk. "I am going to listen to all sides of this story, and there will be no interruptions. You will each have your turn to speak."

"May we go first?" Kylie said without raising her hand.

"No." Mrs. Yeats nodded at Mr. Jett.

Mr. Jett told his story and I had to admit he told what happened when he appeared at the locker just exactly the way it happened. But then he had to add that this was my fifth time not following the lunch period rules.

I would have given up right then if Ginger hadn't slipped her hand into mine. It was sweaty and sticky, but I let it stay there.

Mrs. Yeats had Kylie go next. It was hard to sit there while the Alpha Wolf explained how my friends and I were jealous of her and her friends and how we stalked them and sent Mitch to harass them at lunch and even did a whole science project just to make everybody believe she and her friends were mean.

"When I called her on it," Kylie said in the sweet-like-Splenda voice she'd been using the whole time, "she took it out on poor Heidi and tried to stuff her into that locker. That's when Riannon and I came along and put Tori in there so she wouldn't hurt anybody else." She lifted one of Heidi's arms. "I can show you the bruise she got when Tori grabbed her."

Mrs. Yeats didn't look. She turned her eyes on me.

"Do you want to speak for yourself and your friends?" she said.

"Tori doesn't like to talk in front of people," Ginger said.

"I don't think any of us is 'liking' this," Mrs. Yeats said.

I looked at my tribelet. I didn't want to speak for myself. I was already doomed, so what did it matter? But when I saw all of them holding hands, even Mitch, I couldn't just sit there and let them go down with me. I was the leader.

So I sat up tall in my chair. "First," I said, "I want to make it clear that Ophelia wasn't involved in any of this."

"Really?" Mrs. Yeats said. "My observation has been that the two of you go back to first grade as best friends."

I shook my head. "Ophelia doesn't want to be my friend anymore. Not since Mitch and Winnie and I decided to protect Ginger."

The chins wobbled. "Protect her from what? Is something dangerous going on in my school?"

As I looked into Mrs. Yeats's eyes, I saw two things: (A) she might just suspend you for chewing gum, but (B) she wanted to know the answer to that question. The honest answer.

"Could I stand up there with you?" I said.

She looked a little surprised, but she nodded and motioned for me to join her at the desk. I looked at the Pack with their eyes all innocent, and I let the events of the last exactly thirty-seven days flip through my mind before I started to talk. After that, it was only Lydia and Granna and Mom and Dad and the code I saw and heard in my head.

"I call somebody stuffing somebody in a locker and leaving them in there dangerous," I said.

"I do too," Mrs. Yeats said. "Very much so."

"And I don't ever want to be in that situation again, and I don't ever want anybody else to be either."

"That's why we're here. Before I can make a fair determination of who is responsible, I need to hear your side of the story."

"No," I said.

The chins stopped. "I'm sorry?"

"I don't think it'll do any good to figure out who the bullies are and who the victims are. Somebody will get punished and somebody won't and whether it's fair or not everything will go back to the way it was before." I took a deep breath and wondered for a second why my knees weren't knocking together. "Mitch and Winnie and I have never attacked the bullies. We've only attacked bullying itself. And that's what we're going to keep doing, only we can't do it by ourselves. We need . . ."

I swallowed hard. This was the part I'd never done before. This was the part where my mom would say it was time to stop arguing. But I couldn't. I couldn't just shrug and change the subject.

"We need you and the teachers to know that kids get taunted and intimidated and put down here all the time. We don't care if the people doing it get in trouble. We just want it to stop so we can take back the power to be ourselves. That's all we've been trying to do."

"Why does she keep saying, 'bullying'?" Kylie said, in a tone that, if I'd ever used it with my mother, would have gotten me flushed down the toilet. "Nobody ever bullied anybody until Tori—"

"I beg to differ."

I looked up to see Mrs. Fickus standing in the office doorway. "If I may, Mrs. Yeats?" she said.

"Whatever light you can shed on this would be appreciated," Mrs. Yeats said.

My legs *were* shaking now, and I asked Mrs. Yeats if I could sit down.

After Mrs. Fickus handed Mrs. Yeats a piece of paper, I was glad I did take a seat because Mrs. Yeats silently read whatever was on it, scowled, and then read it again.

"What's that?" Winnie whispered to me.

"I have no idea," I whispered back. But judging from the look on Mrs. Yeats's face when she finished her second reading, it couldn't be good.

"Do you know who wrote this?" she said to Mrs. Fickus.

"No. It was turned in with the other essays." She nodded her helmet head toward the paper. "That is bullying if I ever saw it."

"All right, ladies," Mrs. Yeats said, "and I use the term loosely—I want to know who wrote this. And I want to know now."

She turned the paper around and held it up. It was the paper the Pack had written about me and sent to me via Nestlé, the one I passed in with the one I wrote about Ginger—the person I most admired.

Kylie was the only one still looking innocent. Riannon's face was blank. Izzy and Heidi were both inspecting their laps. Shelby was full-out bawling.

Meanwhile, Winnie was tugging on my sleeve and whispering, "What is it?" I whispered back, "Later," and watched Mrs. Yeats, to see if she was believing this performance.

"This is awful," Kylie said. "Why would someone write that about Tori?"

Mrs. Yeats's eyes narrowed. "Tori?" she said. "Who said this is about Tori?"

It was the first time I ever saw Kylie move her lips without anything coming out. So that was how Mrs. Yeats got to be principal.

"You know what I think?" Kylie said finally. "I think Tori wrote this about herself, just to get us in trouble."

"*No*, she did not! Tori would never do anything like that!"

The room was suddenly full of Ophelia as she stood up and flipped that wonderful braid over her shoulder.

"You wrote it, Kylie," she said. "You planned it at the lunch table with me sitting right there. And you cooked up your whole plot against Tori while I was hiding in the bathroom stalls—just like I was today when you and the rest of your *Pack* kept Ginger in there so she couldn't tell any of the teachers that *you* had Tori trapped in a locker."

The braid whipped as Ophelia turned to Mrs. Yeats, who as far as I could tell, hadn't moved an inch since Ophelia started talking.

"I knew everything that Mitch and Winnie and Tori were doing for Ginger, too, and I'm sorry I never told on Kylie and them, but you know what I'm even more sorry for?" The tears broke through Ophelia's voice. "I'm more sorry that I didn't join Tori's tribelet. And Tori—Tori is still the best friend I ever, ever had."

Then my BFF Ophelia dropped into her chair, put her face in her hands, and cried. The only person in the room crying harder was Shelby. Kylie put her arm around Shelby's shoulders, but Shelby shook her off. That obviously wasn't lost on Mrs. Yeats because her eyes narrowed like laser beams.

"All right," she said, "I'm going to have all of you wait in the outer office while I talk to each girl privately. Shelby, I'll talk to you first."

Shelby sobbed anew.

"Do you want someone to get your inhaler?"

"No," Shelby managed to say. "I don't even have an inhaler."

~

Although Mr. Jett spread us all out so there was a chair between every two girls, Kylie kept whispering to Heidi and Riannon about how Shelby better not "spill her guts." Lovely. Finally he said, "I don't know what Mrs. Yeats is going to do, but I'm giving lunch detention to the next person who opens her mouth."

He stayed there until Mr. V showed up.

When I saw him, I let out all the air I'd been holding in.

The two teachers talked low so we couldn't hear and then Mr. Jett raised his voice and said, "They stay silent until they're called in. That's the only way to quell the girl drama."

I was sure I heard Mitch growl.

When he left Mr. V stood there, looking from one of us to the other. He looked so disappointed that for the first time since I was in the locker, I thought I was going to cry again.

"I'm going to ask some yes or no questions," he said. "Just nod or shake your head."

Kylie looked like she had no intention of doing either one, which was fine because Mr. V turned to Ginger.

"Did you tell Mrs. Yeats about the gingerbread thing?"

Ginger shook her head.

He looked at me, and I shook mine too.

"How about the sabotage on your science project?"

We all shook our heads, even Ophelia.

"Why not?" he said. And then he shook *his* head because (A) it wasn't a yes or no question and (B) . . . he looked like he already knew.

He shook his head again, this time at Kylie. "You don't know how lucky you are that these girls have integrity. But your luck just ran out."

Then he walked straight to Mrs. Yeats's office, tapped on the door, and without waiting for an answer, he went right on in.

The minute he was gone, Kylie marched over to the secretary's desk. "I need to call my mom," she said, flipping her little splashy hair like she was giving out orders.

"No, you don't," the secretary said without even looking up. "All your parents have already been called. They're on their way."

The room erupted in a strange chorus of gasps and whimpers and even one wail. But that all came from the Pack.

The tribelet? We just sat back and breathed. One "Report Alert" successfully called.

Chapter Twenty-Six

I thought it was crowded when Mrs. Yeats had all of *us* in her office. When the parents crammed in there, they spilled out the door so they had to leave it open. That meant we heard almost everything that wasn't mumbled.

We heard that (A) Mrs. Yeats made it clear that the Pack (of course she didn't call them that) were bullies and the tribelet (she didn't call us that either) had tried on our own to protect the victim, Ginger. The only parent who argued was, naturally, Kylie's mother. Something about suing the school.

And (B) that Mrs. Yeats announced that Kylie, Heidi, Riannon, Izzy, and Shelby would all be suspended for five school days. That's when Kylie's mother stormed out and took Kylie with her. The rest of the Pack seemed to shrivel when she was gone.

And (C) Mrs. Yeats said she was going to take every step possible to assure that bullying was stopped at Gold Country Middle School. And she was going to start by taking Shelby's suggestion that my group's Code for Respecting the Dignity of Every Human Being be signed by every sixth-grader.

"*Shelby's* suggestion?" Mitch muttered to me.

But it was okay, because now I knew who had written me that note after our presentation.

I looked at Shelby, but she was crying again. For that matter, so were Izzy and Heidi. Riannon just looked like she needed first aid for shock.

And then came the best part, (D). Mrs. Yeats said, "Any sixth-grader who does not sign it or who signs it and breaks the code will be required to attend some special classes. I'll have to work that out. Mr. Taylor?"

"Yes, ma'am," I heard Dad say.

"This young woman you spoke of earlier. Do you think she would be interested in teaching that for us?"

"She's having some health issues right now," Dad said, "but I can certainly tell her you're interested."

"Lydia?" Ginger said. Even her whisper had a foghorn quality, but I was actually starting to like it.

"Cool," Mitch said.

Ophelia and Winnie did a seated version of the Happy Dance.

Me? For a minute I wasn't sure I wanted Lydia around people like Kylie. But then, when I thought about it logically, if Kylie was around a person like Lydia, maybe she wouldn't have to be a person like Kylie anymore.

~

The tribelet gathered at my house that day after school. Mrs. Yeats was making tomorrow Code Day at lunch—before the Pack went on their suspension—so we decided to make a big copy of the code for people to sign, instead of just a small sheet of paper.

It was very cool having Granna there watching us. She was still in a wheelchair—I couldn't see *that* lasting very long—but she was dressed in her usual baggy pants and dangly green cross earrings and a faded T-shirt that said CELEBRATING THE MAIDU. She chuckled and nodded the whole time we were working.

"Lola Montez would be proud of you," she said, jabbing me gently with her elbow.

"Who's Lola Montez?" Ginger said.

"No one," Mom called from the kitchen.

But I grinned at Granna and said, "She was somebody who dared to be different. Just like us."

When Granna had gone to take a nap, protesting all the way down the hall to the guest room, we made popcorn and admired our poster.

Code for Respecting the Dignity of Every Human Being

Bullying is not a normal part of growing up. It's wrong, and we're not having it at our school anymore. Please sign this pledge to be part of making this a safe place to be.

I will not do any of the following things.
I will help anyone who is being treated in any of these ways.
If I'm being treated in any of these ways, I'll get help from a friend or an adult.

- Negative remarks about other people's appearance
- Threatening looks
- Spreading rumors

- Laughing at others' mistakes
- Laughing when they get up in front of the class (unless their presentation is funny)
- Making fun of somebody's family
- Making mean jokes about someone, especially if that person can hear you
- Damaging or destroying other people's property, including their homework
- Whispering, pointing, and laughing at someone just to make him or her feel bad
- Imitating people in negative ways, especially in front of them
- Giving someone a rude nickname, or insisting on calling them by a name they don't like
- Advertising put-downs of someone (signs, posters, things to sign)
- Organizing a hate club against somebody
- Giving people rude notes that put them down or scare them
- Playing practical jokes designed to make people feel bad about themselves
- Touching people in ways they don't want to be touched (shoving in the halls, poking, stuffing someone in a locker or a trash can, etc.)
- Preventing someone from going where they want and need to go (restroom, locker, lunchroom, etc.)
- Preventing someone from doing their schoolwork
- Deliberately doing something to get a person in trouble
- Threatening someone
- Acting like an angel in front of adults and being mean in the above ways to kids
- Getting back at someone who has bullied you by bullying them
- Any kind of behavior toward others that you have to hide from adults
- Any kind of behavior that takes away people's power to be who they are, even if who they are annoys you

- *Refusing to help somebody who's being bullied in the above ways*

Not everybody is guilty of bullying, but everyone is responsible for making sure every person has the power to be who they are, even if they're different from you.

"Do you think five days suspension is a bad enough punishment?" Phee said.

Mitch grunted.

"What does that even mean?" Phee said.

"It's not an eye for an eye."

"I know, but seriously, Tori could have died in there."

"Really?" Ginger said.

"No!" Winnie's little brow wrinkled. "Right?"

"No," I said. "Because you guys wouldn't have stopped until you found somebody to get me out."

"We're a tribelet," Winnie said.

"You're not gonna cry, are ya?" Mitch said.

Ophelia toyed with a piece of popcorn. "Do you think they'll still be the Pack when they come back from suspension?"

"I hope not," I said. "Isn't that the whole point of stopping them? Not so they'll get in trouble, but so they'll stop . . . being wolves?"

Ginger shook her head. "I don't know about Kylie. She might always be an Alpha Wolf."

"What if we stopped calling her that?"

They all looked at me, like they were as surprised as I was that had just come out of my mouth.

Ophelia said. "What are you going to call her then?"

"Um, 'Kylie'?" Winnie said.

"That's the 'Gold Thumb,'" Ginger said.

Ophelia squinted. "What's that one again? I can't keep them all straight."

"We don't want them calling us names," I said, remembering Winnie the Ninny and Mitch the Witch and all those other things I'd never told the tribelet. "So we shouldn't call them names."

"Oh." Phee suddenly looked shy. If that was possible. "But can we still be the tribelet?"

"Wait." Mitch leaned toward Phee. "Are you in?"

"Can I be in?" Phee said.

In. I wanted us to define *in*. But maybe we'd done enough for now just getting rid of the Pack name.

It was all about "Baby Steps."

And Ophelia and I took one after the rest of the tribelet left. We went to my room and sat on my bed with Nestlé. Mom said she thought I should be rewarded for all I'd done, and that's what I asked for—bed privileges for Nestlé. She also said I was a true lady, no matter how many times a week I wore my Einstein sweatshirt.

"So, Tori?" Phee said.

"Yes," I said.

"You don't even know what I was going to ask you!"

"Was it, 'Can we be best friends again?'"

"It was."

"Then yes."

Ophelia flipped her braid. "But I had it all planned out how I was going to say it!"

Her eyes were all big and sad, so I let her do her whole thing—about how sorry she was and how she should have trusted me, only she let the Pack scare her and how she would never do that again.

I didn't stop her until she said, "I'll do anything you want me to, Tori, as long as you'll still be my friend forever."

"No," I said, and before she could go all drama queen on me, I put my hand up. "Don't ever do anything just because I say it. You have to keep the power to be yourself. And don't let anybody take that away, no matter who they are."

"Oh, Tori!" she cried and threw her long, lanky arms around my neck.

That was the Ophelia I loved, drama queen and all.

~

The next day, Wednesday, a lot of people decided to be "in," if that was what signing the code meant.

Okay, so maybe some people did it because Mr. V said it was cool. And some did it because they didn't want to have to go to the special classes—which Lydia said she'd think about doing. I knew that was why Riannon and Heidi and Izzy finally signed it. In tiny, tiny letters.

Kylie wouldn't, even after Mrs. Bernstein, of *all* people, went over and talked to her. She just sat at her table and bared her teeth. Yeah, it was going to take me a long time to stop thinking of her as the Alpha Wolf.

The coolest thing about the whole code-signing was that Shelby wrote her name on the poster first. I looked at her handwriting. Yep. That was proof. She *was* the person who left me that note, telling me we should have the pledge. Someday I would make sure she got credit.

~

Lydia was proud when I talked to her on the phone that night. I knew she would be. But I wanted to discuss something else with her too.

"You know that prayer you left for me?" I said.

"I do."

"I prayed it."

"Good."

"I've been praying it every night."

"I love it."

"Nestlé prays it with me. I mean, I think dogs can pray, don't you?"

"Yes, I think they do."

"Do you think that's why it worked? Our presentation and the . . . those girls getting caught and everything?"

"That. And the fact that you're following what God teaches."

"I am?"

"The whole tribelet is. Everything I taught you comes right out of the Bible."

"Seriously?"

"Check it out. I left your dad a list of the verses that go with everything." She laughed a gurgly laugh. "You scientists always have to do your own research."

"Well, yeah," I said.

~

When I went to bed that night, with Nestlé snoozing beside me, I did some counting, and I figured out that it was exactly—and I like to be exact—thirty-eight days since Kylie Steppe looked at me and saw something besides, well, nothing.

This day, Thursday, March 5, should be circled in red on the calendar too. Because it was the day I took back the power to be myself.

Who Helped Me Write *SO Not Okay?*

It takes more than just the author to write a book. These are the people who helped me get Tori and the tribelet's story as right as it can be:

Mary Lois Rue, who let me stay with her in Grass Valley and made it come alive for me. She's my mother-in-law, the other Mrs. Rue.

Amy and John Imel, my brother-in-law and sister-in-law who told me what it was like to grow up in Grass Valley, California. (And fed me wonderful food . . .)

My prayer team – **Janelle, Barb, and Lori and her family** – who prayed when it was hard to write about girls being mean to each other.

My editors, **Amy Kerr** and **Tori Kosara**. (We call her "the other Tori!")

All the people who have written books and made films about the problem of bullying. And all the bloggers and website folks who kept me up to date.

And especially the **Mini-Women on the Tween You and Me blog** who bravely shared their stories with me. They're the ones who showed me that "sticks and stones can break your bones, but words can break your heart."

SO Not Okay is only the first of three books that will make up the **Mean Girl Makeover** trilogy. If you would like to help with the next two books by sharing your story of being the victim of bullying or your experience as a bully, please e-mail me at **nancy@nancyrue.com.**

You can be part of the solution!

Blessings,
Nancy Rue

IF YOU WERE DESCENDED FROM ANGELS, HOW WOULD YOU USE YOUR POWERS?

Check out the exciting new *Son of Angels* series!

Jonah, Eliza, and Jeremiah Stone are one-quarter angel, which seems totally cool until it lands them in the middle of a war between angels and fallen angels. As they face the Fallen, they will find their faith tested like never before . . .

By Jerel Law

www.tommynelson.com

www.jerellaw.com

9781400321995-A

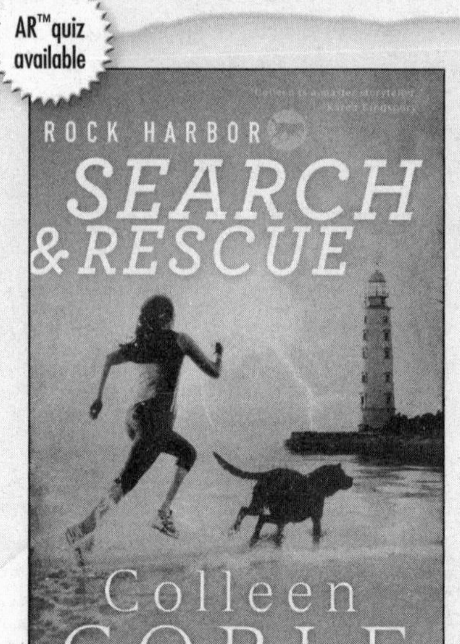

FROM AWARD-WINNING AUTHOR COLLEEN COBLE COMES HER FIRST SERIES FOR YOUNG ADVENTURERS: A MIXTURE OF MYSTERY, SUSPENSE, ACTION—AND ADORABLE PUPPIES!

Eighth-grader Emily O'Reilly is obsessed with all things Search-and-Rescue. The almost-fourteen-year-old spends every spare moment on rescues with her stepmom Naomi and her canine partner Charley. But when an expensive necklace from a renowned jewelry artist is stolen under her care at the fall festival, Emily is determined to prove her innocence to a town that has immediately labeled her guilty.

As Emily sets out to restore her reputation, she isn't prepared for the surprises she and the Search-and-Rescue dogs uncover along the way. Will Emily ever find the real thief?

BY COLLEEN COBLE

www.tommynelson.com

www.colleencoble.com